RAHAB

RAHAB
A NOVEL

Gloria Howe Bremkamp

Originally published as Horn of the Ram

1817

HARPER & ROW, PUBLISHERS, SAN FRANCISCO
Cambridge, Hagerstown, New York, Philadelphia
London, Mexico City, São Paulo, Singapore, Sydney

FIRST HARPER & ROW EDITION PUBLISHED IN 1984.

Library of Congress Cataloging in Publication Data

Bremkamp, Gloria Howe.
    RAHAB.

Reprint. Originally published: Horn of the ram. 1st ed. Chappaqua, N.Y. : Christian Herald Books, c1982.
    1. Rahab (Biblical character)—Fiction.   I. Title.
[PS3552.R369H6 1984]   813'.54   84-47712
ISBN 0-06-061048-4

84 85 86 87 88 10 9 8 7 6 5 4 3 2 1

*In memory
of Lucinda and Bob Howe,
my parents,
who knew long ago
this day would come*

All the great events of history, and all the people who
enact them, move mankind ever closer to the fulfillment
of God's master-plan.

> "And Joshua…sent…two men
> to spy secretly, saying, Go
> view the land, even Jericho.
> And they went, and came into
> an harlot's house, named Rahab….
>
> "And the Lord said unto
> Joshua, See, I have given into
> thine hand Jericho….
>
> "And it shall come to pass,
> that when [the priests] make a
> long blast with the ram's
> horn,…all the people shall
> shout with a great shout; and
> the wall of the city shall
> fall down flat."

Joshua 2:1; 6:2,5

1

On the rooftop of her father's great khan, Rahab sat at her loom and with deft hands plied shuttle through warp. The linen fabric gradually taking shape under her hands was sheer and beautiful. Ordinarily, she would have found satisfaction in the work. But for some reason on this day, there was no satisfaction.

Since early morning, she had been working here with her sister, Tirzah, her body-servant, Ahabina, and assorted slave-women in preparation for the Festival of Harvest. It would soon be upon them. It was the most important event of the year for Jericho, and for her. But this year she felt no excitement, no anticipation.

She paused from her work and stared moodily out over the plains of Jericho. The sun blazed in Canaan's sky. It burnished the River Jordan's fertile lower valley in tones of molten copper and radiated illusive shimmerings across the lush fields and orchards splaying out from Jericho's strong, double-built walls.

For many years, the plains and the city — "the Fragrant One" — had been peacefully fat with the spoils of commerce and complacently confident with the ease of plenty. But now, somehow, under the growing intensity of the late morning heat and her own sense of dissatisfaction, they appeared wilted and vulnerable. It was a disturbing thought.

Shielded on the north and west by the mountains of Samaria, Jericho was keystone to the imperial holdings of Egypt and paraded itself as confident, elegant freeholder of the fertile plains. Date palms and balsam forests girdled her southern boundary and withstood the encroachment of swamps and the Dead Sea's briny marl. As gateway to Egypt on the Jebuz road, the city of Jericho was an important site on a major route of trade.

In considering it now, she realized that such geographic and economic strengths rendered Jericho untouchable. And as Jericho's quedesah — high priestess — she, too, was untouchable. That is why she found the present sense of dissatisfaction and the vague feelings of uncertainty so hard to explain.

She tried to push away the disturbing thoughts by reminding herself that her family possessed the two things most revered by all Canaan, wealth and power.

Her brother-in-law, Yanshuph, as an aide to General Birsha, was a high-ranking member of Jericho's khazianu. Reba, the daughter of Tirzah and Yanshuph, was a beautiful and healthy child.

Her mother, Mozni, was the gentle strength that bound the family close and kept the household running.

Her father, Peridia, acquisitive, shrewd, and highly regarded, owned hundreds of slaves. They worked as domestics in the khan; as dredgers in the salt caves near the Dead Sea; in the fields and forests spreading out from Jericho's southern and eastern walls; and as weavers for her own enterprises.

The beautiful linens, woven here under her supervision, commanded handsome prices from the far marketplaces. Turquoise from Sinai; emeralds and ivory from Nubia; lapis-lazuli, chalcedony, and papyrus from Egypt; magnificent needlework of gorgeous purples from Tyre; cypress from the islands within the Great Sea — all these treasures found their way to her and her family.

All the great merchant caravans made the House of Peridia a regular stop on the trade route from the eastern lands to Canaan. And, except for an occasional tribal skirmish, the entire area was at peace.

She glanced around, gathering other thoughts of reassurance from the sight of closer, more familiar things. Her sister, working at the next loom, was a mosaic of blonde serenity. Beyond, the loyal body-servant, Ahabina, squatted among stalks of flax, preparing them for the looms. Her dark face, with its serpentine scar lacing the left cheek, was intent upon her tasks. Beyond Ahabina, the other slave-women toiled at the dye-vats, making the ceremonial sashes for the Festival of Harvest come alive with brilliant scarlet dye.

From below, in the courtyard and from the workrooms of the great khan, came the sounds of other preparations for the festival. Its rites were both thanksgiving to and placation of Canaan's gods, especially to the great earth-mother goddess Astarte, and to her consort, the god El.

Since she herself was Jericho's quedesah and courtesan to Shatha, the high priest, she was a central figure in these rites. Her share of the tribute riches, brought into the temple by the worshipers, was always satisfying. Whatever regrets she once had over the circumstances that cast her into the role of courtesan to Shatha were compromised and softened by the acquisition of festival wealth.

And someday, she reminded herself, her share of those riches would be even larger. In the meantime, no one in her family wanted for any material thing. Nor would they. Hers was a family blessed by Canaan's gods. Rarely did any of them question their positions or their wealth. Long since, they had paid the price when she was ransomed to Shatha.

Whether ordained by the whims of Canaan's gods or manipulated by the ambitions of men, the House of Peridia, the house of the father of Jericho's quedesah, was one to be reckoned with. And in the same way, Jericho was a city to be reckoned with. Whatever the source of her present dissatisfaction, it couldn't be really important. It would soon pass.

And yet, as she turned again to her loom, she felt that sense of change gnawing deep inside her, a vague emptiness, indistinct yet somehow annoyingly real. And it seemed to have particular reality whenever she heard the khan's guests talk about the Habiru threat.

More and more lately, it seemed that everyone — couriers, traders, merchants, mercenaries, and the odd traveler, as well

— was full of talk about the Habiru. Habiru! Those loathsome, swaggering wanderers who claimed to know only one god — and an unseen god at that!

Worse still, they continually babbled about their 'right' to some promised land. That land was Canaan!

Only the previous evening, she had listened with surprisingly intense interest as her father's guests talked about the Hebrew situation.

"They have their eyes on Canaan," a Jebuzite claimed. "You can be sure of it!"

"Then their unseen god will have to make a miracle to accomplish it!" chortled another. "Canaan's gods are powerful. And Jericho is strong!"

"The man Moses is their god," scoffed a man from Cush. "And he is their so-called miracle-maker."

"But, by the eyes of Baal, Moses is dead! What has Canaan to fear?"

A Midianite agreed. "No one has seen Moses since he went off alone up to Mount Nebo. He's very old, you know. He must be dead. Even a young man would find the climb up Nebo to be a harsh one. Moses must be dead!"

"Well, if he is, then so is his influence over the Hebrew tribes!" The man from Cush turned toward Peridia. "And that's all to the good for us, correct, innkeeper?"

But before her father could answer, the Jebuzite said, "Believe what you like about the death of Moses and his influence. I still say they have their eyes on Canaan. And I still say they are becoming more and more of a threat to all of us!"

With a bit of a shrug, the Midianite conceded a bit. "Their herds are very large, that's true."

"The tribes themselves number in the thousands," inserted an Amalekite.

"Exactly!" The Jebuzite jumped to his feet, nodding emphatically and pointing deliberately at each man. "That's just why they are such a threat. One day, they will confront Jericho for her field and forests and for her water, if for nothing else!"

Peridia then spoke up. A calm authority was in his voice as he reminded his guests that the Moabite kings had refused the Hebrews passage through their lands. "Because of this, those nomads are encamped at an oasis far from Jordan, and even farther from Canaan. I respect your views, my friend from Jebuz, but I cannot feel imminent alarm about this band of beggars."

A murmur of general agreement issued from the group.

But the Jebuzite would not be swayed. "One day, Peridia, you'll be forced to play host to those stiff-necked marauders. And you won't like it. They call themselves 'the chosen people.' Their ways are different. You won't like it a bit!"

Peridia chuckled. "Chosen or not, if they can pay my prices, I'll do business with them, too!"

Persisting, the Jebuzite cut short the ensuing laughter. "If you're that unconcerned, old friend, then why are the other members of Jericho's khazianu now in Egypt, pleading for arms and assistance from Rameses?"

Peridia's eyes narrowed slightly, and it was a long moment before he replied in a still-amiable tone. "Jericho's khazianu are far more interested in the attractions of Rameses' court than in foolish predictions of a war with a band of nomads." He got to his feet, walked to an ornate sideboard, and pulled out drinking cups and a carafe of Jericho's famous balsam rum. "Only our General Birsha has concern for our defenses. And," he added with an uncharacteristic wink, "our General Birsha is often too overcautious."

In recalling the incident, Rahab wondered why the words of the Jebuzite rang with such truth and why the words of her father seemed so careless and unconvincing to her. Even now, in the full, hot light of this morning, they still did.

It was all nonsense, of course. If this question came down to a contest between gods for pasturage and water rights, Canaan and Jericho would remain untouched. Everyone knew the power of Canaan's gods. They could not be surpassed or pushed aside by some mythical, unseen god. Canaan's gods, in fact, should not even be questioned.

Rationally, she knew that. But the stirrings deep inside her were still troublesome. She'd even gone so far as to ask herself if she feared the Hebrews and their unseen god!

It was a dangerous thought, a traitorous thought, especially for one in her position. Involuntarily, she tensed. A thread

13

from the skein she was working through the shuttle snapped under the unexpected pressure of her fingers. A small gasp of astonishment escaped from her. As she fumbled to replace the broken thread, she was aware that her sister and Ahabina were looking at her with puzzlement.

"Fah!" She fumbled again to replace the thread.

Tirzah and Ahabina turned to their work without saying anything. Apparently, they were satisfied that it was only a typical reaction of impatience.

Rahab was glad. She was in no mood for idle conversation, lest it lead to a discussion of the rumors of the Hebrew threat. Someday, after she had sorted out all the talk in her own mind, she might be able to discuss it with her sister, but never with Ahabina. Loyal as the slave-woman was, her suspicious mind would make more of it than was realistic or wise.

The heat increased, pressed down smotheringly, and fumed at the patch of shade offered by the palm-thatch covering over the looms. From below, tree-crickets chittered fitful protest and the courtyard had grown customarily quiet as the sun moved toward its zenith. Rahab continued to fumble with the replacement thread, but it refused to comply.

In frustration, she cast down the shuttle, turned, and glanced toward the city. The dun-colored escarpment of the great temple of Astarte glowered back at her, brooding, ominous, as if in anger that she gave so much as a thought to the rumors of a Hebrew threat.

"Fah!" She stood up and turned her back on the temple. "And double fah!" Tiny explosions of dust swirled up from her sandaled feet. "Senseless heat! Senseless work!"

"It is the same for us, too, my sister," Tirzah said quietly. "We've been at it much too long."

"We'll quit when I say!" Rahab snapped menacingly, and walked toward the dye vats.

The slave-women backed away in deference, their eyes lowered. Rahab brushed past them to where several hanks of ceremonial sashes hung listless in the oppressive heat. She fingered two of them, testing them for dryness. Wet dye oozed out, spattered down onto the hot, dusty roof with a tiny sizzle, and congealed like fresh-drawn blood.

In front of her, the great temple shouldered up, glowering more ominously than before, as if Astarte herself now openly accused her of disloyalty and treachery. She let go of the ceremonial sashes, stepped back abruptly, and whirled toward the weary slaves. "They are badly dyed! What clumsy work! Until you learn to do it right, no food for two days!"

In protest, Tirzah was on her feet. "My sister —" she began. Ahabina's face had gone stone-like with angry surprise.

"They are badly dyed, I said! I will not accept them. And these slaves, these fools — " She waved arrogantly in the direction of the slave-women. "These fools are to be punished. No food for two days!" She whirled to face Ahabina. "See to it! Or you, too, will go without food!" She turned on her heel and in two strides was at the steps leading down to the family's quarters and her own chambers.

In two more strides she left the roof, the heat, and the dark disapproval of her sister and Ahabina. All that went with her into the quiet coolness of her chambers were shifting moods and an emptiness that was beginning to frighten her.

2

Several days journey to the west and south of Jericho, in the city of Ramesseum, a stocky, dark-haired, young man named Joel ben Dishan strode briskly toward the Hall of Counsel in answer to a royal summons. Hebrew by birth in the tribe of Judah, captive and slave-in-bondage, he had most recently been appointed chief scribe to Rameses the Second, great Pharaoh of the land of the Nile and all her imperial holdings.

He was proud of this new job. But at the moment, the royal summons annoyed and puzzled him. The timing was wrong. The day's regular sessions of accepting and recording tribute from provincial governors had long since been completed. Before the sun rose to its zenith, the noisy, milling provincials had departed.

Except for the young page who moved along in front of him, the sun and shadow-laced corridor was deserted. As it should be, he thought with a grimace. This was the time of day when Pharaoh and all other men of good sense should be taking their leisure and their pleasure. That is what annoyed him most about the summons. It interrupted what had been planned as a very companionable afternoon with a favorite maiden of the court.

He passed a clepsydra, scarcely noticing its time-measuring drip of water, and spat in annoyance. Perhaps the great Rameses was finally growing senile. For more than half a century he had ruled. At some point, he must grow senile.

The heat pressed in. Beads of sweat broke and tracked

16

uncomfortably down his face. He pulled a thin cotton square from the green girdle at his waist and mopped at his forehead. He would never get used to this clinging heat — not if he stayed here a lifetime and no more than he would ever completely cease to yearn for his own people.

Ahead of him, the page seemed to scurry faster with the load of scrolls, styluses, the bags of charcoal, and the waterpot for mixing ink. Joel called out for him to slow down. It was too hot to hurry, even in answer to Pharaoh's summons. At once the boy obeyed, and his tunic flapped comically about his knees at the abrupt change of pace.

In spite of his annoyance, Joel grinned. He'd been about this same age when he'd first been brought to Egypt as a captive. He wondered if this lad's life would turn out to be as comfortable as his had been. For even after fourteen years in this place, he still marveled at the chain of events that had made his slavery easier than he'd ever thought possible.

Strangely enough, it all had started with some bits of charcoal and papyrus. He had stolen them and then hid himself away in a remote corner of the palace to draw and sketch. He was so absorbed with his efforts that he failed to hear the approach of the awesome one-eyed priest called Rechibidan — an architect of great merit who held high rank at court. His architectural achievements included the sculptures of Rameses at Abu-Simbel. These enormous full-figure replicas of the king, hewn from red granite bluffs, had been adroitly designed and positioned to catch every trace of sunlight; thus adding to the illusion of the Pharoah's godlike supremacy. A life-long confidant of Rameses, the priest exerted unusual influence in a quiet, unabrasive way. Many felt he was the second most powerful man in the empire.

For several moments, Joel had remained unaware that the priest had stopped and with interest was watching him sketch. When he did glance suddenly around and saw the priest, his first instinct was to hide. But the solid rock wall at this back offered no place.

His second instinct was to run. But the steps at his side were too high to jump onto from a sitting position. His only avenue of escape, straight forward, was blocked by the tall figure of the priest.

So Joel sat rigid with fear staring up at the imposing, unsmiling, one-eyed authority.

"What name do they call you?" Rechibidan asked. Neither anger not threat was in his tone.

But, why should he trust him? He was an Egyptian and full of trickery. He'd tell the page-master; and the page-master had no use for idlers and dreamers, especially if they were Hebrew.

As if reading his mind, the priest gave an almost imperceptible nod of understanding. A smile started to crinkle at one corner of his mouth.

Joel misread the expression as consent for him to flee. He scrambled to his feet and plunged forward.

But one shove of the priest's foot sent him sprawling backward. The sketches and bits of charcoal skittered out of his grasp and fell onto the stone flooring in front of the priest.

Rechibidan chuckled. "Let's hope you sketch and draw better than you hide and run!" He stretched out his hand. "Let me see those sketches."

Joel hesitated; watched warily.

"Pick them up," Rechibidan ordered in a calm tone. "I can't see them where they lie."

Still Joel hesitated, fearful of a ruse that would lead to physical abuse.

Once again the priest assured him. "I mean you no harm. Your drawings look quite good. But I can't see them as well as I'd like to from this distance." He made an almost apologetic gesture toward the patch covering his bad eye; then smiled rather sadly.

Slowly, Joel rose. In the priest's good eye there was no malice, only interest and firm insistence. He moved toward the sketches, picked them up and handed them to the priest.

Rechibidan thanked him and began to study the drawings.

In surprise, still suspecting some kind of trick, Joel stared after the tall figure as the priest moved toward the steps, sat down, and motioned for Joel to join him.

Seated beside him, Joel noticed Rechibidan's hands. They were strong, yet sensitive. Their lines held the expressiveness of the artist and the squareness of the practical craftsman. With a jolt, he was reminded of his father's hands.

They too, had the expressiveness of the artist and the practicality of the craftsman. He remembered them so clearly. Especially when his father was working on the carvings for the sacred Ark of the Covenant that would reside within the secret place of the tabernacle. Thoughts of his mother and sister followed. A pang of loneliness and deep yearning went through him. How good it had been when his family was still all together.

"You draw very well," Rechibidan said, glancing at him. "Perhaps even better than any of the boys now in the priestly school."

Joel blinked in surprise.

"You have received instructions in drawing, haven't you?"

He nodded yes.

"Do you also read and write?"

Again, he nodded.

"Who schooled you in these things?

"My father."

Rechibidan handed the sketches to Joel, then leaned back, rested both elbows on an upper step, and appraised him with a long look that seemed to probe to the deepest corners of his mind.

"What was your father's trade?" he finally asked.

"Scribe — and craftsman-aide to the great crafts-master, Aholiab."

"Ah-h-h-h —" Rechibidan gave a smile of new interest. "Then you are of the tribe of Judah."

Joel straightened and looked at the priest with new respect. "You know of our tribe?"

"I do, indeed."

"You know of Aholiab? Then you knew my father, Dishan ben David?" The questions tumbled out in a spate of eagerness. He hungered for some familiar contact in this awful alien land.

But with regret, Rechibidan shook his head. "I wish I had, my young friend. Aholiab is one of the great designers of our times. And I'm sure your father must have been equally skilled."

Joel glanced away, embarrassed that he had shown eagerness or any other emotion to an enemy.

"I'm truly sorry I didn't know either of them as friends," Rechibidan went on. "But I know you. Or at least I will, if you'll tell me your name." He gave a soft chuckle of tolerance.

After a long moment, Joel told him.

"Very well, Joel ben Dishan, perhaps the priest's school can help you become even more of a master of drawing than you already are." Rechibidan clapped him on the shoulder and stood up. "At least Egypt won't waste your talents if I place you there."

Rechibidan had been true to his word. In the years that followed, Joel thought often of the incident and wondered at the alchemy of fate that had smiled on him that day. It apparently still smiled, thanks to Rechibidan, for he most recently had been named chief scribe to Rameses the Second.

He passed a diorite bust of the Pharaoh, automatically bowed to it, then turned toward the huge wooden doors of the hall of counsel.

The page was struggling with the door, and the waterpot tipped dangerously. Joel moved quickly to keep it from spilling. "Be careful, young oaf!"

Gratefully, the page slipped through the doorway ahead of him and scurried down the long expanse toward the short-legged writing desk positioned near and to one side of the royal dais.

Joel hesitated, finding the contrast between the sunlight and dimness of the hall blinding. His perspiring body welcomed the hall's coolness. He silently praised Rechibidan's genius for designing a clerestory that caught every breeze to best advantage. Even in the hottest weather, more than 2,000 people could be accommodated here in comfort. Equally as important as the coolness was the grandeur and size of the hall. It simply overwhelmed provincial emissaries and kept them subservient, if not loyal, to the throne of Egypt.

Around the periphery of the columned vastness were sculptures of the royal household. Another testimony to Rameses' might and potent mastery. The display included another diorite bust of Rameses, one of his Queen Nofretere, one of each of his four most favored royal concubines, and alabaster busts of two-score of his favorite children. The rest of the one-hundred-and-fifty children he had sired were of little importance and thus ignored in this gallery of the family.

As Joel's eyes accustomed themselves to the soft interior light, he moved forward along the line of statuary toward his writing desk. There were only five visitors. But they were obviously important visitors. For they sat below and facing the royal dais in the loti-form chairs designated for the more important provincial dignitaries. Approaching as he was, Joel could not yet identify them. And because they were involved in a heated argument among themselves, he could not identify their dialects.

On the royal dais, Rameses lounged diagonally across the great throne chair in his customary pose of indifference. His almond eyes were half-closed, concealing his incredible alertness and perception. It was all part of a deliberate affectation to make all visitors feel unworthy in his presence. Observing this disguised intelligence in Rameses once again, Joel realized there was no senility in Pharaoh yet.

Alongside Rameses in the throne chair was the royal cat. Sleek, black, and exuding disdain, it groomed one paw with a crimson tongue. Philo, the vizier, and Riccho, the first chamberlain, were to the left of the Pharoah. Both were staring, in apparent fascination, at the royal cat. Rechibidan sat to the right of Rameses, observing the visitors' argument.

When Joel reached his writing desk, he hesitated, then bowed in the direction of the dais.

Noticing him, Rechibidan leaned toward Rameses and nodded in Joel's direction. The Pharaoh's acknowledgment was a barely perceptible flick of the royal eyelids.

Joel knew the sign well. He motioned for the page to bring him the scrolls that had the records of provincial tribute-tax. They were the current ones, prepared earlier in the day by another scribe. With them in hand, he moved from the writing desk to his customary position closer to the dais. At this point, he got his first good look at the five quarrelsome guests.

He knew only one of them; a bulging Canaanite merchant named Ali ben Azi who was often here in the royal court to barter and to offer rumors to the Egyptian hierarchy. Next to him was a tall, sinewy man with the ramrod posture of a soldier. Of the other three, one was old and wizened. His skin had the look of wet papyrus, but from his manner and dress Joel guessed him to be a provincial king.

Seated next to the old man was a man about Joel's age. He, too, had the bearing of a soldier. The fifth man, his sardonic profile and arrogant bearing clearly evident, appeared to be the most quarrelsome.

From his manner of dress, he also appeared to be the most important member of the group. Unusual scrollwork embroidered his linen tunic and a handsome hooded robe. Suspended about his neck on a golden chain was a spectacular sapphire and emerald amulet.

With his chamberlain's staff, Riccho began to pound for silence. The sound reverberated through the vastness of the hall. The old man glanced toward the dais. The fat merchant swiveled toward his companions in an attempt to halt the argument that continued between the arrogant one and the man with the soldierly bearing.

Again, Riccho pounded the staff against the marble flooring until, at last, order was restored and silence echoed through the hall. Imperiously, the fifth man turned toward the dais. The full shape of the amulet became clearly visible. It was a replica of the Canaanite goddess Astarte. In the same instant, the man's identity became clearly visible, too.

An acid surge of recognition and a thousand painful memories shot through Joel's head and pulsed in his veins. The man was Shatha, high priest of Jericho.

Shatha's despotic looks were unaltered by the years. Unaltered also, Joel realized in the after-shock, were his own bone-deep loathings of the man. His vision blurred. The only thing altered by the years was his own appearance and situation. No longer was he a boy in captivity. Now, he was a man of substance with powerful friends and a position of influence.

Abruptly, Rameses called for the reading of the record of tribute-tax for the province of Jericho.

Joel fumbled with the scroll, nearly dropping it. Rechibidan straightened slightly in his chair. Muttering an oath, Joel fought to regain his composure.

"Come, come, scribe!" Rameses demanded testily, "The records, produce the records for Jericho."

22

"Your Eminence," called out the oldest of the visitors as he struggled onto his feet. "As king of Jericho, I have known you many years. We have always dealt honorably with each other, have we not?"

Rameses nodded, his attention momentarily diverted.

Joel welcomed the interruption. Not only did he need more time to quell the anger inside himself, but he was now discovering that the records put down by another scribe were in a different sequence. To find the information being demanded by Rameses, he would have to search through three scrolls.

Swearing under his breath, he turned and motioned for the page who was scurrying forward with the rest of the scrolls. Together they began the search while King Balaar droned on about old times and about the more recent hard times that had come upon Jericho. From moment to moment, Ali ben Azi the merchant aided the king in his presentation of "lean times" and "trying situations."

"Your understanding, O Rameses," the old king concluded, "is our greatest need and our reason for seeking a special audience with you."

Rameses nodded again, as if considering King Balaar's remarks with unusual generosity. The royal cat yawned.

"My honorable king," protested the tall, soldierly man, coming to this feet. "I don't wish to offend you." He nodded deferentially toward the old man. "But my concern is not the hard times Jericho has seen, but rather, the hard times she may come to see!"

Surprised, the four men on the royal dais turned and stared at him.

"Now, General Birsha," the old king reproved, "We've already had several discussions about this matter and I —"

"I'm sorry, m'lord," Birsha insisted. "But I must use this opportunity to say what I believe."

Shatha started up out of his chair, a dark and dreadful look on his face. Ali ben Azi grabbed his arm, pulling him back, even though his own face was red with chagrin.

"What *do* you believe, General Birsha," Rechibidan prompted.

"I believe that the amount of tribute tax is not the central issue we should be talking about," the general said in a calm, flat tone.

"Then what is?" Rechibidan prompted again.

General Birsha turned slightly, directing his words to Rameses. "The central issue we should be talking about is our greatest need — and yours, mighty Pharaoh."

"And what might that be," asked Philo, the Vizier.

"Defenses!"

"Defenses against what?" Philo asked in astonishment.

"Defenses against the Hebrews!"

The words fell against an abrupt, stunned silence. Joel jerked away from the scrolls and stared. For the second time in as many minutes, shock rolled over him. But this was shock of an entirely different kind. He continued staring at General Birsha, probing for signs of treachery or deceit. But only sincerity etched the granite-like face and radiated from his eyes.

Was it finally to come? Could it really be true? Joel's throat went dry. Was it now in his own generation that the age-old prophecy was to be fulfilled? A sudden rush of memories flashed through his mind. With a spellbinding energy, the indomitable, white-maned Moses had spoken long ago of the Holy presence of one God and of His promise to His chosen people. *The day shall come when we shall again inhabit the land of our fathers' inheritance,* Moses had said.

A tremor went through Joel. He turned and found Rechibidan looking at him as if he was reading his mind.

Philo broke the tense silence with a hard laugh. "Rubbish!"

Birsha was unmoved.

"You forget my dear general," Philo went on, "it was the great Rameses who let the Hebrews leave this valley of life in the first place. Do you think he would have if they were a threat to any part of the imperial holdings?"

"The exodus occurred many years ago," Birsha countered without raising his voice. "Today, the Hebrews are a threat!"

"And an imminent threat, honorable vizier." It was the young man who rose to his feet. He was nearly as tall as the general, but there the resemblance ended. For he was about Joel's age, and he was as smoothly handsome as the general was lined and worn. "Only recently," he said in a clear, steady

24

voice, "the Habiru defeated the Canaanite king, Arad, at Hormah. Then, they moved to the Valley of Zared where they parleyed with the chieftains of Moab."

Philo and Rechibidan exchanged questioning glances.

"Captain Yanshuph is right," General Birsha inserted. "When the Moabites refused the Habiru passage through their lands, they made war on Sihon and took his lands."

The scroll sagged in Joel's hands. The prophecy was coming true. It was, indeed.

Pharaoh's eyes flicked open in genuine astonishment.

"Most recently," Captain Yanshuph continued, "our most trusted couriers told us the Habiru will assault the craggy stronghold of Bashan within a short time. They also told us that even if the Hebrews defeat Og of Bashan, they will not be satisfied."

Rechibidan turned his head in order to fully scrutinize General Birsha with his good eye. "How say you to this, general?"

Birsha paced forward a step or two, then carefully stopped, as if reminded of the distance that protocol dictated he must keep from the royal dais. "I agree with the couriers, honored priest. The oases and unpredictable watering places where the Habiru have been are now too small for them. Their flocks are large. Their people are large in number. Canaan's pastures, fields and water beckon them."

Philo leaned forward, scoffing: "Pastures and water may beckon them, but not Jericho. It's a fortified, double-walled city. It's a stronghold!" He glanced about looking for confirmation among the others on the royal dais and found it only in Riccho.

"Shepherds and wanderers may be able to win tribal skirmishes in Moab," the chamberlain offered, "but they have no means to assault a stronghold like Jericho."

Shatha made a guttural sound. His face was a mask of stony anger.

Birsha walked slowly back to his chair. But instead of sitting down, he walked around it and traced one sinewy finger along the polished arm and back-rest. "Jericho tempts the Hebrews for three reasons," he said in a patient tone. "First, she shoulders heavily against some of the richest land in all of Canaan.

25

Only Tyre and Phoenicia have more natural bounty to offer."

Uneasily, the merchant Ali ben Azi shifted his considerable bulk in the chair and mopped at his forehead. Riches were not the thing to talk about.

"The second reason Jericho tempts the Hebrews," Birsha continued, "is that while she may be a stronghold, she's also gateway to the eastern flank of Rameses' great empire; and thus, it appears that a threat against Jericho is also a threat against Rameses!"

Shatha could no longer contain himself. With a muttered curse, he started out of his chair.

But the thin, blue-veined hand of Jericho's king detained him this time. The old king had been watching Rameses and had notice the look of admiration that filtered across the royal face.

Joel also noticed it, and found it unusual. Generally, Pharaoh's opinion of provincials was one of disdain. Their posturings and subservience galled him. Rechibidan had once observed that Pharaoh encouraged such fawning by his own demeanor. But since he was Pharaoh, that was rather beside the point. In this instance however, Birsha's straight-forward logic apparently had generated admiration.

"Your logic is excellent, General Birsha," intoned Rameses. "But your information is questionable."

"How so, my lord?"

"The Hebrews are now encamped at Kadesh-Barnea. Since this is some distance from Jericho, the threat you fear is not imminent." He stroked the head of the royal cat and added, "In fact, it may never go beyond an unlikely threat."

Birsha demurred, but Rameses cut him off. "It's also known to Pharaoh that the Hebrews have shaved their beards in mourning of Aaron. They will not make war against anyone as long as they are mourning the brother of Moses."

Joel glanced at the monarch in surprise. Aaron's death had occurred months before, and his people mourned their dead for only thirty days. The old prophecy called for Aaron's death to be the signal for the march through Moab and on into Canaan. Surely, the Jerichoans knew as much.

"But sire," Birsha protested, "there must be some misunderstanding. Our couriers report the Hebrews in Moab at this time."

"So you have told us, General Birsha," Rameses conceded in a voice mildly condescending. "And you were telling us your reasons for believing the Hebrew threat to be real. But you've mentioned only two of the three reasons you hold such belief. What is the third?"

Without hesitation, Birsha responded: "Their God! Their Jehovah, the unseen one!"

A tremor went through Joel.

Philo and Riccho stiffened at the insult.

"The Hebrews believe this Jehovah leads them to an age-old destiny."

Rameses and Rechibidan remained motionless, as did the captain, king, and merchant from Jericho. But Shatha exploded onto his feet with a curse. It reverberated through the great hall of counsel.

"What rot!" he spat at Birsha. "There is no god greater than Canaan's great goddess Astarte! She is even worshipped in Egypt!"

Resentment slid into Rameses' great almond eyes at the inference that some other power — any other power — was or could be greater than his. And for it to be proclaimed that he was outranked by a Canaanite goddess compounded the insult.

Ignoring the forbidden distance between Rameses and visitors, Shatha angrily strode toward the royal dais. The royal cat hissed and arched its back defensively.

"The Hebrew god is nothing!" Shatha scoffed. "He's invisible. He has no statues. The goddess Astarte is more than a match for that." With an obscene gesture, he added, "And as for leading the Hebrews, this so-called god of theirs has only led them into forty years of desert wanderings."

Rameses' eyes narrowed to serpent-like slits. This was the ultimate insult.

Birsha and the other Jerichoans stood thunderstruck. For now, Shatha was inferring that Rameses had never heard of the Hebrew God. Not only that, but Shatha had rubbed salt into Pharaoh's most sensitive wound. Rameses' stubborn refusal to permit the Hebrews to leave Egypt, despite crop failures, destruction of herds, plagues of frogs, locusts, and boils, had cost him his first-born son. Only then had he relented and secretly, by night, told the Hebrews to leave. When they did so, an angry outcry arose in Rameses' court. "Why have you done this? Why have you let Israel go from serving us?" To placate them, Rameses pursued the Israelites to recapture them. But the hand of the Hebrew God prevailed and sorely defeated Pharaoh with the miracle at the Red Sea. The episode had almost cost Rameses his throne. It had taken him years to fully recover the respect and authority he had previously enjoyed.

And now, an arrogant, provincial priest dared to broach the subject once more. For Shatha to have dredged up the past was a disastrous blunder.

Resentment flaring into open anger, Rameses straightened in the royal chair. In doing so, the royal cat was dislodged and unceremoniously dumped onto the dais. Rameses stood up, left the dais and disappeared through a private doorway.

Shatha misread the intent of the departure and moved even closer to the dais.

Rechibidan remained unmoving. But, the royal cat arched its back and hissed a warning.

Shatha was undeterred. His eyes, glittering with self-importance, were fastened on Rechibidan's astonished face. When he was barely a stride away from the very edge of the dais, the cat hissed again, and with a screech hurled itself at the arrogant figure of Jericho's high priest.

Attempting to fend off the sharp-clawed attack, Shatha hit the cat with an awful blow. It dropped to the marble floor, lifeless.

Silence dropped over the men. In horrid astonishment, they stared at the sleek, black, unmoving form at Shatha's sandaled feet. Lengthening and deepening, the silence seemed to match a growing animosity toward Jericho's high priest.

It was Rechibidan who finally broke the stillness. He stepped down from the dais and went toward Joel and the page. "Did you find the record of Jericho's tribute-tax?"

Joel nodded and held up the scrolls. The amount was a

pittance. Even the poorest of the poor provinces contributed more. In fact, the list was so short he wondered why the other scribe had recorded it on three separate scrolls.

"Is this all?"

Again, Joel nodded.

A reflective frown crossed Rechibidan's face. "It appears our visitors may have paid someone to confuse this!" He ran a questioning finger down the lists.

500 cubits linens
6 cor dates
50 cabs balsam rum
17 ephah assorted grains
14 beqas lapis-lazuli
2 large casks spices
3 live ostriches
2 pairs peafowl
12 lion skins
5 baskets assorted pots with Royal Crest
6 bags (small) turquoise nuggets

"What kind of fools do they take us for?" The frown on Rechibidan's face darkened. "The tax collectors we send to this fat whore of a province regularly meet with disaster. Her king comes here playing on friendship and claiming poverty. Her general talks of war with the Hebrews. Her tax records are made confusing. And her high priest —" Voice trailing off, he handed the scrolls back to Joel and abruptly returned to the dais, pausing only to look again at the lifeless form of the royal cat.

The Jerichoans remained rooted in silence and in dread anticipation. Behind them, a squad of palace guards had stealthily appeared and stationed themselves around the columned periphery of the great hall of counsel. The action went unnoticed by the Jerichoans.

"Your insults, men of Jericho, come in many forms," Rechibidan thrusted. "But they do not go unanswered. In the name of Rameses, I issue this decree." He motioned for Joel to record the edict. "All future tribute-tax levied against the Province of Jericho will be three times greater than the largest of former contributions!"

An involuntary gasp escaped from King Balaar. Shatha's slate-gray eyes darkened dangerously. Ali ben Azi went pale. And the faces of Birsha and Yanshuph acknowledged denial of their pleas for men-at-arms.

"Further, I decree in the name of Rameses, that a new rabiser, a new tax-collector, will return to Jericho with you this very day. Any attempt whatsoever to thwart his work will result in the imprisonment of all five of you."

The Jerichoans shifted with sullen uneasiness.

Rechibidan turned with a forceful motion. "Write in their names individually, scribe." He turned again to face the Jerichoans and momentarily stared at the unmoving form of the royal cat. He stepped off the dais to directly confront Shatha. "I further decree that if any danger befalls the new rabiser, he will be avenged — avenged by the execution of Jericho's high priest!"

3

Night canopied the Land of Canaan. Under its star-embroidered velvet, Ali ben Azi's caravan wound down from the hills toward Jericho's waiting walls. The procession was quiet. Only the sounds of plodding hooves, the creaking of harness, and occasional mutterings of the drovers and herdsmen intruded.

A night bird screeched, momentarily breaching the silence. Joel stirred and adjusted the leather pouch inside the girdle at his waist. It contained the seals and official documents of his new position, rabiser to the province of Jericho, and a free man. The mighty Pharaoh Rameses the Second had proclaimed it within an hour after the scene in the great hall of counsel.

"I understand your enmity toward Jericho and her high priest," the old monarch had said to him. "Rechibidan reminded me of your past experience. You should make a good adversary to those fellaheen. We need a rabiser in Jericho with a personal interest in holding those Canaanite jackals in line!"

The monarch had risen and walked to him. "You will have several duties other than collecting my rightful tax. This talk of the Hebrews disturbs me. If we do have to fortify Jericho, I want to be prepared. You are to make drawings of every fortification, every watering place, and give me details on how they are sentried."

Joel made a deep bow of both appreciation for the new job and to hide the admiration he felt for Pharaoh's grasp of the Hebrew situation. His reactions in front of the leaders of

Jericho had made him appear disinterested and even senile in his assessment of the threat, but just the opposite was true.

"One thing more, Joel ben Dishan," the old emperor had said placing a surprisingly strong hand on his shoulder, "You go back to Jericho free of your bondage to Egypt. Because of your loyalty to Rechibidan, I proclaim you a free man and I bid you well."

He had been outfitted with all the proper trappings of his new position: clothing, foodstuffs, herds, two large travel litters, pack animals, a large trail-tent, and a chest filled with papyrus scrolls and writing tools. The young slave-page who had served him well and who reminded him of his own plight years before would accompany him. He had also been supplied with pouches of gold coins, the seal of official documents, four lackeys, four porters, twenty men-at-arms, and his long-time friend-in-captivity, the Nubian slave Hejaz.

A free man! The reality of the idea soothed him even now. He luxuriated in the thought even here at the rear of ben Azi's caravan where the stench of the trail overwhelmed his nostrils. A free man. And all thanks to Rechibidan. He had tried to thank him. But when the time had come for farewell, he had found no words for the feelings that crowded his heart. As if reading his mind, the one-eyed priest had smiled and nodded. And then with a sudden turn to seriousness, Rechibidan had counseled, "Retain your conscience, my son. Walk with patient wisdom, and carefully weigh the values of freedom and servitude.

"All men are slaves. All serve some master. Only the names of the masters differ. Now that you are a free man, you will realize this more clearly. And you will realize, too, that no man can silence his own heritage. Its demands cry out even more loudly than those of friendship or of loyalty."

The words moved him so deeply that he could only grasp the strong hand that had set him free, cling to it briefly, and then turn quickly away. He would miss his friend. He would never forget him.

With a heavy sigh, he stared out into the black night of Canaan. The caravan progressed through the last of the foothills. The sandy roadway spilled out onto a plain. In the distance, torches flared a grudging welcome at Jericho's west gate. The walls seemed smaller than he remembered. But it had been fourteen years. He was only a lad then, a captive headed into bondage.

As the caravan moved closer to the gates, Hejaz came up to walk protectively at the right side of Joel's litter. Two men-at-arms flanked the left side. "The lackeys, the page, and the pack animals need your protection more than I do," Joel laughed, directing Hejaz to dismiss the men-at-arms.

Other caravans now were converging on the maw of Jericho's gate. Voices, animals, and movement festered, swelled, and erupted into shouts of recognition for the litters bearing Jericho's khazianu. Soldiers barked out orders to let the royal and priestly litters pass through the gateway first. And then, almost before Joel realized it, his own litter was into the confines of the gate itself. He straightened to get a better view.

The maw was as long in distance as the city's double-walls were wide. Between the walls was a space wide enough for two people to walk side-by-side. It was impossible in this crowd to gauge exact measurements, but he made a mental note to check this out for his drawings. More men and animals blocked his view. The only thing he could accurately describe was the heat and the stench. Swearing under his breath, he grabbed for a linen square. The Whore of Canaan still wore the same perfume!

As suddenly as they had entered, they now exited the narrow maw. Torch-bearers and a cordon of palace guards formed about the litters of Balaar and Shatha. Orange-yellow flames flickered in the shadowy streets. Drivers and herdsmen cat-called; bearers cursed; mercenaries and beggars shouted; and music filtered through the din. The noise inside the city matched her insufferable smell.

Her houses weren't much better. Built of libn, the sun-baked plaster so common to all construction, they were ugly and close-packed. Too poorly-based to stand alone, Joel decided, they possessed mutual walls and leaned in precarious support of each other. Like the weaknesses of the people they sheltered, if one should fall, all would go.

Nowhere could he see a building with the strength or the

33

grace that Rechibidan could build of the same materials. On the rooftops of these ugly houses, the people of Jericho peered down at the incoming caravans. They waved torches and shouted greetings to them. But in comparison to the huge outpourings of humanity that greeted Pharaoh's arrivals, this welcome to Balaar and Shatha was pitifully thin. Jericho, it seemed, was in many ways a poor mimic of Egypt.

The caravan slowed. Balaar and Shatha's litters disengaged and moved off in a different direction. Joel glanced about, checking on his own retinue. All seemed in order. As he straightened, a sudden movement in the shadows of a nearby house caught the corner of his eye. A beggar, shapeless and hooded, pressed toward his litter.

Before he could act, Hejaz intercepted the man. With a single swift motion, he sent the ragged creature flying back into the shadows. A heavy thud resulted and Joel winced. "That's one fellow who'll beg no more this night."

"Nor will his companion," the Nubian replied.

"What companion?"

"This one." Hejaz handed him a long, slender knife. "In spite of Pharaoh's edict, they'll make your stay here a short one, if they can."

Joel examined the knife as best he could in the dim light. It seemed crudely made, yet its blade was as deadly as that of a fine Persian dagger. A shiver of caution traced between his shoulders. Carefully, he placed the dagger inside his waist girdle, determined to examine it more thoroughly in better light.

Once again, the caravan moved forward. Balaar's and Shatha's litters had disappeared in the direction of a large structure surrounded by sycamores and palms. Joel hoped it was the khan where he'd been told he would stay. The journey had been tedious. He was ready for a bath, if there was such a thing in this forsaken, stinking place. And he looked forward to sleeping on something other than the desert floor.

"Where's Captain Yanshuph's litter?" he asked Hejaz.

"Still ahead of us. Going the same way we are." Hejaz turned, pointing to the large structure surrounded by the sycamores and palms. "Is that the palace?"

Joel peered again through the dimness, brightened only by the flickering torches. A fleeting sense of recognition went through him and he gave an involuntary shudder. This was Jericho's temple; it loomed menacingly. Flames of torches glowered at its entrance and bathed the immense, crudely-carved image of a nude woman in weird, unnatural shadows.

The figure's great bulging abdomen, signifying the fruit of life and the fertility of the female, was distorted by the torch-light. Massive stone hands cradled huge breasts from which writhed a graven image of the serpent god, El. Two other vipers circled the thighs, their heads uplifted as if in praise of the loins. On one massive toe rested the image of a dove. This was the statue of Astarte, great earth-mother goddess of fertility and abundance.

Joel shuddered again as old memories flooded his mind. He pushed them aside. He was not ready. "Walk with patient wisdom," Rechibidan had counseled him. He would try. He must.

"The khan," Hejaz called out. "It must be just ahead. I see the captain's litter turning into a large courtyard."

"Good. We can all use some hot food. And Hejaz, remember our plans for precautions. I want no one eating from the khan's pots or drinking from its supply of rum or water. We'll use our own as long as possible."

Joel leaned back in his litter, closed his eyes and his mind to the temple and to Astarte. There would be time enough to exact retribution — time enough later.

As the porters set down his litter inside the courtyard, he stepped out, stretched and savored the feeling of solid ground beneath his feet. The place was crowded. Large as it was, people and animals were almost as close-packed as in the maw of the gate moments before. Captain Yanshuph was nowhere in sight.

"Jericho is well-named," Hejaz growled, coming alongside him and sniffing the fetid air.

Joel nodded, remembering the Akkadian word for Jericho meant 'fragrant.'

"Only for you, my friend," the Nubian grumbled, "would I have come to this place. Only for you."

"Only for me would I have come," Joel grinned, looking about for the young captain, and wondering what sort of lodgings his hosts would provide.

Slave-women tended meat at three huge cooking fires. Everywhere, groups of hungry travelers hunkered in close groups. Other slave-women scuttled back and forth from a pantry-like room at one side of the courtyard. They were laden with great square loaves of bread and steaming bowls. One slave scurried in front of Joel and Hejaz almost spilling the contents. They quickly backed up.

"Probably full of lentils," said Joel. "That's the mainstay of a Canaanite's diet, you know."

Hejaz grimaced.

"You'll have to get used to them."

"Neither of us will ever get used to anything Canaanite," Hejaz retorted, his brow wrinkling in distaste at the surroundings. Son of a Nubian king long since defeated by Rameses' armies, Hejaz had been the property of the royal court for more years than he claimed to remember. In reality, he had been a slave-in-bondage only a few months longer than Joel, and was only a year or so older. Tall, brawny, scholarly, and a superb athlete, he and Joel had been friends since the day Joel entered the priestly school. Abruptly, he motioned toward the main building of the khan.

Joel turned and saw Captain Yanshuph bearing down on them. "If he wasn't Canaanite, he might be a good man to have for a friend," Joel mused, remembering the young captain's conduct in front of Rameses.

Hejaz grunted.

Yanshuph stopped before them and gave a curt nod.

"What's this?" Hejaz challenged. "You give no salaam of welcome to Pharaoh's rabiser?"

Yanshuph reddened and gave a quick bow. "This is the khan of the honorable Peridia," he announced, straightening. "He is one of Jericho's most influential and respected citizens."

"Then why is this most prominent landlord not here to greet my master?" Hejaz pursued.

"The honorable Peridia is also the father of my wife," Yanshuph shot back. "As his son by marriage I bid you —" He paused, glanced nervously over his shoulder and up toward the roof of the main building.

Joel followed the look. Two women stood on the rooftop intently watching them.

"I — I — bid you —" Yanshuph began again. "I bid you welcome in the absence of my father-in-law."

With a straight face, Joel accepted the explanation. No one in Jericho would willingly house an Egyptian tax-collector. The owner of the khan would be more unwilling than most. A rabiser was bad for business. From Yanshuph's actions, Joel surmised he had been recently and heatedly reminded of that. But from his personal viewpoint, the khan was the safest place for him and his retinue. It was so public, the Jerichoans would be forced to take every precaution for his safety.

He glanced about, realizing the very location and architecture of the khan provided several protective advantages. It appeared to be situated at the edge of the city. A high libn wall with the entry gate separated the complex from the street down which they had so recently traveled. Its two-story buildings formed a rough rectangle on three sides of the courtyard. The main building and the one to its left appeared to be set flush against the city's walls.

This was far better than being housed in the king's palace amidst loyal palace guards, or in a private residence along Jericho's ugly, crowded streets. Considering the duress of Pharaoh's edict, the Jerichoans had chosen well. A flicker of approval started through him, but Yanshuph's next words quickly extinguished it.

"Your lodgings here are temporary. Other arrangements are being made for you elsewhere."

"No need for that," Joel demurred easily. "My men and I will be quite comfortable here, and quite safe, too. I'm sure you'll see to that."

Yanshuph appeared to pale a bit and once again glanced nervously over his shoulder. The two women on the rooftop began to descend the flight of steps cut into the face of the main building. Halfway down, one woman turned, moved along a second floor passageway and disappeared through a door. The other woman continued down the steps.

Yanshuph abruptly hurried to intercept her at the foot of the steps. A heated argument ensued. Over the noise in the courtyard, their words were indistinguishable. From Yanshuph's gestures, however, it was clear that he was being out-talked.

Joel found it curious that a mere woman could, or would, so hotly defy the captain's authority — especially since he was a member of the landlord's household. But Canaanites were odd in many ways, and women were always unpredictable. "Help him out, Hejaz," Joel ordered, "or we'll never get any food in our bellies, let alone a place to settle into."

Hejaz stepped forward a few paces. "Honorable captain!" His voice boomed out over the noise. "Honorable captain, my master's lodgings, are they in that direction?"

Momentarily, the argument halted as did the crowd noise. But before Yanshuph could reply, the woman stridently took up the argument once more.

"Honorable captain!" Hejaz urged even more loudly, "Your actions betray your words of hospitality."

Several people in the courtyard now stopped eating and talking and turned with curiosity.

"Can it be," Hejaz shouted in feigned amazement, "that we are not welcome here?"

The woman grew still more adamant. Yanshuph held up his hand as if asking for a truce. Laughter rippled through the crowd, and Hejaz warmed even more quickly to his task of humiliating their host. "Good captain!" As a general's aide isn't your authority good everywhere in Jericho?"

The laughter in the courtyard swelled. Joel, arms folded across his chest, leaned back against the side of his travel-litter enjoying the whole situation.

"Well, isn't it?" Hejaz insisted. "Everybody else knows that a general's aide is supposed to have authority. Don't you know that?"

Supportive catcalls rose over a wave of new laughter.

Hejaz made yet another thrust. "A general's aide should command obedience, too!"

"Especially from a woman!" shouted one of the travelers, and a general roar of agreement bounced raucously across the courtyard.

By this time, Yanshuph and the woman were standing motionless, staring at the jeering scene.

"She's either his mistress or she owns the place," someone scoffed.

"What she owns is a sharp tongue!" scorned another.

"And she owns the captain too, from the looks of it!" Hejaz jousted with a booming laugh.

Roughly brushing past Yanshuph, the woman stepped down into the courtyard. Light from the cooking fires now fully revealed her identity to the ridiculing crowd. The reaction of recognition was instantaneous, and to Joel, quite surprising. For like water disappearing into sand, their laughter and jeering drained away and vanished.

Fear invaded the courtyard. In fact, so rapid was the change of mood, and so unexpected, that Joel glanced around to see if he had imagined it or if some personage of great authority had entered the gate. But the crowd's reaction apparently was for the woman.

In subdued respect, they slowly backed away and opened a path for her. An appreciative murmur escaped from Hejaz and Joel well understood why.

She moved toward them with the easy grace of a person of royalty, head held high and arrogantly defiant. Her hair, the color of a raven's wing and shoulder length, was burnished with dancing refractions of firelight. She was of medium height, and the outline of her lithe figure beneath the clinging folds of her linen gown was more than acceptable. She was a beautiful woman. Appreciation stirred in Joel.

Only a few paces from him now, he realized she wore no cosmetics except for a hint of vermillion on her lips and a touch of antimony drawn in fine lines about her eyes. Her features were regular and her skin unblemished.

It was her eyes though, that gave the fire and excitement to her personality. In color, they were the startling blue of lapis-lazuli. In expression, they appraised him with direct and open dislike. He found it amusing, and at the same time strangely disturbing. It was if she considered herself his equal, or perhaps his superior.

Yanshuph, frowning and embarrassed, came up clearing his

39

throat. "I — uh — rabiser, this is the daughter, the eldest daughter of Peridia and sister to my wife. She is called by the name Rahab."

Joel instantly recognized the name. Every gaming room in Egypt had heard of Rahab. She was rumored to be one of the most beautiful women in all of Egypt's provinces. She was also called the Harlot of Jericho. Many men claimed to have known her. Joel acknowledged the introduction with a slight nod.

She remained motionless, her direct, uncompromising gaze not wavering. She appeared to calculate his worth and the measure of his intent in terms of her own convenience. The idea bothered him. Abruptly, he wondered if the stories about her were true.

"My master's name is Joel ben Dishan," Hejaz announced loudly enough for the whole courtyard to hear. "He is rabiser of the mighty Rameses, supreme ruler of all the lands of Egypt."

The crowd murmured in annoyance at their identities and turned away to the more important activities of eating and talking.

"Unfortunately," Joel observed, "the lands of Egypt also include this odorous place."

Resentment flashed hotly in Rahab's eyes. "We supply your ruler with many things of value. Are they odorous, too?"

"Your accounting of them has a very bad stench," he parried, quickly realizing why Yanshuph had trouble arguing with her. She was a woman to be reckoned with. "Less tribute arrives from Jericho than from the poorest of the poor provinces."

Rahab's confident expression faltered. Genuine astonishment filled her eyes as she searched his face for a long moment. Then, she cast such a sharp questioning look at Yanshuph that Joel realized she knew nothing of recent events in Ramesseum. Apparently, Yanshuph had told her nothing of the edict.

"The journey has been long and tedious," Hejaz inserted impatiently. "My master desires his lodgings at once."

"We are very crowded," she said in a wooden tone, still eyeing Yanshuph's masklike face.·

"Your crowd is made up of fellaheen," Hejaz shot back. "My master is the personal envoy of Rameses. You owe him the courtesies of his office."

"I owe him nothing," she said flatly. "We have no lodgings for your master."

"Then where is your master?" Joel thrust. "Where is the master of this khan?"

"Or someone with real authority," Hejaz sniped.

With a quick, conciliatory gesture, Yanshuph reported, "This woman does have authority."

"Oh?"

"Aye! She is quedesah."

"A high priestess?" Joel straightened with surprise. "Well, then, why all the argument? She will make room for us here."

She swiveled toward him.

He laughed. "Oh, yes, quedesah. You will make room for us." He turned reprovingly to Yanshuph. "Why, good captain, why didn't you tell her?"

"Tell me what?" she snapped.

"That your consort, Shatha, offered me the hospitality of this khan." It was a lie, of course. Not a single word had passed between him and the high priest since their departure from Ramesseum. But someone had given instructions to Yanshuph to bring him here. Now that he had seen the place, he was determined to stay and make the most of the protection it would offer. "Now that I know you are Shatha's quedesah, I understand why he wishes me to lodge here."

Angry suspicion and confusion fled through Rahab's startlingly blue eyes. In a way, Joel almost felt sorry for her.

But he considered that unexpected emotion only for a second. Then, he reached for a pouch in his waist girdle, opened it and pulled out a gold coin. "You'll be paid of course, for your hospitality." At arm's length, he offered her the coin.

Yanshuph abruptly objected. "We have a custom of housing special guests for three days without payment. It's — uh — it's just common Canaanite courtesy."

"What do either of them know of courtesy?" Rahab snapped, taking the coin. With deliberate insult, she tested the coin between her teeth. She then spun about and swiftly walked away toward the main building. Yanshuph was left the chore of showing the rabiser to his lodgings.

Their quarters were on the second level. Small and poorly furnished, they obviously would not do as a base of operations. Tallow oil burned in a clay saucer on top of a scarred wooden chest and provided the only light in the room. Near the door was a rough wooden bench with a water jug. In front of it, a small roughly-tiled depression in the earthen floor was meant to serve as a foot-bath. The bedding consisted of two reed mats covered with goatskins piled in one corner. Only a single window relieved the prison-like, mud-baked walls.

It was a very poor room, indeed. Certainly not worth the gold coin. But for the time being, it would have to do. The lackeys finished stacking luggage in one corner under the watchful eyes of Hejaz and then disappeared to bring up food. Joel pulled the official document pouch from his waist girdle and tossed it onto the wooden chest. "These lodgings are scarcely better than those of my first visit to this miserable stink-hole."

"Except there are no bars on the windows and bolts on the doors," Hejaz reminded him. "And — no ropes on your wrists, my friend." He moved to the wooden bench, picked up the water jug, and sloshed some of its contents into the foot-bath. "Come wash your feet. You'll feel better."

"You go first," Joel countered, walking to the window. "Your feet are bigger than mine."

The Nubian gave a good-natured laugh, sat down and undid his sandals.

The window was only wide enough for a medium-sized man to get through but it opened to view the plains of Jericho spreading south from the town. Joel peered out. The Jebuz Road meandering eastward to the River Jordan and back westward to the hill country through which they had just come, shimmered in the soft light of a late-rising moon.

He leaned out farther, glancing up and down to satisfy his assumption that the khan was built on, and was part of, the city's wall. The ground was thirty feet below, and a sheer drop. Not much of an escape route, he thought. Above him, the wall appeared to stop. He assumed it was at that juncture where the broad rooftop of the khan began. It was only a short distance above his head. He would have to investigate further in daylight.

"Is all secure?" asked Hejaz, sloshing his feet in the shallow water of the foot-bath.

He started to pull back from the window to reply when he heard an odd noise. It was a sharp hissing sound, almost like that of a viper. He stopped suddenly, listening. The sound came again. As he focused his attention more intensely, he realized that he had picked up the sounds of a conversation. He motioned for Hejaz to join him at the window. For several seconds, they both remained alert and unmoving, straining to hear the words.

But the conversation was very low-toned. "Hejaz, lift me up through the window so I can hear better." With the Nubian's support, he twisted and wedged himself into the window opening as far as he dared. Now he could make out five different voices. Three of them he knew — Rahab, Yanshuph, and General Birsha. The other two voices were unfamiliar. One of them rumbled with a tone of authority. The fifth one had to be a courier. His words identified him clearly.

"They did not come by the king's highway."

"Then how?" the rumbling voice asked.

"Through the lands of the border tribes. No settled kingdom would allow passage. But since the tribes on the border move as the wind, too, they have no worries about this blight of Israelites!"

Joel's pulse quickened.

"Were they heavily armed?" asked Yanshuph.

"Aye! With swords, sledges, and shields. There were thousands of them. They stormed the mountain strongholds of Bashan as if running across an open plain."

"But the armies of Og withstood them, did they not?" queried the rumbling voice.

"Nay, innkeeper," the courier replied. "Og is defeated. His cities are destroyed. The giant men of Bashan lie dead, and their widows and children wail and weep."

Joel's heart thumped against his chest. The prophecy was coming true.

"Where do these Hebrews go now?" Rahab asked.

"Who can say?" came the reply.

"But what about Edom and the other kingdoms of Moab?" questioned General Birsha. "Didn't they go to the aid of their kinsmen?"

"They had no chance, sir. The Hebrews are very clever. Moses is a shrewd leader."

"Moses?" Rahab gasped. "I thought he was dead!"

"Nay, my lady. Moses still lives. His years have made him a wise leader. He bypassed the other Moabite kingdoms, stayed out of their lands. Therefore, they had no quarrel with him."

"It's the same strategy he used so many months ago," General Birsha explained, "when he led his people to Kadesh. Even though it was a much longer route, he skirted forbidden Canaanite lands rather than do battle. It was in obedience to his God that he did so."

"Obedience to his god?" exclaimed Rahab. "Fah!"

"It is said to be true, my lady," the courier concurred. "But what they found in Kadesh was a wilderness. Its watering-places were filled with thorns. It would not sustain any human life."

"It is as General Birsha predicted earlier," rumbled Peridia. "The wilderness in Kadesh would prompt Moses to move his Hebrews on a march through Moab."

"But I had hoped that Og of Bashan would stop them." General Birsha's tone of disappointment was clear.

A blunt silence ensued. Joel waited tensely, scarcely daring to breathe. The prophecy was coming true, all of it. One day Jericho would also feel the wrath of God's chosen people — his own people, he reminded himself.

"A blight on the Hebrews!" Rahab hissed. "A blight on all of them!"

"Have you reported these things to King Balaar and to Jericho's high priest?" General Birsha asked.

"Nay, sir. I am courier to the honorable Peridia and to the quedesah, not to the temple and the palace."

"It is well," Peridia rumbled. The sound of coins passing from one hand to another was followed by the muffled footsteps going away. Then, all was silent on the rooftop and in the mean, little room housing Joel and Hejaz.

4

As the first pale gold began to spill from the cup of morning, Rahab carefully made her way through the almost-deserted courtyard toward the gate of the khan.

Events of the previous evening weighed heavily upon her. The news of the defeat of Og of Bashan by the Hebrews was as disturbing as the arrival of the Egyptian rabiser had been irritating. How dare Shatha saddle her with him!

She could do nothing about the Hebrews, but she intended to confront her consort and demand relief from the loathsome burden of the rabiser. Reaching the gate, she paused and glanced around to make sure she was not followed. She especially did not wish to be observed — nor accompanied — by Ahabina. In fact, the less she had to do with Ahabina these days, the better. The body-servant still sulked over being ordered to withhold food from the sash-dyers. No matter how much loyalty existed between them, there was no time now to mollify and coddle a sulky slave.

Satisfied that no one was following, she slipped out of the gate and scurried through a stand of sycamores toward the temple. Shatha had not sent a single message of his return. He had not called for her to come to him, nor had he indicated that he even wanted her to know he was back from Ramesseum.

"Fah!" With good reason, she thought irritably, since he had the gall to dump the Egyptian rabiser on her doorstep without a word of warning. Even more bothersome was the rabiser's claim that Jericho's tribute-tax was smaller than the poorest of the poor provinces.

She knew better. Personally, she had checked the tribute list before the caravan left for Ramesseum. It was so large she had complained to her father. Uncharacteristically, he had sided with Shatha. The purpose for this uncharacteristic attitude, she had discovered later, was to help General Birsha persuade Rameses to supply men-at-arms for Jericho. And, after the most recent news from the couriers last night, that need for extra men-at-arms seemed more real than ever. But at the moment, that was beside the point. Shatha owed her an accounting for the presence of the rabiser.

She reached the side of the temple, pulled a wooden key from her scarlet sash, unlocked a half-hidden door, and slipped inside. Stale, musty air assailed her as she made her way carefully down the narrow passage leading to Shatha's private quarters.

He doted on secrecy and privacy. "They enhance the mystery of my position," he had once told her. Later, she had learned that those same qualities also enhanced his wealth. He possessed treasures so rare as to draw the envy of even a Rameses. Long since, she had learned to bargain with him for her share of that wealth. In some ways, she did very well. In other ways, she knew he simply let her collect trifles to compensate for her subjection and her servitude as his courtesan. She also knew he used her as a defensive pawn whenever a threat to his possessions appeared. The most recent — and the most rankling — example of this was the unannounced arrival of the rabiser. Until now, with only one exception, she had put up with it because she had no other choice.

Her one attempt to flee from Shatha occurred on the day she was to become his courtesan and sacred virgin to the temple of Astarte.

On that long ago day, in one fleeting instant, she had recognized what her future with him was to be. With animal fear, she had run from him. For three days she had eluded capture by hiding in Jericho's alleyways and in a riverside grove — with a filthy slave-boy who also sought escape. The runaway slave had given her a strange, worthless amulet — a ring made from a bit of ram's horn and carved with an odd, roughly-beautiful cherubim. She hadn't thought of the ring for years, nor of the meaning it once held for her. Strange she should think of it now. It was a token of a time when she was a different person. She reached the entrance to Shatha's private quarters and went inside without hesitation. The place was very quiet. If he was here at all (and not off sleeping with some temple maiden) he must be sleeping. She paused, taking jealous inventory of the rich furnishings around her. A series of low couches covered in rich fabrics and three magnificent rugs of exquisite design dominated the largest of the rooms.

Brilliant-hued tapestries masked the dun-colored walls and softened the massiveness of hand-carved teak chests. Beyond, overlooking the sacred temple grove, was Shatha's ornate sleeping balcony. Only one other Jericho household could match this grandeur. She had no intention of being robbed of her treasures by an Egyptian rabiser. She hurried on across the large room toward the sleeping balcony. No sound issued from behind the brocaded richness of its curtains. She pushed them open. Her consort sprawled nude and asleep on the great bed.

Pale sunlight scattered across his face and up onto the life-sized statue of Astarte that was carved in the headboard. With a start, she realized Shatha no longer was a young man. The difference in their ages was becoming more obvious all the time. He was nearing forty-five years. His shoulders and upper arms, once taut as saddle leather, were now flaccid-looking. Gray showed clearly in the patch of hair on his chest. His clean-shaven head lolled against the pillow in such a way that his jaw and neck muscles slumped together in fleshy folds and hid the golden chain about his neck. Blue-veined eyelids covered his piercing eyes and gave the mighty Shatha an appearance of vulnerable innocence.

"Innocence, indeed!" she muttered, shaking him roughly by the shoulder.

The eyelids flew open. He struggled upright, one hand groping for the dagger lying at his side.

"You don't need that!" She snatched away the weapon and threw it aside.

The slate-gray eyes came fully into focus and immediately

47

darkened with annoyance. He yanked the coverlet up over himself and turned his back on her. "Leave me be! Begone! Leave me to my peace!"

"What peace do you deserve, m'lord?" she asked in acid sweetness.

"Begone, I say! The trip from Ramesseum was a tedious one!"

"It was also an expensive one!" she snapped back. "You befoul my father's house with an Egyptian tax-collector without even a word of warning!"

A muscle tensed in his shoulder.

"You could have at least sent a messenger, m'lord!"

He said nothing.

She strode angrily around to the other side of the bed and leaned close. "You could have given us some warning — some time to prepare!"

"I have my reasons."

"No doubt!" she flared. "But I want him removed — and now!"

He turned away from her again. "I have my reasons!"

"Fah! on your reasons." She moved again to directly face him. "I want him removed — removed — removed!"

With a muttered oath, he threw back the covers, swung out of bed, and reached for a scarlet robe lying nearby.

"Why thrust the vulture of taxation on me?" she charged. "Why thrust him on my father's household?"

"He stays!"

"No!" She stamped her foot. "I will not have it. It is not reasonable!"

"A high priest does not have to be reasonable!" He shrugged into the robe.

"Neither does a sheep running before a jackal!"

He spun around and eyed her with a warning look of calculation. A vein pulsed angrily in his neck. "The rabiser remains. He stays, I say, at the khan. He is your penalty!"

"Penalty? For what?"

"Failure and carelessness!" he snapped, pulling tight the sash of his robe.

"What failure?"

"Your failure to give your proper share of the tribute-tax we carried to Ramesseum."

In utter astonishment, she watched him pace away. Five hundred cubits of her own fine linens had gone on that caravan, to say nothing of what was sent from the temple storehouses, half of which was hers.

"Jericho's tally was a pittance when we arrived," Shatha charged. "A mere and embarrassing pittance."

In typical fashion, he was turning the blame. How she wished she had questioned Yanshuph more closely about the details of the trip last night. But the appearance of the Egyptian with his retinue had so unsettled her that she had not thought to pursue all the details. One thing she did know. The shorting of the tribute-tax was none of her doing. She walked to the balcony railing and stared down into the temple grove. If the shipment didn't arrive as it had been planned, there could be only three possible explanations. She whirled about and watched her consort search through a jewel case on a far table. He glanced at her, a peculiar, guarded look overlaying the anger in his face.

Slowly, she walked toward him. "Could it be," she accused, "that your share of the tribute was short?"

He gave a mirthless laugh and continued to search through the jewel case. "Or, could it be that there is some other reason?" She moved closer. "Could it be that Jericho's high priest has done something foolish and as a result has lost his influence in Pharaoh's court?"

He said nothing, but his fingers momentarily halted their search through the jewel case.

"That's it, isn't it?" She closed in. "That has to be it. Otherwise, you would not have returned with another rabiser at your heels!"

He stiffened.

"Or were you at his heels?"

He spun around, fear raging darkly in his face and the amulet on the golden neckchain swinging out in a vicious arc.

"That's it, isn't it?" she pursued. "You are at his heels!"

With an oath, he slapped her full in the face. "Leave it be, woman. The rabiser stays in the khan unless you want us all

49

executed!" In a stride, he crossed the room, brushed aside the brocaded curtains, and disappeared.

Executed? The word hit her as hard as had the blow in the face. Momentarily, she sagged against a nearby table. A death edict? What for? What had really happened in Egypt? And why hadn't Yanshuph told her?

The carving of Astarte on the headboard of the great bed glowered down at her much in the same fashion as the temple had seemed to glower at her only a few days before on the roof of the khan. A death edict? Why?

By the time she reached the khan's gate once more, a trembling urgency pushed her to find Yanshuph and question him. The courtyard was now astir. New smells of the day's first meal spiraled up from the cooking fires. Travelers laughed and chattered as they packed their animals for the trail. From the weaving rooms came the traditional slave-chant as the women began to work at the looms. She rushed past them all, intent on finding Yanshuph.

The main room's spacious handsomeness was empty. "Yanshuph?" Wall tapestries deadened the hollow pitch of her voice. "Yanshuph!"

"He is not here, my daughter. He's at the palace with General Birsha." Her father came toward her from the terrace. "They are reporting the news, brought last night by our couriers, to the king."

"Well, has he bothered to tell you yet of the trip to Ramesseum?"

Her father looked puzzled.

"Has he bothered to tell you any of the details of the trip? He certainly left me ignorant of them! There is trouble — with Shatha."

Her father's eyes, strikingly like her own, darkened with dislike at the mention of the name. "What's he done to us now?"

Rahab grasped his forearm. "We must question Yanshuph about the details of the trip, my father. About every detail," she urged. "And quickly!"

With only a moment's hesitation, he summoned a slave to fetch Yanshuph from the palace.

Rahab walked on into the sanctuary of the terrace. Remote

from the clatter of the courtyard and safe from prying eyes and ears, it was the family's favorite meeting place. It nestled in the central part of the khan in an enlarged area between the inner and outer walls of the city. Flowering shrubs colorfully guarded its perimeters. An immense palm tree shaded the area. The tree had been a gift to Peridia from the citizens of Jericho, signifying their respect for him as a man of integrity. As Rahab stepped onto the terrace, her mother, Mozni, smiled up at her. "May your day be golden, my daughter." The small woman was seated on a comfortable divan, a basket of mending in her lap.

Rahab kissed her mother and sat down. Before her was a low table set with baskets of fruit and cheeses, fresh breads, and a pitcher of goat's milk.

"Have you broken fast?" her mother asked.

"She's just returned from the temple," her father explained, coming to join them.

Mozni's smile faded. Her gentle, dark eyes questioned them both.

Peridia eased himself down onto the divan next to his wife and protectively patted her hand. "There's some new trouble with Shatha. But no cause for you to worry."

Mozni set aside her mending basket and held up a small tunic. "This is for our grandchild. A fitting is in order. I must go and find her."

Her reaction was typical. Mozni was of that class of women to which tradition denied any involvement in politics or religion. Compliance with the universal custom had created terrible conflicts for her when her eldest daughter had been thrust into the position of quedesah, and, therefore, into the vortex of Jericho's politics and religion with its overtones of intrigue and malevolence. Over the years, Mozni had contended with the situation in the only way she knew — by totally avoiding any direct knowledge of what went on between her daughter and the high priest. She gathered up her sewing, kissed Rahab, and left the terrace.

Resettling himself on the divan, Peridia asked, "What is it this time? What new trouble does the peacock of the temple bring to us?"

"The rabiser."

51

"Oh-h-h-h —"

"Doesn't it disturb you?"

He shrugged. "A rabiser is much like a burr in the foot, my daughter. A nuisance, but not a permanent threat."

She resented the fact that her father seemed so unperturbed. "Well, this one may prove more than a nuisance!"

"But we'll be rid of him shortly. What damage can he do in just three days? That's all Yanshuph is planning for, surely — the customary three days lodging for a special guest."

"Special guest?" she rasped. "Yanshuph misleads you, my father!"

Peridia scowled in surprise.

"The rabiser is here as a punishment to us." She went on to tell him about the argument with Shatha. The only thing she left out was that her consort had slapped her. It was too humiliating; and besides, she feared what Peridia might attempt to do in retaliation. She would get her own vengeance with Shatha later. For now, the problem was to rid the khan of the rabiser. "We must do something, my father," she concluded. "Shatha's orders are for the rabiser to be lodged here permanently!"

Peridia pushed onto his feet and walked away in anger. But his next words made it clear that he had missed the point she was trying so hard to make; for he said, "The tax we sent to Ramesseum was enormous! Whelp of the devil. Shatha probably had it stolen!"

"Or else he didn't put in his rightful share, after all. But that's not the point, my father. The point is how to get rid of the rabiser. Except, of course, for the details of what Yanshuph didn't tell us!"

"What details?"

"There may be a death edict involved!"

Peridia pulled up short. A heavy frown wedged onto his rugged face. "A death edict? For whom?"

She made a gesture of frustration and shook her head. "Maybe for all five who went to Ramesseum — including Yanshuph — who knows?"

"Nay, Rahab. The death edict does not include me." Yanshuph strode into the room.

She and her father swung around to face him.

"It is only your consort who is under the edict of death," her young brother-in-law declared.

Anger gouged at her. "Why didn't you bother to tell me this last night?"

"You gave me no chance."

"Well you have the chance now," she snapped.

"Yes, Yanshuph," Peridia confirmed sternly, "there is a chance for you to tell it now. And we want to hear it all!"

Yanshuph glanced sheepishly at them both, then made an apologetic gesture and began to relate in full detail what had happened at Ramesseum.

As his report progressed, Rahab sat transfixed with angry astonishment. From her father's face, he was experiencing the same feelings. Under threat of imprisonment for five of Jericho's most important leaders, they were now coerced into paying three times more tribute-tax than ever before and were bound to give a free-hand to the Egyptian rabiser in collecting the tax. The decreed execution of Shatha insured the rabiser's personal and professional safety!

What was worse, the onerous responsibility for the rabiser's safety had been placed squarely on the khan of Peridia. Shatha had seen to that. There was no way to fight back against either the rabiser or Shatha. There was nothing they could do.

Except submit. Once again — submit! The revolting idea pushed her to her feet. "Blasphemy of the gods!" she spat, pacing away. "Fah! upon that rabiser! And Fah! upon that son of a jackal, Shatha!"

Peridia walked to the far edge of the terrace, slamming one fist into his open palm again and again. "Greed — Shatha's damnable greed — and his temper! Why, in the name of all the gods, did he have to kill that cat!"

"You should have told me all this last night, Yanshuph." Rahab accused afresh.

"I tried to," he bristled, defensively. "I tried to — but you were so —"

"I was so what?" she demanded.

"You were so angry at everyone."

"Hold, my children!" Peridia commanded, coming back to

step between them. He grabbed them each by the arm and pushed them apart. "Fighting among ourselves solves nothing. We need ideas, not invectives!"

Rahab relented first. She returned to the divan, picked up a pomegranate from the table in front of her and a small knife.

"Now you're quite sure, Yanshuph," Peridia probed, "that no one else is involved in this death edict?"

"Quite sure, sir," he responded in a much-subdued tone.

"And there is nothing more of importance that needs to be told about this trip?"

"No, sir. Nothing more."

"And what about the rabiser? Does he know all these facts?"

Yanshuph nodded. "In Ramesseum, he recorded the edict. And once arrived here, he reminded me that he was confident we would make it safe for him."

Peridia rubbed his hands together as if figuring new odds for a bargaining position.

Rahab grimaced and savagely slit open the pomegranate. Juice spurted from it and coated her fingers in sugary wetness.

"Perhaps we should see to the rabiser's safety," her father rumbled thoughtfully. "Perhaps, indeed, we should."

"Fah! He'll steal us blind."

"That may be," her father conceded. "But considering all the possibilities, Shatha may have done us a favor by lodging the rabiser with us." He walked away, still pondering the situation. "Yes, perhaps he has unwittingly done us a favor."

"Shatha does no favors for anyone — even unwittingly!" Rahab snapped, wiping her fingers. "Let the king's palace guards oversee the Egyptian."

Peridia shook his head. "That won't do. The times are too unsettled. Loyalty is not what it once was. My old friend Balaar and I have spoken of it often. He does not trust his guards." He sat down on the divan beside her. "In this present situation, I am more concerned for Yanshuph and for Balaar and Birsha than I am for the potential thievery of the rabiser."

She shook her head, not understanding.

"As long as we protect the rabiser, we protect our own leaders," he explained. "That is especially important right now."

"You're referring to the news about the Hebrew threat?"
He nodded. "Whether we like it or not, Jericho is on the threshold of vast change. Unwelcome as that might be, we cannot meet it without leadership."

She started to protest. He waved her off with an authoritative gesture. "King Balaar, old and sick as he is, is still king. Ali ben Azi — however we may mistrust him — is a merchant of worth with many contacts beyond these walls. And, he is as loyal as his kind can be. Besides, if things really get bad, ben Azi will disappear. On the other hand, General Birsha is a man of courage and foresight. We may come to see we should have listened to him more carefully — and much sooner." He leaned back, staring with a brooding sadness across the terrace.

For the first time, Rahab realized her father seemed old and tired — tired with the weariness that goes beyond physical age. The realization startled her. In an automatic reaction, she placed her hand on his arm and smiled at him.

He responded in kind, then pointed to Yanshuph. "And this young man has great influence with young soldiers and merchants. That, too, is important for Jericho." Again, he patted her hand. "What I'm saying is that as long as we protect the rabiser, we are protecting all our leaders. And that we must do." He gave her a searching look. "Do you understand?"

His reasoning was clear. She respected it and realized that, at some point, she might fully accept it. But it was hard to do so now. "What about Shatha?" she asked quietly.

Her father's expression abruptly changed. The eyes, so like her own, darkened with dislike. Color rose in his rugged face. "It is now we, not Rameses, who hold the threat of death over him!"

5

Five days had passed since Peridia had made the decision that they should house and safeguard the rabiser and his retinue of Egyptians.

On the morning of the sixth day, Rahab hurried alone through Jericho's narrow, noisy streets to accomplish the first of two missions. The first mission dealt with the rabiser and how to better control his wanderings in and around Jericho. The second mission concerned Shatha and was of a more personally-avenging nature.

She had not seen the arrogant priest since the morning after his return from Ramesseum. Word had come to her, however, that he was cloistered in meditation. The very idea was laughable.

She pulled the common, homespun burnoose more closely about her face. She had told no one that she was leaving the khan. And once again, she had taken special care to avoid the sharp-eyed Ahabina. More and more frequently, she had noticed subtle changes of attitude in her body-servant. At times, she would look up to find the slave-woman staring at her in sullen puzzlement. At other times, she caught a glint of active hatred in the woman's gaze.

As she approached the street of Nahshon the seeress, her intended destination, she became aware that the noisy street crowds had thinned, as if avoiding traveling too close to the seeress's house. An old rhyme — one on which two generations of Jericho's children (herself included) had been raised — rang in her ears.

"Astarte, El, Baal and Mot
The gods lead us as they are wroth!
Eyes for the living, eyes for the dead,
Be very good, lest Nahshon takes your head!"
She turned into the street where the seeress's house was located and paused with misgiving. Was she really wise to come here? Her father had warned against it. In reconsidering his warning, she had to admit that she, too, actively feared Nahshon.

From an outward appearance, there was nothing frightening about the woman — no evidence of her mystical powers. Past fifty, she was short, plump, and her features were quite ordinary. Most of the time her metallic-colored eyes gave no hint of supernatural vision. Nor were there any indications of magical sensitivity in her blunt, work-lined hands. She neither dressed nor carried herself with any special grace. In fact, Rahab decided, Nahshon was as ordinary as hundreds of other Canaanite women who made love to their men, bore children, kept house, cooked, worked in the fields, carried water from Jericho's abundant springs, and performed the other assorted trivia of daily living.

But in spite of this commonplace outward appearance, Rahab knew the woman to possess a deep underlayer of mystery. She had often witnessed it during temple rituals. And she also knew that the seeress held enormous influence over Shatha. In fact, all Jericho knew that. It was whispered in the streets that she held more influence over the high priest than did his quedesah.

With a troubled sigh, she paused again and debated whether to go on, or to return to the khan and try to find another solution to the problem that brought her on the first of the morning's missions — the safeguarding of the rabiser.

In the five days since her father made the decision to house and protect the tax collector, the actual performing of that onerous chore had fallen to her. Yanshuph had gone off with General Birsha in a search for men-at-arms because of the Hebrew threat. In so doing, he had taken with him several household servants she had planned to use as guards for the rabiser. Her father was supportive, but of little actual help since he was busy with the management of the khan and all the other holdings. That left only her.

Any other time she could have managed the added chore with no difficulty. But this was the time of final preparations for the Festival of Harvest. In fact, the event was only a few days away. Much remained to be done. She simply could not reassign trusted manpower just to guard that meddling Egyptian.

And he was unpredictable! She fumed inwardly just thinking about how he and the big Nubian roamed everywhere, prying and probing into everything. They had even gone beyond the city's walls to gape at crops and at the salt mines, to observe the forests, the fields, the herds, and to inspect the watering places and the general lay of the land. They talked with slaves, with overseers, and with free-men. They asked countless questions and made countless written notations. One way or another, she knew they would steal Jericho blind. She knew it in her bones. And it was impossible to safeguard them except by one-on-one surveillance. She simply could not spare the manpower for that — not now.

That left her only one recourse. She had to find a way to reduce the rabiser's wanderings — without him knowing it, of course. Any overt move to restrain him would result in a claim of interference and a demand to be moved to different housing. Her household could not afford that possibility.

At last, she had thought of Nahshon. She could help. So in spite of her father's warnings, and her own fear, she had come to the forbidding place just a few feet in front of her. After all, the only thing she needed from Nahshon was a simple, harmless potion that could be mixed discreetly with the Egyptian's food — something harmless to slow him down for a few days. It was as simple as that.

At the door of the seeress's house, a sudden contrary wind-gust gyrated into a miniature cyclone. For an instant she wondered if it was a sign to proceed no further, but she pushed away that thought as quickly as it had come and rapped loudly on Nahshon's door.

No response came. Impatiently now, she knocked again and glanced about the street in both directions. It was still deserted. When her third knock received no response, she tried the latch. She found it unbolted, opened the door and slipped inside.

Like many other Jericho homes, the unoccupied room was meagerly furnished. It held two wooden benches, a rough table and chest, and in the earthen floor was a crudely-carved foot-basin. She disdained the thought of removing her sandals and washing her feet in such a place. Why Nahshon didn't make more of a show of her powerful position was another mystery. The cheapest rooms in the khan were better than this one. The heavy musk-like incense permeating the room was overpowering.

Rahab quickly moved on to an inner doorway covered by a ramskin hung from the lintel. Pushing aside the covering, she called out. When there was no answer, she began to fear she had made the trip for nothing and would have to return later. She was not sure she could make herself come here again.

As common as the first room had been, this inner one was unlike any other room in all of Jericho, she told herself. Its furnishings were ordinary enough — a work table, benches, a large firehole in the floor, and a stairway leading up to Nahshon's living quarters. But everything else in the room was quite extraordinary.

Around the walls were hung amulets of every size and description. Beneath them, carefully stacked against one wall, was a series of clay pots containing some of the supplies for Nahshon's awesome craft. Fascinated, she inspected them: mangrove roots, hyssop, swallowworts carefully clipped and shredded, bats' wings, and spider dust. Slightly separated from these were swatches of human hair and a jar of human fingernail clippings. When finely-ground and mixed with certain secret potions, they were reputed to be an unfailing aphrodisiac. With a flash of humor, she decided she certainly didn't want the rabiser's potion mixed from those ingredients.

She moved on to another area where a series of carefully sealed jars were marked myrrh, anise, and with the names of other treasured spices from the far eastern kingdoms. These were gifts to Nahshon from Shatha. They were probably his greatest gesture of generosity, Rahab thought acidly.

59

On the side of the room away from the stairway, a variety of herbs hung drying from wooden pegs. From one large peg dangled a cluster of mandrake roots, their tendrils resembling miniature human forms in the final agonizing throes of death. Immediately adjacent hung Nahshon's famous and fearsome fetish-of-destiny. It was a chain of solid silver laced with the tail feathers of ravens. During temple rituals, Nahshon wore it about her waist. In ceremonies calling for predictions of the future and the sacrifices needed to make them come true, she brandished the fetish with frightening violence. Its location adjacent to the mandrake roots seemed gruesomely appropriate. With a quiver of distaste, Rahab backed away and turned to leave when Nahshon's resonant voice came from behind her. "Don't go, quedesah."

She wheeled around, surprised and immediately curious about how long the older woman had been standing at the stairway watching her.

"I'm honored to have the beautiful courtesan of the mighty Shatha visit my lowly house." The mouth smiled pleasantly enough, but the metallic-colored eyes scanned her with uncomfortable calculation. Nahshon was dirty and dressed in a rumpled khurkah with a torn bodice. She was also barefoot, a sign of humiliation for one in her position of power.

Rahab wondered again what attracted Shatha to this creature. Black snakes rustled nervously in their reed baskets near the stairs. Albino mice in a nearby hopper scurried round and round as if seeking escape. To hide a similar feeling, Rahab made a low bow.

"An important reason must bring you to me." Nahshon came toward her, arms outstretched offering an embrace of welcome.

The gesture was unnecessary and unwanted. Rahab steeled herself to accept it, knowing that refusal or evasion would be taken as insulting and automatically defeat the purpose of the visit. But as she was pulled up tightly against Nahshon's plump, soiled body, the closeness and the smell of balsam rum repulsed her. With a forced laugh, she resisted and shrugged free by pushing Nahshon back and holding her at arms' length. "You are right, as always, great seeress," she said in a tightly controlled voice that covered the shudder of revulsion going through her. "An important reason does bring me here. But my request is very simple and should not cause you any great inconvenience." She let go of Nahshon's arms and walked away.

The piercing eyes followed her with something akin to longing. "What would you have me do?"

Rahab turned. "I need to purchase a simple, harmless potion to induce drowsiness."

"For yourself?"

"Oh, no!"

"For your consort, then?"

She hesitated, choosing her words carefully. She was reluctant to discuss the rabiser with Nahshon. It was possible she knew nothing of the situation and in her apparent rum-filled state, it was better that way. "Nay, seeress. The potion I seek is not for my consort. He sleeps well without aid. The potion is needed at the khan."

"Peridia sent you to seek *my* help?"

"Nay. I came on my own."

Nahshon ambled to a table on which were cups, a jug of balsam rum, and a bowl filled with fly-specked fruit. With a hand motion, she offered the refreshment.

Rahab declined with a shake of her head. "Do you have such a potion?"

But Nahshon was not to be hurried. She poured rum into one of the cups, sipped at it, and then, with maddening slowness, carried it to a bench and settled down. "Why is such a potion needed at the khan?" she asked.

"Please, seeress, I really haven't much time to visit. There's much work to be —"

"Is the potion for a member of the khan's household?" Nahshon persisted. "Or for a guest?"

"It's for a guest — for an unwelcome guest —" Rahab conceded.

Nahshon sipped thoughtfully at the rum.

"Do you have a potion I can — "

"Then this guest must be very important."

"Not especially," she hedged.

"That's odd!"

"Odd? How is it odd? My request is a simple one."

Nahshon drained the cup and wiped her mouth with the back of her hand.

"How is it odd?" Rahab insisted in open irritation.

Nahshon fixed her with an accusing look. "It is odd that you, quedesah, come here yourself — alone — in behalf of a healthy and unimportant traveler."

The logic caught Rahab off-guard. However rum-filled Nahshon had appeared, it was obvious that her drinking had not affected her reasoning. And it was equally obvious she would not fill the potion without knowing who it was for. Rahab hesitated yet a moment longer, still reluctant to discuss the rabiser.

But she hesitated too long. Nahshon set down the cup, pushed her plump body up off the bench, and moved with surprising speed to the inner doorway. She pushed aside the ramskin covering and looked sternly at Rahab. "I have no potion of the kind you seek. I cannot help you, quedesah."

Only one reason could cause Nahshon to so brusquely refuse such a simple request and rudely dismiss her. And that would be to protect Shatha. Of course! She should have thought of that before. It had been utter foolishness to assume Shatha had not confided in the seeress about the death edict should any harm come to the rabiser. And it had been equally foolish not to approach Nahshon directly with the facts that brought her here.

As it was, her cautious approach had brought her danger-ously close to revealing her hatred for Shatha. The hard suspi-cion in Nahshon's tone of voice clearly spoke to that point.

A shiver raced through her as she realized how dangerously close she had also come to revealing the advantage Peridia felt they had over Shatha by the presence of the rabiser in the khan.

Tentatively, in a placating gesture, she extended her hand to Nahshon and said cautiously, "I have tried too hard to guard Shatha's secret. And as a result, I have offended you, great seeress."

The suspicion on Nahshon's face was unrelenting.

Rahab gave a shrug of defeat. "The potion is to protect my consort."

The ramskin door covering sagged slightly as Nahshon began to relax her grip on it.

"Indirectly, the potion is for Shatha's protection," Rahab went on to explain. "It is hard to guard the rabiser when he wanders so. And when the rabiser is unguarded, he is in danger. And when he is in danger, so is Shatha." She went on to describe in detail the situation, being careful to emphasize her concern for Shatha.

As Rahab's words began to take effect, Nahshon slowly released the ramskin covering until it smacked softly against the sides of the doorway. "You should have spoken truthfully to begin with, quedesah."

With feigned apology, Rahab nodded.

"These are dangerous times. We must, at all costs, protect the high priest."

Rahab nodded again. "Do you have the kind of potion I'm looking for?"

Nahshon moved toward a far shelf and retrieved a small jar filled with a powdered substance.

Rahab followed, pulling a pouch of gold coins from the scarlet sash at her waist. She emptied its contents into Nahshon's outstretched hand. In exchange, the seeress poured the powdered substance into the now-empty pouch.

"It will not take much of this to make your Egyptian drowsy. Use it with care, quedesah."

Rahab murmured a word of thanks, slipped the pouch back into the scarlet sash, and with a sense of relief left the house.

Once more on the street, she paused only long enough to clear her lungs of the awful smell of incense and rum. It was an enormous relief to have the first errand of the morning finished. She had come close to failing. She would not be as foolish on her second mission, a mission to the court of temple maidens that would give her far more satisfaction. For Shatha would soon find himself in a situation as frustrating and insulting as she found the presence of the rabiser to be.

6

Joel sat with Hejaz in their new and larger quarters at the khan recording tribute lists. The young slave-page sat cross-legged on the floor nearby preparing extra rolls of papyrus. Two of the lackeys lounged just outside the doorway gaming with bones. Preparation for the first shipment to Ramesseum under Joel's authority was going smoothly. It was a rich shipment of tribute-tax. And he knew the next month's shipment would be even richer, coming as it would after the Festival of Harvest.

He paused and stretched, feeling satisfied that Rechibidan and Rameses would approve of his work. Maybe he was beginning to really feel like an officer of the empire. At least, he was trying to make the best of it.

Surprisingly enough, he had discovered the Jerichoans, too, were apparently trying to make the best of it. On the day after his arrival, they had moved him into these more comfortable and larger quarters. In addition to this room, there were two sleeping areas and a storage area, and there were two windows instead of one as in the squalid little room on the south wall in which he had first been housed.

Yes, he thought again in surveying the quarters, these were far better than the first room, even though there was still a prison-like quality about the place. These rooms were isolated in the east quadrant of the khan's second floor and surrounded by storerooms. Directly below were the weaving rooms.

He and Hejaz had decided the move to this location indicated two things. First, his hosts were avoiding a possibility that he would demand quarters in the palace or the temple. Second, the isolated location clearly implied a sheltered and guarded environment. They were aware of constant surveillance by members of the household staff. But no one interfered with their duties. Because of this, Joel had decided not to object to the surveillance. After all, the more effort the Jerichoans put into safeguarding him and his men, the better he liked it.

With the exception of an incident that occurred during the first few days after his arrival, his new situation had been surprisingly uneventful. That one incident, however, had to do with his health. Within a week of his arrival, he began to experience strange spells of lethargy. At one point, he became violently ill.

Hejaz had summoned the women of the house to attend him. Though Joel's memory was dim, Hejaz later told him that Rahab had been among the women who had come and that she had appeared the most agitated over his condition. In that strange Jericho dialect, she had thoroughly tongue-lashed her body-servant, Ahabina, and had threatened to have her punished for her carelessness. After that, he had quickly recovered. He had had no more difficulties since then.

He and Hejaz debated whether the illness was caused by some drug. Rahab's obvious concern, and her anger toward her own slave-woman, seemed to confirm that possibility. Whatever else the Jerichoans were, they were not foolish. They could not afford another dead rabiser.

Stretching again, he got up and walked to the doorway. The courtyard below hummed with activity. Great sacks of grains were carried in by sweating field hands. Potters, smelters, and stone masons went about their tasks with unusual urgency. Household slaves hurried back and forth from the weaving rooms to storerooms ladened with great folds of beautiful linens and bundles of scarlet cords.

From the emerald forests beyond the walls came the sounds of adze and paring chisel mingling with the slave chants of the fruit pickers and the salt bearers.

"The City of Palms girds herself for the Festival of Harvest, Hejaz. It will undoubtedly be quite a celebration."

"It'll be no celebration for us, my friend," he lamented.

"We'll be too busy counting the tribute for Rameses!"

Joel gave a mirthless laugh. The Nubian was right. They had nothing to celebrate — no social life, no personal companionship. While celibacy was not a natural part of his belief, a sense of caution had constrained him from seeking the companionship of a Canaanite woman. And he had warned Hejaz against it, too.

As a result, their main activity, aside from their work, was in visiting with travelers staying at the khan. But even those contacts did not relieve the sense of sameness or offer any special cheer. For the talk always turned to the Hebrews and their marauding and killing. The travelers were full of such talk. And not a single one had a good word to say for or about the Hebrews. They were a threat, a very real threat. After one of these conversations, Joel always went away with a heaviness of heart.

Lounging against the doorway thinking of these things, he realized that with the exception of Hejaz and of Reba, the child who had befriended him, he experienced no light-hearted or companionable relationship in this place.

The friendship with the child had come quite by accident. She had chanced on him one morning on the walkway in front of his rooms. He had been sitting there sketching the courtyard scene. The child was fascinated with the swift, dark lines that became faces and architectural features so familiar to her.

"You are an Egyptian," she had greeted him.

He agreed with a smile and a nod.

"I'm not supposed to talk to you," she announced gravely.

"Then why do you?"

She shrugged and looked intently at the sketch of the courtyard coming alive on the papyrus. "Can you draw birds?"

"I suppose I can. Any special kind of bird?"

She considered it for a moment. "What does a — a — vul — a vulture of — tax — tax —"

With a startled laugh, he helped her. "A vulture of taxation?"

She nodded. "What does that kind of bird look like?"

He laughed again. "You are looking at one!"

She searched his face with large, solemn eyes. "But you aren't a bird — are you?"

"I am whatever anyone wishes to see," he replied gently.

The child reminded him of his own sister. She had been about this age the last time he saw her. "Come, sit beside me," he invited the youngster. "I will draw something just for you — a bird that really looks like a bird."

And so began the first real friendship he had found in Jericho. The child sought him often after that. She was a lively and lovable youngster. He amused her with sketching and began to feel a sense of protective interest toward her.

But it was not enough. It only seemed to whet his appetite for adult friendship. He turned away from the door with a deep sigh, realizing all over again that friendship was a treasure forbidden him in this place. He was as much of an enemy to his hosts as they were to him. Even pleasant, friendly conversation was not to be found.

Even conversations between Canaanites were not friendly. Most of them seemed to be restricted to skirmishes for authority or jousts of cunning. One that had occurred just the night before was a typical example.

In a remote corner of the courtyard, he had come upon Rahab and Shatha involved in a heated argument about a load of contraband goods on a newly-arrived caravan. Their argument was so violent they were unaware of anything else. He had quickly gathered up Hejaz, the lackeys, the porters, and his men-at-arms and had confiscated the entire load and locked it in Pharaoh's storehouse. By the time he had returned to his rooms, Rahab was already there.

She confronted him swiftly and directly. "You steal, rabiser!"

He denied it and discovered he rather enjoyed her agitation. Her blue eyes sparked with fiery anger.

"You steal!" she snapped again. "The goods from the caravan of Tegush the Amalekite are meant for Samaria, not for Jericho. You have no right to them. Pharaoh has no right to them. They belong to Samaria."

"A thousand pardons, spirited hostess," he salaamed with a sarcastic flourish. "But I overheard your — ah — your — ah, conversation with the high priest. And from what I heard, the goods appear to be contraband."

Fire flashed again in the blue eyes. "Raca! They are *not* contraband. They belong to —"

He gave a hard laugh, cutting her off. "Contraband or not,

you should thank me, quedesah. If I have the goods, you are spared another argument with your consort."

She tensed like a wildcat ready to spring. He braced. But the impact of the lithe, beautiful body flinging itself against him didn't come. Instead, disdain quickly covered her anger. And just as quickly, he felt something akin to disappointment.

"You will regret this, rabiser," she warned. "Jericho has no room for Egyptian thieves in the guise of an official."

"I shall be happy to remove my party to the palace or the temple," he replied. "You have only to tell me when, my hostess."

"Fah!" She whirled and left.

He had won the verbal joust. But it had left him with an empty feeling. He would never be anything but an enemy in this place. Apparently, that was the way it was to be. He sat down at his writing table and affixed the royal seal to the scroll Hejaz handed to him before he had vanished into the storeroom.

The lackeys, tiring of the gambling game, now dozed outside the doorway. The young slave-page was immersed in his chore of preparing extra papyrus. The substance was precious and the boy worked carefully with each sheet. He laid thin strips of pith from the papyrus reed side-by-side and then placed a second layer at right angles over them. He wet them down with small dabs of water and worked them together with a pressing motion. Finally, he covered the sheets with a thin layer of paste and carefully impressed the royal emblem in one corner of each sheet. Dried, trimmed, and polished, each sheet was about five by ten inches. Pharaoh's trade and tribute records, however, required rolls of twenty sheets. This was the preparation over which the young slave-page now worked so diligently. He was good at it. He snipped, fitted, and pasted the sheets together with consummate patience. As Joel approvingly watched the painstaking work, it suddenly occurred to him that material riches caused an indescribable and tedious burden at every level of society.

The more a man possessed, the more he wished to possess, until finally, he became enslaved to possessions. Unless he had as much as Pharaoh did, of course. Then, possessions simply enslaved other human beings. Dissatisfaction washed through him.

Tax-collecting was not really the job for him, J el decided. How had he ever deluded himself with its advantages of prestige? Wasn't he really simply another of the endless line of men sent on an endless task to preserve a portion of Pharaoh's endless possessions?

He glanced over into the storeroom where his own meager possessions were housed: clay jars stuffed with rolls of papyrus, his official leather pouch with the seals of his office, and his personal wardrobe. They were pitifully few, especially when compared to the obvious wealth he had seen here at the khan and in certain areas of Jericho. And in comparison to Pharaoh's incredible world of possessions, they were even more pitifully meager. But in spite of their meagerness, it astonished him to discover how deep was his sense of pride in them.

Even more astonishing was the realization that he could understand why the Jerichoans felt proportionately larger pride in their possessions, and why they would pursue any course to hold on to them. Rahab epitomized that attitude — and he understood it!

He picked up a new stylus and began to sharpen its nib with a small knife. He, too, was as much a part of the eternal circle of pride-in-possessions as were Jericho and Rameses.

Taxing and haggling, gathering and cursing, thieving and hiding, and even killing, to possess more. Losing and regathering to start again the eternal circle. And for what purpose?

For what purpose, indeed, he thought with frustration. Did all men wield their energies to the possession of goods?

He got up and went to the window that looked eastward toward the River Jordan and beyond to Moab. The flow of water in the Jordan was beginning to get louder. He could hear it even at this distance, and he could see the far-off green haze of vegetation lining the banks of the river. In his imagination, he could almost see the white water of springtide begin its downward rush to the Dead Sea. And for what purpose? It would simply be captured there for all eternity, except for that small part that vomited itself up to be possessed as briny marl on the Dead One's callous shores.

Where, then, was fulfillment? With his own people? Or were they also simply searching for possessions? He recalled his talks in the courtyard with travelers who claimed his people were marauders, killers, and stiff-necked thieves. Was the talk true? Were his own people now like this? Did they no longer search for the intangible beauty that fed a man's soul? Did they no longer follow the Law given by God to Moses? If they did not, then what was the worth of man's descendants? What, in fact, was the worth of any man's strivings if not to diligently search out something other than himself?

The distant view blurred as tears misted his eyes. Roughly, he rubbed them away, dismayed at the depth of his feelings. They contradicted reality. A man could not eat unless he had possessions to trade for food. Nor could he clothe himself and his family without leather and fleece. He quickly turned away from the window and started back toward the writing table.

A shadow fell across the doorway. "Rabiser?" The lackeys scrambled to their feet to block the entry. Hejaz appeared from the storeroom, one hand on the dagger at his waist.

Tegush the Amalekite halted, held up his hands in a sign of truce, then made the familiar gesture of greeting by touching his right hand to heart and mouth.

Joel responded, motioned the lackeys out of the way, and dismissed the slave-page. Hejaz relaxed his grip on the knife but did not completely withdraw his hand.

Tegush hesitated and made a second gesture of greeting to the Nubian before entering the room.

Joel motioned for the Amalekite to come and be seated on a nearby hassock. As the trader crossed the room, Hejaz stationed himself just inside the doorway.

Instead of taking the offered seat, the Amalekite hunkered down on his heels beside it and extended his sinewy arms from the sleeves of his orange-striped robes to embrace his bony knees. It was a habit born of trail life.

Out of courtesy to his unexpected visitor, Joel came from behind the writing table and assumed a similar position.

A thin beard scraggled unimpressively at the man's chin.

But the eyes were powerful, almost hypnotic. Even the perpetual sun-squint could not hide their curious depth. "I have come to inquire of your intentions, rabiser." He spoke in common Akkadian.

Joel responded in the same tongue. "My intentions?"

"Aye, your intentions for the use of my caravan goods. For what reason do you hold them and delay my journey to Samaria?"

"Because they now belong to Pharaoh."

"But honorable rabiser, the goods you hold do not belong to Pharaoh. In Edom I paid Pharaoh's caravan levy on them. At Jericho's gate, I paid for use of this province's road." He spread his hands in a futile gesture. "And doubtless I will pay again — if I get beyond this odorous place and to my destination without being robbed of them again!"

"Perhaps I have done you a favor." Joel said.

The trader frowned.

"You have no goods," Joel explained, "thus you have no need to further risk the dangers of the road."

Color rose in the Amalekite's leathery face. "Does this mean I cannot retrieve my goods from unlawful possession?"

Joel bridled. "Unlawful possession is a serious accusation, trader."

The man shrugged with hands held wide, palms up. "You have my goods. Yet, I have paid the tax as prescribed by Pharaoh's law. I paid at Edom and I paid at —"

"So you've already said," Joel cut in. "But you forget the other law concerning this matter."

A look of puzzled wariness crept into the Amalekite's eyes. "What other law?"

"The law of contraband."

"Contraband?"

"Aye! The law that says contraband goods are fair game for anyone, trader!"

"But I carry no contraband goods, rabiser!" His fingers flexed and tightened around his knees. "I carry consigned goods, consigned goods for the markets of Samaria!"

Consigned! The word jarred him. He glanced at Hejaz for a look of support, but found no reaction. He stood up, shook the

cramps from his legs, and thought back to the argument between Rahab and Shatha. They had been so angry with each
other, that their words had come in a torrent. And they had
mixed common Akkadian with that peculiar Jericho dialect
that he found so hard to understand. Was it possible he had
confused the words "contraband" and "consigned?" He
turned and walked back to the writing table, considering the
possibility.

"The honorable Peridia will vouch that I carry only consigned goods, never contraband."

Joel found this bit of information interesting, but beside the
point. If he had confused the words "consigned" and
"contraband," the trader's protest was valid. It also meant, he
realized, that Rahab's protest last night was also valid.

But even so, to return the goods to Tegush might mean
giving Shatha a second chance to steal them. On the other
hand, to keep the merchandise for Pharaoh would be stealing,
too. That was not part of his duty as rabiser. "Another's need
and rightful property should not be an occasion for profit." He
said the words more to himself than to anyone else.

The Amalekite however, quickly responded. "That's an odd
attitude for an Egyptian, especially an Egyptian tax-collector."
The piercing eyes probed at him. "That is more the attitude of a
Hebrew!"

Hejaz abruptly stiffened.

"Each man must cast his own shadow," Joel said with a soft
laugh, refusing to waver under the man's probing look.

In half-apology, the trader shrugged and got to his feet. "I
meant no offense, rabiser. My words are often blunt."

"It is nothing," Joel reassured, still pondering what action
would be best to take in this situation. Since he was determined not to let Shatha have a second chance to steal the
property, only one other recourse seemed apparent. Slowly,
he walked toward the Amalekite. "Will you *sell* your *consigned*
goods to a rabiser?"

The leathery face looked at Joel in astonishment.

Behind the trader, Hejaz broke into surprised laughter.

The Amalekite glanced in confusion from one to the other.

"It is no trick," Joel grinned. "Will you let me buy your goods
for Pharaoh?"

"The whole load?"

"Why not? The whole load is already in Pharaoh's storehouse."

A wide smile cracked across the trader's face. "The price will be high, rabiser!"

With a laugh, he reached for the scroll on which was listed the entire contents of the caravan and motioned for Hejaz to fetch a pouch of gold coins. "Do you read, Amalekite?"

The trader nodded.

"Then come, check this inventory and we'll strike a bargain."

The trader came to the table, braced both hands on it, and bent over to carefully scan the listing.

Joel walked away, satisfied with the handling of the situation. Hejaz returned and gave the money pouch to the Amalekite, who poured out the contents onto the scrolls, counted it, replaced it, and slowly stuffed the pouch into the folds of his orange-striped robes. "May your days be long and prosperous, rabiser."

Joel turned back to acknowledge the closing of the deal. As he did so, Peridia appeared in the doorway. In sharp surprise, Joel halted. It was the first time his host had come to these quarters. Tegush, he decided, must be more important than he had realized.

"It is well-settled, innkeeper. The rabiser is an honorable man, too." Tegush salaamed to Joel and quickly left.

Peridia came forward and in a rumbling voice explained, "My reason for coming here is not to spy on your dealings with the Amalekite, rabiser." He made a conciliatory gesture. "Though of course I am aware of those dealings."

For the first time, Joel noticed the similarity between Peridia's eyes and those of Rahab. They were the same startling blue color, and they gazed intently. "Then how *can* I help you, innkeeper?"

"You can do me a favor, if you will."

"A favor?"

Hejaz stared in disbelief.

"How can I, an Egyptian tax-collector, do you a favor?"

Peridia's laugh was as rumbling as his voice. "It is because you *are* Egyptian and because you *are* Pharaoh's tax-collector."

Peridia went to the hassock and sat down. "Tonight, King Balaar is giving a dinner at the palace honoring General Birsha. He has just returned from a trip to northern provinces seeking men-at-arms. He will report on the trip tonight. He will have information of value to Rameses as well as to Jericho.

"I want you to come to the dinner and hear what will be said. And I hope you will find it important enough to relay all you hear to the mighty Rameses and let him know how serious our situation is. The Hebrew threat is real, very real. It is only a question of time."

Joel walked toward the writing table, hedging for time to quell his astonishment, rather than out of a need to consider the ramifications of Peridia's request. They were obvious.

Idly, he began to roll up the scroll listing the Amalekite's goods and in the process dislodged a hard, round object. He picked it up. It was a ring made from a bit of ram's horn. On its surface was carved a roughly beautiful cherubim. In disbelief, he stared. Only two such rings had ever been made. He had given his own away many years ago. The other one had belonged to his sister!

"Well?" Peridia intoned. "What's your answer, rabiser? Can you grant me this favor?"

Forcibly, he shook off this new astonishment at this most personal discovery. Tightly closing his fist around the ring, he turned and gave a low bow of deference to Peridia. "I will come."

The innkeeper got to his feet. "Good! Bring your manservant. He will be welcomed, too. I will send my household guards at the sundown hour to accompany you both."

As Peridia left the room, Hejaz rushed toward him and slapped him on the back. "By Isis and Osiris! We finally got a dinner invitation!"

When Joel did not respond, the big Nubian bent down awkwardly and peered into his face. "What's wrong? You look as though you have seen a spirit from the dead!"

Slowly, he opened his hand to reveal the ring cradled in his palm. "Perhaps I have, Hejaz. Perhaps, I have!"

7

A few hours later, and a few hundred cubits from the khan, Shatha stirred from his late afternoon respite, unaware that fate had drawn together Tegush, Peridia, and the rabiser, and that eventually the fabric of the Amalekite's destiny would include him, too.

He yawned and stretched. His hand met the warm flesh of the temple maiden who still slept at his side. Startled momentarily, he drew back. Then the memory of his newest conquest came to him freshly and fullly. He raised up on one elbow and looked at the girl. She wasn't as beautiful as Rahab. Nor did she have the same fire and spirit. But she would do. At least this one, he thought with a tinge of irritation, could not put him off with excuses of being too busy preparing for the festival. Nor would her mood sway with distracting concerns about Egyptian tax-collectors.

But most important, the girl lying here beside him would never have the shameless insolence, nor the opportunity, to write outrageous edicts to the other temple maidens in his name!

He sat up and with renewed irritation recounted all the ways Rahab had found to agitate and spite him since his return from Ramesseum. She had caused one disturbance after another. First, she had helped to instigate Birsha's trip to the northern provinces for mercenaries. It was a foolish excursion, one that would have to be paid for out of the temple treasury. The royal treasury was depleted under the impact of Egyptian tax.

In the second instance, Rahab had misused the sleeping potion prescribed by Nahshon and had caused the Egyptian to become violently ill. It was as if she didn't care that his own life depended on the safety of the Egyptian's life. The fact that she had persuaded Balaar to supply additional palace guards for surveillance of the Egyptian did not ease the knowledge that his own life was under constant threat, and that she was taking every possible advantage of the situation. Always acquisitive and stubborn, she had grown more openly rebellious since his return from Ramesseum. As recently as last night, she had argued so vehemently over a fine load of consigned goods that she had attracted the notice of the Egyptian, who confiscated the entire load from beneath their very eyes.

But most irritating of all was his certain suspicion that she was behind the outrageous edict written to the temple maidens several days past in his name. In his name, he fumed, recalling that it had read: "At the dictate of Jericho's high priest, no temple maiden shall lie with him until after the festival of harvest." It had gone on to describe stringent punishment for anyone disobeying the edict.

Of course, none of the maidens had dared violate it. It had taken a few days for him to unravel the mystery of their strange obstinancy. Finally, Nahshon had proved most helpful in resolving the problem and in restoring proper behavior among the maidens.

He swore under his breath. He had no proof that Rahab was behind it, but his gut feeling told him she was. He swore again. He would deal with her properly for that incredible insult. And he would begin tonight. King Balaar was hosting a dinner in honor of Birsha's return from the northern provinces. Rahab would be forced to sit with him at the priestly dining couch for the affair. She could no longer avoid him or hide behind the protection of preparations for the Festival of Harvest. He would find a way to avenge himself for her insulting behavior.

Angrily determined, he swung out of bed. His foot brushed across the garments he had earlier discarded. He stooped, picked up one of the garments and stared at it. It was a mantle of sheer, white, expensive linen. It was his favorite. Rahab had woven it for him. An intricate design of pomegranates and lotus was embroidered on its hem. Precious stones repeated these symbols of power and life on the brocaded neckline. On the cuff of the right sleeve, embroidered in blue and gold, was the serpent form of the powerful god El, consort of Astarte. It was his trademark, the symbol of his rank and of his total superiority over Jericho and over Rahab!

Admiringly, he rubbed his hand over it. No king had anything so handsome, not even Rameses. This mantle was a special treasure. When he wore it, it set him apart. He considered it singularly appropriate as an enhancement of his high rank. His fingers traced across the embroidered outline of the god El and a new, darkly intriguing thought came to him.

Rahab deserved to be humiliated with a special kind of humiliation — one that would settle any lingering doubts she might have about who was the real power in Jericho, and who held final authority over the court of temple maidens.

He remained motionless a moment or two longer relishing the new thought and the peculiar meaning it held for him. Then, he moved around the bed and laid the mantle over the nude body of the sleeping girl. With a mirthless laugh, he went off to dress for dinner at the king's palace.

An hour later, deliberately late, he entered the royal dining hall feeling arrogantly confident that his most recent idea for humiliating Rahab would cause her considerable embarrassment in the court of temple maidens. And without question, it would reassert his authority over her. He found the thought particularly pleasant, and he intended to add to his sense of pleasure by publicly humiliating Rahab in this place, too. He had to admit, in fact, that the only reason he had even come to this dinner was to publicly humiliate his quedesah.

Since he strongly opposed Birsha's views on the supposed Hebrew threat, his absence from tonight's affair would have made that opposition abundantly clear to all Jericho. But the pull of Rahab's presence, and the chance to take retaliation, was too tempting to let pass. And so he had come, deliberately late as an open breach of custom and courtesy and, as an affront to General Birsha.

He took a deep and satisfying breath, realizing that for the first time since his return from Ramesseum he felt again the familiar sensation of being in control. He liked it.

Dismissing his escort of temple guards, he moved toward

the privileged seating area at the far end of the hall. Elaborate decorations visually testified to the importance King Balaar imputed to this occasion. Military banners hung from each of the main columns in the hall and were bathed in an orange glare from huge bronze torchiers.

Hand-picked squads of palace guards, resplendent in breast-plates and helmets, walked the perimeters of the hall as a living backdrop. Interspersed in front of them were dozens of slaves wielding ostrich-plume fans on long ivory handles to fend off the heat of the torchiers. All the guests, except for Jericho's khazianu, were seated in an at-random fashion in the fore part of the hall. In the center of the hall was a wide open space reserved for musicians, dancers, and other entertainers.

The privileged seating area was in a U-shaped configuration made up of handsome dining couches — gifts to King Balaar from Rameses in an earlier and better time. Low tables, finely-wrought in silver and gold, were placed immediately in front of them. These also were gifts from Rameses. Each couch was covered with a purple and gold throw. And — except for the royal dining couch — each one accommodated two people. The royal couch could seat seven. Customarily, Jericho's high priest and his quedesah were among the seven.

For this occasion, however, only General Birsha and Phelga, his wife, were seated with Jericho's king. The rest of the khazianu were seated in no apparent order of distinction along either side of the royal couch.

But Shatha realized that his own couch, with Rahab already seated, was two removed from King Balaar and on his left, rather than on his immediate right as was customary. His sense of satisfaction vanished. The unusual seating arrangement meant exclusion. It was insultingly obvious. Resentment cut through him as he recognized yet another rebuff from his peers. Such incidents had been occurring with alarming frequency ever since the return from Ramesseum.

He moved on, despising the situation, reviling the turn of fate, and wondering if Rahab had a hand in this, too. But he did not dwell on the thought.

Now greetings from the crowd came from every side. Many stood and bowed to him. He responded automatically and kept going. A quick, loud burst of music brought forth the appearance of a dozen brilliantly-costumed dwarfs juggling over-sized swords.

As they began their performance in the center of the hall, he approached his own dining couch. Rahab, dressed in a dazzling white tunic embroidered with the scarlet ornaments symbolizing her rank, glanced up.

Uncalled, a pang of desire went through him. Roughly, he dismissed it, reminding himself that he would find satisfaction from her in other ways. He turned, gave a thin greeting to Peridia and Mozni seated to his left, then turned again to acknowledge the royal couch, the magistrates of the royal treasury, Yanshuph, and Tirzah. Almost directly across from him, beyond the performing dwarfs, sat Nahshon and Ali ben Azi. He nodded to them.

Then he spotted the Egyptian!

Shock froze him. The stocky, dark-haired man and his big Nubian friend sat alone at the far end of the privileged seating area. Their dining couch was slightly removed from the others, in accordance with that irritating Egyptian custom that banned them from eating at the same table with foreigners lest it imply equality.

Equality, indeed! Arrogant scum! Quickly, he sat down and leaned close to Rahab. "How did that contemptuous Egyptian get in here?"

"You mean Pharaoh's rabiser?" she replied playfully.

"By the gods, you know who I mean!"

"Why, I'm surprised, noble Shatha," she smiled with acid sweetness. "I thought you'd washed your hands of him. Think of it no more."

He grabbed her by the wrist, pulled it down so the action could not be seen by the others, and gave it a hard twist.

A small sound of pain escaped from her.

"I say again, how did he get here? Did that doddering Balaar quail at the sight of him and ask him to stay?"

"I know nothing of Balaar's fears," she bit back angrily, trying to free herself. "The Egyptian has been left in my care. You commanded it!"

He straightened with surprise and loosened his grip.

She struggled free. Defiance burned in her eyes. "You put him in my charge. You said to watch him."

"By the eyes of Baal, Rahab, I never meant —"

"You said that was the penalty I had to pay."

"But, I didn't mean —"

"You said it was the penalty I must pay to save you from sacrifice," she snapped, rubbing at her wrist.

"Enough!" he blazed, glancing about to make sure they were not being overheard. "I didn't mean you should have the Egyptian jackal at your side constantly."

"What else would you have me do?" she snapped, ignoring his warning. "Since Nahshon attempted to poison him, what else can I do?"

"Nahshon?"

"Or did she fail to tell you that, my noble Shatha?" Her tone took on an acid sweetness again.

A servant approached with wine goblets for the royal toast. Shatha chafed at the interruption, fuming at Rahab's accusation against Nahshon. Nahshon was the one person in Jericho who had not rebuffed him since the return from Egypt. The servant moved away. "That's an open lie!" he hissed. "Nahshon would not be that careless."

Rahab gave a scornful laugh. "You're a fine one to judge carelessness."

"Be careful of your tongue, woman!"

"As careful as you were of Rameses' cat?" she charged cuttingly. Rage, dark and dreadful, overwhelmed him. Savagely, he grabbed for her to jerk her toward him. But she recoiled, fear spilling into her eyes.

It was then that Peridia placed a warning hand on his arm. Angrily, he swiveled around. His right hand bumped against the freshly-filled goblet and sent it hurtling through the air to clatter loudly on the stone flooring in front of the dining couch.

The dwarfs halted. The music trailed to silence. Every eye in the place turned toward him. With an oath, he scrambled to his feet and brushed at the wine staining his robes.

Peridia was right beside him, still grasping his left arm. "Are you hurt, priest?"

Shatha shook him off.

But the rumbling voice came again, this time with a heavier tone of warning. "Are you hurt? Or are you just as surprised at such an unfortunate accident as the rest of us are?" He gave a sweeping gesture indicating the staring crowd.

Shatha glared at the innkeeper, brushed again at the wine stains on his garments, and fought to control the rage hammering inside him. The pleasure of slapping Rahab's insolent mouth might not be worth the risk of the crowd's disapproval — not now. Already, he felt his reputation and authority had suffered enough by the positioning of his dining couch. The royal insult could not have gone unnoticed by the crowd, even though their greetings on his arrival had been respectful.

However justified he might be to put Rahab in her place, he was unwilling to risk the crowd's disapproval. Rahab was popular with them. The odds were too great. He would deal with Rahab later.

With reluctance, he turned to face the assembled guests and forced a thin smile onto his face. Fingering the amulet of Astarte that hung from the golden chain about his neck, he gave a magnanimous gesture of reassurance to them all. They appeared to accept it. Then he turned and bowed low to King Balaar. "My apologies, sire. It was an unfortunate accident."

Balaar sat unmoving, eyeing him with suspicion. Surprised quiet settled over the crowd. Balaar's delay lengthened. Shatha began to feel like a schoolboy awaiting admonishment. Bile rose up in his throat as embarrassment poured through him. The crowd's eyes were on him again. The old fool! Would he never acknowledge the apology?

The delay continued. The flaming torchiers sputtered against it. Finally, the old king did respond, but indirectly. He raised a thin, blue-veined hand and motioned for the dwarfs and musicians to resume their performances.

Shatha hesitated, expecting at least a nod. None was forthcoming. Hot with embarrassment, he sat down. Servants scurried forward to mop up the mess and to replace and replenish the wine goblet. With a reassuring word to Mozni and to Rahab, Peridia reseated himself.

Shatha felt closed in. Rahab did not look at him or break her stony silence. It was just as well, for he could not retaliate either verbally or physically. Peridia was alert and listening to anything that might pass between them. Across the crowd, the rabiser appeared to be laughing at him.

He felt shackled — subjugated — trapped!

He picked up the fresh wine goblet and drank deeply from it. Only one persistent thought comforted him now. He would find a way to avenge himself, to reassert his authority. Somehow, some way, before this night was over, he would prove to Rahab and to the rest of Jericho that he was their true lord and master.

By the time General Birsha began his report of the trips to the northern provinces, Shatha had withdrawn into brooding sullenness. On the surface, he seemed totally disinterested in Birsha's blunt account of how he had bargained for men-at-arms to help defend Jericho against a Hebrew attack — and what it would cost in goods and gold.

"Regardless of the cost," Birsha said, "our need for help is great. Our northern neighbors feel we have a common enemy in the Hebrews, who are led by the legendary Moses, but whose victories come by and through the great power of their God, Yahweh."

"Rot!" Shatha muttered to himself, expecting an audible protest from the crowd. It did not come. Rather, they seemed to stir with uneasy acceptance. Even Rahab appeared to accept Birsha's utterances without question. And across the way, the Egyptian and his Nubian friend were leaning forward, raptly intent on Birsha's chronicles of past Hebrew victories. Shatha shook his head at the foolishness of these reactions.

"After the death of Aaron, high priest to the Hebrews and brother to Moses, the tribes went through their customary period of mourning. Then they marched on and defeated the mighty Amalekite, King Arad," Birsha recounted. "They burned his cities and took women and children prisoner. Then, bypassing the strongly fortified land of Edom, they journeyed toward Kadesh-Barnea. But when at last they arrived at Kadesh, they discovered no water and no pasturage. You can imagine their discouragement.

"It is related that in their discouragement, they cried out against Yahweh. He did not like this, for He is a jealous God.

Our northern neighbors call him El Qanno — the God who brooks no rival. This God of the Hebrews, they say, is the one God. Present everywhere and all-powerful. And, they say, He is 'The only God!'"

Shatha glanced in dismay at Birsha. What kind of fool was this general of Jericho? What did he know of the power of gods? A murmur of concern stirred the crowd.

"Perhaps this is true, my friends," Birsha went on in a commanding tone. "For when the Hebrews complained and turned to their own devices and began to trust themselves, their God, Yahweh, sent fiery serpents among them. Many were bitten and many died. When this occurred, the people went to Moses and asked him to pray to Yahweh to take away the serpents. Moses did so.

"And after Moses prayed, the God Yahweh instructed Moses to make a fiery serpent of brass and set it upon a pole. Then He decreed that every one who was bitten should look upon the serpent of brass to be saved from death. Moses did as he was told. So did the people. And those who had been bitten lived!"

Disbelief rippled through the assemblage and found its counterpart in the alert faces of the rabiser and his Nubian friend. Rahab trembled. A fearful look shrouded her face. It was as if Birsha's words had conjured up some dreadful memory. Shatha noted the reactions and with a scornful mutter, motioned for a servant to bring more wine.

"I tell you truth," Birsha proceeded steadfastly. "We must not make light of the Hebrew threat. For after this occurrence, the tribes moved without barrier into the Valley of Zared and parleyed with Sihon, king of the Amorites, for passage through his lands. He would not give them passage. And so they fought with Sihon. And they defeated him.

"Then, they turned and marched in the direction of Bashan. Og, king of Bashan, marched out to meet them with all his people to give battle at Edrei. It is reported that the God Yahweh told Moses not to be afraid of Og, but to deal with him and his people as they had with the Amorites. They obeyed. They defeated Og, his sons, and all his people. Not one of the people of Bashan escaped. And so the Hebrews took possession of that country.

"Following this, the sons of Israel set out and pitched their camp in the plains of Moab beyond the Jordan opposite Jericho. This was also done at the instruction of their God, Yahweh."

Birsha paused. The impact of his words was revealed in the uneasy faces of the assembled crowd. He turned to King Balaar. "For the moment, sire, the Hebrews seem peacefully settled in the Plains of Moab. But if I know men, it is a false peace. The Hebrews thirst for cool, pure springs. Their flocks — very large in number — hunger for the lush pastures of this verdant valley." He turned again toward the crowd. Sadness now overrode the stern tone of logic. "My friends, I fear that soon the Hebrew God, Yahweh, will lead his people here to the plains of Jericho and to the very walls of our city. If we are as wise as we are wealthy, we will prepare at once to defend ourselves. It is very important to bring in mercenaries from the northern provinces. We ourselves will have to make sacrifices, but, believe me, no cost is too great. The Hebrew threat is real — very real!"

His words fell heavily into a hush broken only by the sputtering flames in the torchiers and by the softly rhythmic swish of ostrich-plume fans brushing against the air.

Rahab had turned quite pale. The fearful look still masked her face. To Shatha, her reaction was uncharacteristic. It both puzzled and annoyed him. So did the reaction of the rabiser and his slave. They sat scrutinizing the crowd's awed silence much as lions calculate the moment to attack their prey. The thought pushed Shatha to his feet.

"This Yahweh, General Birsha," he questioned with unconcealed scorn. "What does he look like?"

Birsha had started to reseat himself beside King Balaar, but Shatha's tone caused him to sharply straighten and face his challenger. The mood of the crowd wavered.

Instantly, Shatha sensed it. He drew himself up to full height and imperiously fingered the amulet of Astarte hanging from its golden chain. "Does your silence, General Birsha, mean that your northern friends don't know what the Hebrew god looks like?"

Birsha's face darkened.

·

King Balaar glowered disapproval and started to speak.

But Shatha ignored the old man. "Could they not show you a statue of the Hebrew god, General Birsha?" he pushed.

"As you already know, high priest, there are no statues of the Hebrew god. He is an invisible god. He has decreed against statues of Himself."

The crowd stirred with uncertainty.

"No statues?" Shatha scoffed. "Invisible? Then how do these Hebrews know they have a god?"

"Through their leaders — Abraham, Isaac, Jacob — and through their present leader, Moses."

"Ah, yes — Moses."

"It is the same with Canaanites, priest. We know our gods through our leaders."

"This Moses must be a remarkable man," Shatha rasped.

"He is a great leader," Birsha replied with open candor. "He is thoughtful in judgment, courageous in battle. His wisdom is legendary. And his obedience to his God is unquestioned. But all these things are known to you, priest. Why do you pretend otherwise?"

The crowd liked Birsha's thrust.

But Shatha was not to be put off. This was the moment he had waited for. He stepped away from his dining couch and walked out into the center of the hall. "It is true, worthy general. I do know these things. And because I know them, I must oppose your report."

Birsha tensed. Balaar came up halfway out of his chair. The mood of the crowd once again grew expectant, but this time, its interest and attention were with the high priest.

"I oppose your report — and your opinion of Moses — because I do know this invisible Hebrew god. I believe such a god is fictitious. And I believe the man called Moses is a charlatan!" He turned to the startled, superstitious crowd. "Or else the Hebrews are men of little sense. How else could this Moses coerce them with decrees from a god they can't even see?"

A titter of agreement came from the back of the hall where some of the lesser priests were seated.

Shatha played up to it. "How can anything be powerful if

85

you cannot see it or touch it?" he challenged. "All powerful gods have statues."

Again from the back of the hall came agreement. And from two other directions, voices picked up the sentiment and echoed it.

"If this Hebrew god is jealous, he should be!" Shatha declared, parading in a half-circle before the guests. "He should be very jealous of the powers of Canaan's gods!"

More voices joined in affirmation. The crowd's mood was openly shifting, being calmed after the dire predictions made by Birsha. Shatha felt his pulse quicken as he realized he was snatching the honor of the night away from Birsha.

King Balaar came to his feet with surprising agility and even more surprising authority. "Silence!" he admonished. Stunned, the crowd hesitated. "General Birsha is no boy with his first sling. He is your general — a man of courage and good judgment. Your behavior, high priest, is insulting to Jericho's general and to Jericho's king! And so is the behavior of you who are guests in my palace!" He pointed an accusing finger at the crowd; his glare and his stance commanded their silence and their respect. Old and doddering as he was, he was still king and held the power of life and death in his quavering hands. Therefore, he was dangerous when angered. The crowd backed down.

But to Shatha's mind, a far greater danger lay elsewhere; in Pharaoh's edict, in his own deflated authority, and in the potential drain on Jericho's treasury for unneeded men-at-arms. In quick, deferential defense, he bowed to Balaar. "My king, sincerest apologies for the second time tonight." He straightened and came forward. "I do not oppose General Birsha as a person. But I do oppose the report he has given to this gathering."

Balaar was listening, but not convinced.

"It is possible," Shatha went on, approaching the royal dining couch, "that our worthy general is being made to play the fool by his northern friends!"

Balaar's face reddened. Birsha stood stiffly silent.

"In what way?" Balaar demanded. "In what way?"

"By trusting the northerners too much," Shatha suggested,

coming even closer to the royal dining couch. "It is possible the northern provinces have reasons of their own for painting such a dire picture of the Hebrew danger — reasons that have nothing to do with Jericho's destiny."

"What would those reasons be?" Birsha asked.

"To extract a better price for their mercenaries," Shatha said carefully.

A startled hush fell across the hall and was reflected in the faces of the king and the general.

"Birsha, as you say, sire, is a man of honor," Shatha went on skillfully, trying to reassert his influence before king and crowd. "He is open and direct and expects others to be the same. They are not. Birsha thinks in terms of weapons, as he should, and not of costs. But —" he plucked the dagger from his girdle and casually tossed it down onto the stone flooring in front of the royal dining couch. "Weapons, regardless of the cost, are useless unless directed by the hand of man. And in turn, man acts acts on his own to please the whims of the gods."

He stooped, picked up the dagger, and held it out toward Birsha. "You'll notice I said 'gods,' General Birsha, not one 'god.' Many gods are needed to wield the weapons in the hands of man." He paused, expecting a comment. But Birsha fixed him with a steady look and said nothing.

Shatha shrugged, "You, general, know all about weapons. But I know about the gods. And I tell you, and the people of Jericho, that this Hebrew god you speak of is not our concern. He has less power than the jackals of the forest."

He had spoken very softly, but the assemblage had grown so quiet that the sound of his words drifted to the far corners of the hall and came back to him in a twice-repeated echo.

Slowly, he turned and walked away from the royal dining couch, surveyed the crowd, and tried to gauge the effect of his words. Every eye was on him with a look of approval. Even a strange, new light had entered the eyes of the rabisher. Rahab was visibly trembling. He gave a sardonic smile and replaced the dagger in his girdle. He was in control again.

"The Hebrew god — the one you cannot see — in no way compares with Canaan's gods. We have all seen the marvels of El, serpent-god of the universe, who lives a thousand plains and ten-thousand fields from Canaan in the midst of the fountains of the two deeps." He held out his arm to let the folds of his cloak reveal the symbol of El to his listeners. "This all-powerful god who brings the seasons and orders his children, Shahru, the dawn, and Shalmu, the sunset, to give us light and darkness, also fights victoriously for us to turn aside the blights and plagues of Mot, the black god of death. Can the unseen Hebrew god do this?"

The crowd was leaning forward, enraptured by the descriptions of their familiar gods. Only Rahab stared vacantly across the openness of the hall. He turned from her, his scarlet robes swaying hypnotically.

"There is Baal — great god of the storm — who brings lightning to frighten away evil spirits. When his voice rumbles from the sky, he joins with Astarte as the giver of fertility. Can the Hebrew god claim such power?

"And, people of Jericho, there is still an even greater god under whose protection this City of Palms is sheltered. It is Astarte, the great earth-mother goddess for whom we are productive, to whom we propitiate sacrifices to assure our wealth, from whom we receive the bounty of the fertile plains of Jericho."

Except for a small group, relief and assurance glistened from every face as Shatha recited the powerful characteristics of Astarte. In his voice was a tone of persuasive authority that wrapped his listeners with the comforting sense of the acceptable and familiar. He viewed their reactions with sardonic pleasure, recognizing that through him, each person was assaulting the strangeness of the unknown, unseeable Hebrew god.

"Citizens of Jericho, hear me well." He no longer spoke softly but with a strident passion that stirred the hearts of his listeners. "There is no more powerful force than the gods of Canaan. They don't lead us through forty years of wilderness wanderings. Our bellies are full. Our storehouses bulge. And" — he tore the amulet from the golden chain and brandished it above his head — "our gods are not invisible!"

The crowd came to its feet.

"Jericho thrives!" Shatha shouted. "Astarte reigns! Blasphemies on the Hebrew god! He cannot touch us! He dares not even show his face!"

The crowd surged toward him shouting, "Balu! Balu!" Shatha was their god, their will, their salvation. Hebrews, be damned! Shatha, the high priest of Jericho, was the power of plenty! In a reaffirmation of faith in what could be seen and touched, they swept him up onto their shoulders. "Balu! Balu! Master protector!"

Music burst forth, spontaneously joining the shouting, frenzied chant. The boisterous crowd wound through the royal dining hall and out into the streets of Jericho.

Fear and anger traced twin paths of acid through Rahab, and left her with the same drained emptiness she seemed to be experiencing more and more frequently.

Arrogant deceit and a persuasive tongue had prevailed. General Birsha's logic and sense of caution, as well as King Balaar's support of him, lay shattered and broken as the wine goblet Shatha had destroyed earlier in the evening.

King Balaar trembled with rage as he left the hall, followed by a grim-faced general and his wife. Yanshuph and Tirzah stood very close together, hands tightly clasped, watching the king and general make their departures.

A menacing memory went through Rahab:

"Astarte, El, Baal, and Mot
The gods lead us as they are wroth."

Involuntarily, she shivered and turned to her parents. Her mother's eyes held an incredulous expression. Her father's eyes were troubled and his words were angry.

"The lion within our gates roars mightily, my daughter!"

She pulled the scarlet cloak about her shoulders and tried to stop shaking. "Can it be that he has discovered some new prey?"

"More likely he is feeling the pressure of the old prey turning on him," Peridia rumbled. "He is mad. You know that, don't you?"

She nodded, pulling the cloak even more tightly around her shoulders. Yanshuph and Tirzah joined the family group.

"He is dangerous!" Peridia intoned. "We must keep you

away from him. We must —" His voice trailed off. With a heavy sigh and shake of his head, he guided his family across the now empty dining hall.

Near the entrance, Rahab dropped back to pick up the palace guard escort arranged for her, the Egyptian, and his Nubian.

Joel came up alongside her and said quietly, "Honorable hostess, I am in your debt, and that of your father as well, for inviting me to come here tonight."

The tone of sincerity surprised her. Considering all that had taken place, she expected sarcasm.

"In truth," he repeated, as if reading her mind, "I *am* in your debt. We both are." He indicated Hejaz, who bowed respectfully.

She mistrusted his change in attitude, but did not reply. Something in his eyes — a depth she had never before noticed — kept her from it.

Joel bowed and slowly straightened. As he did, the folds of his vestment fell away revealing a silver chain about his neck. Clasped in its links was an odd-looking talisman.

She stared at it first in curiosity, then in astonishment, and finally, in alarm. It was made from a bit of ram's horn and carved with a roughly beautiful cherubim, an exact duplicate of the talisman she had received from the dirty, wildly-frightened slave-boy so many years before.

8

Three days had passed since the dinner at the palace and the alarming revelations about Shatha, about the Hebrew god, and about the rabiser. It was now the day of the full moon nearest the spring equinox.

Tonight, the temple rituals for the Festival of Harvest would begin. As quedesah, Rahab would preside in opulence and authority in honor of Astarte. And from a practical standpoint, she would share in a huge amount of tribute and sacrificial offerings being brought into the city. This should be a day of excitement, a day of spirit.

The hillsides were covered in spring blossoms. They helped to hide the nakedness of the freshly-harvested fields. The River Jordan was beginning to course full from the snow-melt of the northern mountains.

But Rahab felt no excitement. She was nervous and short-tempered. Not once had she felt the usual enthusiasm for the forthcoming rituals. She had risen early and watched the day come awake. Then, as custom dictated, she had summoned Ahabina to walk with her in the dawn's cool freshness to enjoy the sights of Jericho adorned for the festival. She had considered not calling Ahabina at all, but she still had need of her. Besides, had she not done so, there would have been questions. How could she have answered them? — That Ahabina was changing and she mistrusted her? It was just easier to do what was expected, for the moment. And so they walked.

But there was no joy in the customary exercise. Instead, the sights of Jericho disturbed her. She seemed to view everything through the vivid specter of the stirring of change deep inside her. And memories of recent events did not help: Birsha's belief in the power of the Hebrew god, Shatha's egomania, and the rabiser's possession of the odd-looking ram's horn ring. She forced the memories back and sternly reminded herself that more important things needed her attention on this special day of days. But even now, late in the morning in the khan's main storeroom where she gave the final check to the supplies for the temple ritual, the specter still hung over her.

She finished counting the last set of ritual linens for the temple maidens and motioned for Ahabina to have the lackeys close the chest. She glanced about making sure all other cases were properly secured. From outside came the din of activity anticipating the festival. The khan bulged with travelers. None had dickered over prices or accommodations; profits were excellent; foods and wines were plenteous.

Even Jericho's crystalline air shimmered with festive sounds. Why should she worry about the Egyptian? The fact that he also had an odd-looking ring similar to hers proved absolutely nothing. He probably had stolen it from the poor young wretch she had befriended so many years before. There was absolutely no proof that the two were the same person — none at all. What she did know was that the man now wearing the ram's horn ring was Egyptian and was a rabiser, Rameses' tax-collector, her sworn enemy. What happened years ago, whatever she might have felt then, no longer mattered.

What *did* matter was that rabiser was constantly underfoot. Every word had to be spoken carefully lest his ears pick it up. Every business transaction had to be hidden from his sharp eyes. Carelessness already had cost her the load of goods from Tegush. And because she wanted to spite Shatha, she had encouraged her father to invite the rabiser and his Nubian to the dinner for Birsha. As a consequence, she had made the accidental and uncomfortable discovery that he wore the odd-looking ring similar to her own. Ever since that night the rabiser had been more assertive than ever, almost as though Birsha's views of the Hebrews gave him some supernatural confidence. She had watched him closely during the dinner at the palace and noted the absorbed interest showing openly on the square planes of his face. It had seemed to her that he not only believed Birsha, but that he had listened to the reports as if he was hearing a familiar and well-loved story. She found the reaction curious.

With annoyance, she moved back along the row of cases for final inspection. The storeroom was hot and dark. And the heat was not eased by the foot-lamps carried by Ahabina and the lackeys.

Fah upon the heat! Fah upon the rabiser! How really irritating it was to have him constantly underfoot.

It was an irritating as General Birsha's reports of the Hebrews and of their strange and invisible god. These Hebrews were reported to account full measure to every man and to be as hospitable to strangers as to kin. What nonsense! They were also said to possess endless resilience to the inroads of pestilence, war, and wandering. They called themselves the chosen people.

Chosen for what, she wondered acidly. To kill and maraud? It sounded as if that was all there was to their strange god. If so, then what of the stories of his mercy and kindness and his love for his people? Was that a myth? Or was it real? Real or not, what did it matter?

Even if General Birsha was an alarmist as Shatha had proclaimed, his reports of the Hebrew's one god were less pleasant to consider than the chosen people themselves. "I am what I am." "I cause to be." How utterly ridiculous! An invisible god? Impossible! Yet the idea clung to her like a relentless and unwelcome guest.

She instructed Ahabina to refold a dozen of the scarlet ceremonial sashes; she then closed the last of the packing cases and ordered the lackeys to take them to the court of temple maidens under Ahabina's watchful eyes.

All that remained now was to gather a mantle and a small case of jewels from her rooms. The royal escort would soon come for her.

She quickly left the storeroom. The rites of the Festival of Harvest would cleanse her mind of all these disturbing thoughts, even though it would be difficult to once again consort with Shatha. Fah on the Hebrews and their strange god!

As she stepped inside her rooms, Tirzah greeted her. The

younger woman's usually serene face appeared flushed with uncertainty. "A word with you before you leave, my sister."

"Something wrong?"

"I am as tangled as a fox in a bramble," Tirzah said with a thin laugh.

"For what reason?"

"The Egyptian."

Rahab gave a snort of impatience and went toward the dressing area.

"How much longer is he going to be here?"

"Who can say?" She rummaged through a chest for an appropriate mantle.

"Is he truly our enemy? He seems so — so — Oh, I don't know."

She straightened in surprise. "He seems so — what?"

"Well, what I mean is — maybe we're not doing the right thing. It's just that it really doesn't seem to be his fault."

"What's not his fault?" Rahab demanded, closing the lid of the chest and returning with a mantle.

"He draws so well," Tirzah said, helping Rabah adjust the mantle around her shoulders.

Exasperated, she turned. "In the name of Astarte, what are you talking about, Tirzah?"

"You know — drawing — sketching."

"So the Egyptian draws. He also snoops and pries and collects tax tribute."

"But don't you think it is a great talent to be able to draw, Rahab? Don't you think a man must have some good in him to have such a talent?"

"I do not!" She went to the wall where her jewel-case was hidden and took out the ritual jewels. The odd-looking ram's horn ring lay at the bottom of the case.

A reflective look came onto Tirzah's face. "It would be wonderful to do something like that."

"What?" On impulse, she picked up the strange ram's horn ring and dropped it, along with the ritual jewels, into a small leather pouch.

"To draw and sketch," Tirzah went on. "What fun it would be to make objects take shape with charcoal and pigments. What fun, indeed."

"So he amuses himself with games — good." She went to the polished bronze disc and glanced at her reflection. A whisper of breeze caught at her hair, dislodging it. She straightened it and adjusted the mantle more firmly about her shoulders. "It will keep him occupied. He'll have less time for annoying the household."

"He is really quite clever with his hands."

"He is clever in other ways, too."

"He sketches all manner of things. Birds in the sky, people, the streets and buildings of Jericho, the fountains, the courtyard. And he has done a remarkable likeness of Reba."

Rahab glanced sharply at Tirzah's reflection in the polished bronze.

"But I do hate to see her growing so attached to him if he is truly our enemy."

Rahab whirled. "What do you mean attached?"

"Oh don't be alarmed. It is nothing, really."

"Nothing? When has Reba been around the Egyptian?"

"Several times, I guess. But I only saw her today. She sat with him on the walkway in front of his rooms, watching him draw. She was fascinated by it. It amused her, as it would any child. And he seemed so kind. Very gentle and protective. I watched them for quite a while. They laughed together a great deal. It's as if he feels some real affection —"

"This is impossible! I cannot believe my ears!"

"But, my sister —"

Rahab exploded. "No one, including Reba — especially Reba — is to have anything to do with him. You know that, Tirzah!"

"But — but —"

"It is dangerous. How could you let this happen?"

"I cannot watch the child every single moment." Tirzah defended quickly. "It is like trying to catch a rabbit without a snare."

"Without a snare? Don't you see, this is the Egyptian's snare?"

Tirzah looked puzzled.

With a resigned shake of her head, Rahab went to her sister. "My foolish one, don't you see that the rabiser feels no affection for Reba. It is a trick."

"But, but what kind of trick?"

"A trick to learn what else he can about our goods and our wealth."

Tirzah's eyes widened.

"Oh yes, he is very kind, very gentle with Reba," Rahab said softly and sarcastically. "Why shouldn't he be? He has made her trust him completely. I'll wager she talks to him with utter innocence about everything that goes on in this entire household. And no doubt she also answers all the questions he might ask of her."

"Come now. What can a child know of things that would be of interest to an Egyptian rabiser?"

"Tirzah, you're more innocent than the child!"

Stubbornness set itself on her sister's usually smiling lips. "The child is amused by his sketching and drawing. And he finds pleasure in amusing her. He means no harm."

"I'm astonished! You are defending him!"

"No — I — I — just —"

"You speak as if he is as good as any Jerichoan."

"He can't be all bad," Tirzah protested. "He could not pretend such kindness to a child if he did not feel it. The child would sense it and withdraw from him. This I know!"

"You know? You know?" Rahab snapped irritably. "You know nothing. Especially about men like this. You've lived in the shelter of this khan and in the protection of Yanshuph's arms. You cannot know about men like the rabiser. You're as innocent as Reba."

"Perhaps I am," came the tense reply. "And then perhaps you are not innocent enough."

The rebuff was unlike Tirzah.

"As each day passes, Rahab, you grow more suspicious and more grasping. Even your eyes have begun to offend you. For they no longer see the unmeasurable qualities in people."

Hurt ripped through her.

"Some things can never be bartered and traded. Shekels and ephahs can't measure human qualities. You used to know that."

"You scorn shekels and ephahs?" Rahab snapped back.

"I scorn what they have done to you."

"Shekels and ephahs protect our positions of prominence," she defended, angry now over Tirzah's unexpected frankness. "You enjoy their fruits as much as I. So don't question the actions that lie behind their accumulation."

Tirzah came toward her, surprisingly stubborn. "But I do question — and I grieve — for you! Your blood and mine are one. I grieve for you, my sister, because you have no compassion."

Rahab's heart lurched.

"There was a time when you valued the qualities of the human heart," Tirzah went on, her eyes beginning to brim with tears. "You cared for the beauty that only the soul can tell of. You would have understood that even a man such as the rabiser can enjoy the innocence of friendship with a child. But that has changed. You have changed, Rahab. Shatha has done this to you.

"You scorn and ridicule him. You protest his arrogance. And I don't blame you. He is arrogant and he's cruel. Yet, you are still greatly influenced by him."

Defenseless before the truth, Rahab turned away.

"But more than that, you are influenced by your own passion to possess. The price of our prominence is very high — for all of us. But you, my sister, pay more than anyone else."

The words cut deep, slashing open old wounds of conscience, wounds that had been carefully sealed in order to exist as Shatha's courtesan. Now, Tirzah's candid accusation laid them bare and forced her to reckon with them at a time when she could not afford to face them. Not on this day of all days. In the long, silent moment that followed, it was the irony of the timing that rallied her defenses and made her pride gather up its shredded image.

"I am well-rewarded," she said, slowly turning to face her sister. "And so is the rest of this household. You, for instance, would be hard-pressed to search for your living from the land. You and Yanshuph both!"

Tirzah paled, but did not back off.

"What's happened to you?" Rahab quickly pursued, going toward her. "You defend a man who is our sworn enemy. You speak ill of me. What's happened to you? You might as well say also that you believe those ridiculous stories about the Hebrews' unseen god. I would be no more shocked than I already am."

A strange light flashed into Tirzah's eyes. "Perhaps I could say that. And perhaps I would, if I knew that this Yahweh was a God of mercy and compassion."

Incredulous, Rahab stared.

"I am not as clever as you, Rahab. Nor do I know the ways of men nor the ways of the temple. But I do know it is wrong to mock the beauty that only a husband and wife together can know. The temple rituals do that. I know it is wrong to kill children in the name of religious sacrifice. And I know it is wrong to take food from a starving man just to appease a statue!"

"Tirzah!"

Her sister did not waver. "These things are wrong, and you know it."

"But," Rahab protested, "it's our custom. It's decreed by Canaan's gods."

Tirzah shook her head. "I should like to know what the Hebrews' God thinks about such things. Some say he frowns on them. If this be true, then, yes, it is possible I *could* believe there is such a God. And it is possible I could believe *in* Him — even if He is unseen!"

Rahab groped for a response and found none. Instead a cold tracing of fear went through her. The room grieved with an oppressive stillness. Pity crept into Tirzah's eyes, and once again Rahab felt the deep cutting ache in her own conscience.

She stood helplessly pinned by the unswerving accuracy of her sister's disapproval. For in truth it matched her own. But she was tied to custom and to convenience and to the comfortable. And that was far more practical.

She wanted to cry out; to deny the pity, to refute the anguish that was steadily creeping through her own soul.

Snatching up the leather pouch of ritual jewels, she turned away and hurried toward the court of temple maidens.

In the bone-wearying, sun-blistered heat of the land of Canaan, the court of temple maidens was a paradise of shade, silks, and subtlety. Luxury and color promenaded only less beautifully than the maidens themselves.

As quedesah of Jericho and courtesan to the high priest, Rahab's authority over all the distinctive ranks of temple maidens was second only to Shatha's. Customarily, her word was indisputable, her actions unquestioned. For she was the human representative of the great earth-mother goddess, Astarte. Worship of Astarte was Canaan's umbilical cord to prosperity.

Rahab entered the cool shaded splendor of the court still distressed about the confrontation with Tirzah, and still fighting to reseal the wounds of her own conscience.

She stopped in front of a large statue of Astarte and lit an incense pot. Baskets filled with tiny amulets of the great goddess were placed at the foot of the statue. These would be sold later to the festival worshippers by the temple maidens. How simple, easy, and really quite practical the worship of Astarte was. There was no foolishness about an invisible god. Canaan's gods were very visible.

Ahabina approached and salaamed. Rahab returned the greeting and then as Ahabina lay garlands of flowers at the base of the statue, Rahab prostrated herself before it. Practicality was the key to Canaan's rituals, she reminded herself. The symbolism and representative acts that would occur later tonight would clearly prove it without any maddening haze of moral questions involved.

Tirzah had spoken as if somehow religion and morals should be interwoven. What rot! Moral values were the concern of Canaan's social laws. They had nothing to do with religion. What a goose Tirzah was.

Propitiation of the gods was the purpose of the festival and the passionate acts it encouraged. Whether those acts were divine or mortal, religious or moral was simply not relevant.

As quedesah, she only had to approve, to participate, to influence. No rule of giving to the poor was needed to justify a Canaanite's avarice during festival. No prayer for forgiveness had to be made to dull Canaan's common ambition to possess. It was a simple matter of bargaining.

Worshippers bargained with their possessions for more of Astarte's fruits of plenty. And at the same time, they boasted of their already-accumulated wealth before the envious eyes of their neighbors. If a man brought two goats in tribute at festival time, he expected six in return. If he got them, Astarte was divine. If he did not, it was an evil omen that his envious neighbor had poxed the two goats. In due time, the affronted worshipper made off with six of his neighbor's goats as just recompense.

It was as simple as that. It was practical. Wealth meant a good life — now — in the present. Possessions were vital here and now. They were the baksheesh to the hereafter, the necessary gratuity to the world beyond the veil of mortal sight. Once in that nether world, a person's two souls — ka, the wanderer and ba, the protector — found sustenance through the wealth buried with them. Canaan's religion was practical. Why didn't Tirzah accept this fact of life?

As Ahabina finished laying all the flowers about Astarte's statue, Rahab arose and, with Ahabina following, made her way across the main court. All the maidens, in various states of dress, and their body-servants gave her greetings and obeisance. She accepted them with a growing sense of satisfaction. Her spirits began to brighten. A sense of festive anticipation was in the air. Slaves hurried about with bath water, perfumes, and soothing lotions. Chatter and laughter abounded.

She had no need to feel disturbed or fearful, she reminded herself. Even the strict classification of the temple maidens seemed to take on a special kind of comfortable practicality. The most select group, her own group, were the divine courtesans who represented the virginal qualities of the great goddess Astarte. These were the exclusive property of Astarte's imposing rank of priests.

In the second order were the maidens who gave pleasure to all citizens who sought santification in the eyes of Astarte through acts of coalescence. The third group were the childbearers. And the last group was composed of the distinctly homogeneous souls who gave santification to those of their own kind.

The ranks of the male prostitutes were likewise as practically organized. The services enacted by all were considered sacred.

A sensation of the familiar and comfortable swept over her. As quedesah, she was Astarte's most important human representative. Her power was great. Whatever might lie in the future, it could not touch her here and now. In this setting, she was an absolute authority. The fawnings of all the others attested to it.

Reaching her own special and private dressing area, she tossed her mantle to one slave, gave the jewel case to another, and motioned for a third slave to draw her bath. It was then that Ahabina reappeared in an obvious state of agitation.

Curiosity aroused, she watched the once-loyal body-servant summarily dismiss the other slaves with a wave of her hand. Quickly then, she came close, leaned down and whispered the news that a certain temple maiden had in her possession the sheer, white mantle belonging to the high priest.

As the words tumbled from Ahabina, Rahab quelled the anger and jealousy coursing through her and muted it with the wary caution of calculation. This could be the moment she had been waiting for to test the real power of her consort versus her own. She looked up, searching Ahabina's scar-laced face, and wondering if she could trust her just once more. The recent attitude of sullenness and suspicion seemed to have vanished before the onslaught of genuine distress.

"It is said this maiden has had the mantle since the night of General Birsha's dinner. She is telling everyone it is a gift from the noble Shatha!" Ahabina finished. "What does this mean? Is my mistress to be replaced as quedesah? If that happens, what will become of me?"

For another long moment, Rahab studied the face of her servant. The fear of displacement could reassert loyalty in many people. But status was an even greater motivator for one such as Ahabina. Carefully, in a controlled tone, she began to reassure the slave. "I am still quedesah. And you, Ahabina, are still the most important slave in Jericho, because you are my loyal body-servant. Nothing will happen to you as long as I remain quedesah." She reached out and placed her hand on that of the slave's in a gesture of approval and trust. "It is not the noble Shatha we need to fear," she asserted. "It is the maiden who has the mantle."

Ahabina reacted exactly as she hoped. Anger seeped into

101

the dark eyes. The strong brown hand clenched reflexively, and she straightened as if to go at once to confront the interloper.

"The statue of Astarte darkens with displeasure at this news, Ahabina."

The slave turned, following Rahab's gesture.

"What shall we do to appease Astarte's anger, Ahabina? What can we do?"

No answer was forthcoming.

"The temple maiden who has the mantle is a threat to you, as well as to me, Ahabina. She is the only maiden who defied my edict that none should lie with the noble Shatha until after the festival."

A look of decision now clearly showed in the slave's face.

"What should be done about it, Ahabina?"

"We should fulfill the punishment of the edict, my mistress. We should fulfill it at once." She pulled a short dagger from the girdle at her waist.

Rahab nodded. "Be discreet, Ahabina. And when you've finished, take the mantle to the khan. It must be carefully washed and mended before his eminence, the Noble Shatha, again adorns himself in it."

She watched the slave move away, satisfied that Shatha would long remember the results of his attempt to humiliate her and belittle the power of her position.

9

The day's shadows lengthened into twilight across the City of Palms. The Festival of Harvest was underway. Torches began to flicker up and down the crooked length of the Street of Shops where Joel and Hejaz, accompanied by a squad of palace guards, were being pushed along in the carnival-like press of a boisterous crowd of celebrants.

Perspiration plastered Joel's yellow linen vestment to his back. He paused, mopped at his face and glanced at the Nubian. The powerful ebony body, clad in a short green tunic, seemed untouched by the stifling heat. "The khan would've been cooler," Joel repeated for the third time.

"That is now a passing regret, my friend. You, yourself, said we have three reasons for coming to this hellish Canaanite festival."

"And all good reasons," Joel said, mopping again at his face.

"Ah, yes," Hejaz recited. "First, we must measure Jericho's true wealth. Second, we must try to find the Amalekite trader and ask about that ring of yours. And third," he chuckled, "Is this third reason a good one, oh noble rabiser?"

"Why not? Seeing the performance of our innkeeper's eldest daughter should be worth this heat and the smell of this place."

Hejaz wrinkled his nose. "I'm not so sure. Besides, if it is to be such a worthwhile performance, why isn't her family attending?"

"Greed, my friend!"

"Greed? from a Canaanite?" Hejaz feigned surprise.

"Aye," Joel came back, "Some Egyptian might steal the khan if they all went to this hedonistic ritual." The crowd jostled and shoved. Rags and silks pushed along side-by-side. But the cordon of palace guards kept a closed-rank buffer from everything except the smells and the noise. "Besides, she's a beautiful woman," Joel shouted. "And I make a study of them, you know. So my interest is purely investigative!"

"As is mine." Hejaz laughed, "with any Nubian maid I can find!"

Shops were crammed with merchandise: pottery, ornamental work, hides, skins, colorful bolts of cloth, jewelry, metal goods, and leather work. One shopkeeper hawked gum arabic and rose-paste candies. Another, being swarmed by children and grownups alike, was selling helawi.

"That's Jericho's most popular confection, Hejaz. It's made of sesame and sugar cane. It's good."

The Nubian grinned and shoved through the cordon of palace guards to make a purchase. He returned, like a little boy at this first carnival, offering pieces of the confection to all the guards as well as to Joel. Further down the street, it was Joel's turn to stop the small cavalcade, this time in amazement at the mounds of foodstuffs for sale under a bright-striped awning. Lebn, the cheese-like substance that stayed fresh for days in the heat of the valley and the deserts, hung like ponderous over-ripe melons on upright sticks. Flat loaves of fragrant coarse brown bread pyramided beside them. Salted fish from the River Jordan were piled high in baskets. And next to these were more baskets — dozens of them — filled to overflowing with fruits and vegetables and herbs.

"Look at that!" Joel said, with a shake of his head. "And in a land forever hungry."

"It almost equals the bazaars of Pharaoh," Hejaz agreed.

"Aye!" Joel responded. "It is small wonder the Festival of Harvest is so important. Even an unpracticed eye can see why Jericho parades as elegant mistress of the lower Jordan valley." He did a quick, rough calculation. "How much of all this do you think will actually be reported to us for the next shipment of tax to —"

Hejaz tugged roughly at his sleeve. "The Amalekite — over there —"

Joel swiveled in the direction Hejaz pointed and saw the striped robe of the trader disappear behind a stack of hides at the tanner's stall. Quickly, Joel elbowed his way through the palace guards and tried to push through the crowd to get to the trader. He had so many questions about the ring. Particularly where Tegush had gotten it. How long ago? Under what circumstances? After all these years, the Amalekite could be the first real link with his family.

But the crowd closed in and flowed around him like quicksand. The harder he shoved, the closer packed the crowd became. It was impossible to move except as the crowd moved.

The Amalekite had disappeared. And now looking around, Joel realized that Hejaz and the palace guards had disappeared, too, in the packed mass of smelly bodies. With a curse, he tried to push back to the spot where he'd veered away from them. But the pressing crowd would not yield.

Abruptly, a strident burst of horns and drums pounded across the din announcing the start of the festival's opening ritual. The crowd paused; then with a new, rough urgency, it shifted and moved toward the open plaza and temple grove. Joel found himself shoved along with it. And in the same moment, he realized he was vulnerable from every side, if anyone in the crowd recognized him as the hated rabiser. He had no wish to die in Pharaoh's service. Panic caught at him. In fact, he had no wish to die at all — from whatever cause.

At the entrance to the sacred grove, the giant statue of Astarte, distorted by torchlight, bid them grotesque welcome. Once inside the grove, the press of the crowd eased somewhat. Joel could see that it was a roofless, four-sided enclosure sentried by sycamores, ancient and tall, and a bevy of womanish tamarisks. Throughout Canaan, the tamarisks were highly valued as trees of good fortune. Any acts performed under or near them were thought to be especially blessed by Canaan's gods. A tremor went through him as he suddenly remembered the law given by Moses that banned the use of such idolatrous groves. He briefly wondered if what he was about to see might be more than he'd bargained for.

He looked around again for Hejaz and the palace guards, but to no avail. A parade of naked children, garlanded in flowers, tumbled and frolicked in front of the crowd now leading it toward the altar room at the far end of the grove.

Here, more torches blazed, their ponderous orange flames accenting six large window-like openings carved just below the top of the wall. Hundreds of temple doves perched in these openings. Around him, the crowd began to throw grain up into the air. It was an act of benevolence designed to bring special concessions of good fortune from the sacred birds.

Other celebrants allowed large snakes, living symbols of the god El, Astarte's consort, to stick their heads out of their tunics. Many of the crowd moved closer, trying to touch the snakes, visibly eager for the blessings of such symbols.

Joel watched with disgust. Tarnished as his memory was of the Hebrew rites of thanksgiving and atonements; unfaithful as he had been to his prayers; the behavior of the Canaanites angered him. He suddenly realized how strongly the teachings of his youth were still with him.

Familiar words of Mosaic law coursed through his mind.

"I am the Lord Thy God. There is no other god before me!"

He paused momentarily and looked at the focal point of the altar room. It was another statue of Astarte. This one was a low-relief figure carved in the wall itself. A glazed decorative tile delineated the entire figure. The headpiece was raven black and adorned with a crown of lapis-lazuli. The eyes were sapphire.

On the body, the sexual aspects of Canaan's great earth-mother goddess were clearly depicted. Pearls encrusted the huge breasts. The right arm crossed beneath the breasts and on it nestled a graven white dove. From the dove's mouth issued the smoky pungence of incense. Carved in the clutched right hand were stalks of over-ripe grains, their heads heavy with amethysts.

Below the statue's right arm, the distended belly folded down to a triangular field of glistening emeralds. Below this, entwining one leg of the statue, was the serpent-form of the god El. Embossed in rubies and opals, its head was uplifted as if in praise of the loins. The head, however, was not that of a serpent, but rather, that of a human with the features described in onyx and obsidian.

106

The left arm of the statue was outstretched. From the hand cascaded miniature human forms. Beneath, positioned as if to catch them, waited the form of Mot, the black moth, Canaan's god of death.

It was a sensuous and blasphemous portrayal.

"Thou shalt make thee no graven images."

Though the old commandment sprang to his mind, Joel couldn't escape a sense of appreciation for the beautiful workmanship of the statue. In fact, it surprised him. Canaanites were notably poor craftsmen. Old as Jericho was, and as many cultures as she had known, her present citizens contributed no creativity to her. They were too absorbed in trading for wealth and in seeking the animal pleasures of life. The statue in front of him had to be the work of a foreign artisan. It was too beautiful a piece of work to be otherwise.

The crowd edged forward once more, pushing Joel directly in front of the altar platform and at the feet of Astarte. He was separated from her only by a cordon of half-a-hundred men-at-arms. The four corner blocks of the platform were in the design of open lilies. On top of the platform was a strange clay object that appeared to be a hollow cylinder some two cubits tall. He'd never seen anything like it before and wondered what it was used for.

But before he could pursue the thought priestly trumpets rent the air with two shivering blasts. The crowd quieted. The chant of female voices could be heard, and within a matter of seconds a procession of five-score temple maidens came into view from behind the wall of the altar platform. All were identically dressed in diaphanous white linen sashed with scarlet. Joel recognized the costumes as those woven in the khan and wryly wondered how much Rahab and Peridia had made Shatha pay for them.

Each maiden carried a basket of small clay figurines of Astarte. The maidens were followed by two priests clad in dun-colored vestments. Their heads and faces were clean-shaven in Egyptian style.

One of the priests carried a magnificent electrum bowl filled with wine. He placed it on the strange looking cylindrical object in the center of the altar. The other priest carried four immaculate white doves and placed them in the openings on the sides of the stand. Now, Joel recognized that the strange looking stand was a miniature version of the temple itself.

The temple maidens moved on across the platform and out into the crowd where they began to sell the small clay figures of Astarte. Other priests now appeared with leavened loaves, jars of wine, and still smaller versions of the clay stands. When all of these objects were set in place, a drum beat sounded. It was loud and commanding. Everyone turned to face the left side of the altar.

From the darkness beyond the torches came more priests carrying baskets of planted grapevines. They were followed by a short, plump woman dressed in a vivid green cassock. The hem of the cassock was gold-embroidered with the symbols of long life and prosperity, the lotus and pomegranate. Her ample waist was encircled by a silver chain, from which were suspended two raven's wings and a golden pouch. Around her neck, she wore a talisman of five symbolic bats wrought in silver and set with precious stones. And on her head, she wore a fiery red wig!

Joel stared in surprise. Egyptians considered red wigs an abomination. They were said to possess the powers of the spirits of evil! But apparently, from the chant springing up from the crowd, the Canaanites did not hold the Egyptian belief. "Nahshon! Great seeress! Nahshon brings good fortune! Praise the seeress! Praise Nahshon! She is all-powerful!"

Rythmically, the chant continued, and Nahshon began the rites of fertility for Canaan's fields and vines. First, she went to one of the stands holding the leavened loaves. She took one of them, moved on to a wine jar, and dipped it in. Two priests repeated her actions. Now, she came forward scattering bits of the wine-soaked bread in all directions. The crowd pushed forward, eager to be touched by this enchanted sprinkling. It would mean good crops in the coming season.

When the leavened loaf had been disposed of, she plucked a handful of powdery substance from the golden pouch at her waist and scattered it over all the priests, the grapevines, the wine, and the electrum bowl.

"Fortune smiles," she intoned. "Fortune smiles! Fortune

108

smiles greatly on Jericho and on her people! The great goddess Astarte smiles on Jericho and favors her with bountiful crops and vines. I, Nahshon, predict it! I, Nahshon, command it!"

Scornfully, Joel looked away, recalling another old ordinance.

"Listen not to the soothsayers.

I, Jehovah, am giver of the Law —"

The Canaanite crowd was enthusiastic over Nahshon's pronouncement. They picked it up, echoing it again and again while the priests helped Nahshon to get down from the front of the altar and move among them. She reached into her golden pouch once more and cast its powdery susbstance far and wide over everything and everybody.

Joel tried to step aside, but the crowd was too closely packed. She was coming directly at him, and he wondered if she planned to identify him to this volatile crowd.

But then he could see the trance-like glaze in her eyes. She had not recognized him. An odor of peculiar sweetness clung to her. He identified it as a strange drug known in Egypt that was used to produce hallucinations. Still uncomfortable at her closeness as she passed directly in front of him, he tried again to step back. But the throng held him as they tried to get close to her to touch the abominable red wig. Only when a third priest appeared suddenly on the altar did they relent.

This priest was covered in ashes and held a broken reed in his hand. At the sight of him, the mood of the crowd instantly altered. The chant of approval for Nahshon became a warning for her; and then, in another instant, it became a roar of disapproval for the priestly representation of Mot, the black moth, the god of Death. He responded to their disapproval by brandishing the broken reed at them and lunging threateningly in their direction. Then, he turned on the priests who were tending the grapevines and the remaining leavened loaves and wine. Pantomiming dire threats to them, he almost succeeded in snatching away one of the young vines.

But Nahshon had hurriedly clambered back up on the altar and immediately accosted Mot with the powerful raven's wings suspended from the silver chain at her waist. He dropped the young vine and backed away. Then ensued a

109

thrust-and-parry pantomime of the ancient battle between fertility and barrenness, between good and evil.

Joel was fascinated. Nothing he had ever seen rivaled it for sheer animal emotion. But, at last, Mot was vanquished. The symbolic charade was completed. A deafening shout of triumph went up from the crowd and rang through the pagan grove. Before it subsided, the priestly trumpets again sounded. This heralded the arrival of the herdsmen-priests, and the beginning of the ritual to assure the bounty of herds and flocks.

One priest carried a small kid in his arms. A second led a she-goat. A third and a fourth brought on a clay stove and a bronze cauldron and set them up on the altar. A charcoal fire was started and fanned into eager flames with the use of an eagle's wing.

"Thou shalt not seethe a kid
in its mother's milk."

As a boy, he had never understood this instruction. Now, he did. In dire times, when all other pleas to Canaan's gods failed, the Canaanites practiced child-sacrifice. The act now in preparation on the altar would symbolize that desecration of life!

The crowd grew more boisterous. Scuffling broke out. Bawdy jokes and obscenities bludgeoned the grove and rebounded from the altar and from the bejeweled statue of Astarte. As he suspected, the herdsmen-priests milked the she-goat and placed the milk in the bronze cauldron over the fire. They killed the kid, dressed it, and merrily boiled it in the milk of its own dam. Odious steam rose in a cloud, hovered over the altar, and mingled with the smell of fresh blood and pungent incense. Joel grabbed for the linen square tucked in his sash and held his nose against the stench of the unholy sacrifice. A temple guard noticed and made an obscene gesture at him. Joel responded in kind.

More torches, carried by more priests, were brought to the altar and placed in heavy staunchions near the statue of Astarte. Flames bathed the statue with living fire. The music sharpened. The priests began the song of sacrifice, urging the crowd to join in.

"As to the fields and vines,
They are the fields and vines of Astarte.

Merciful Astarte, who banishes Mot, makes them
   productive.
As to the flocks and herds,
Astarte makes them prolific because we sacrifice to her.
Now, the fire is removed from the ashes.
The kid is slain and rests in the curds of its dam's milk!
Now, gods of Canaan, be pleasured by our offerings.
Come, gods of Canaan,
Be pleasured by our offerings, and pleasure us in return!
Come, gods of Canaan! Come! Come!"

"Come, gods of Canaan! Come, come." The crowd shouted
and stomped, swayed and clapped, and shouted again and
again for their gods to come forth and lead them to pleasure.

Adjacent to the statue, a concealed doorway opened. As if
issuing from Astarte herself, Jericho's high priest and quedesah appeared. Regal, arrogant, untouchable, they stood in full
view of the frantically-shouting crowd. Rahab's white gown,
sheer and gossamer, was sashed with scarlet. Pearls embroidered its bodice. Her dark, lustrous hair was drawn back and
tightly bound under a golden loti-form headpiece set with
lapis-lazuli. The similarity to Astarte's statue was unmistakable.

Something wrenched at Joel deep inside.

Thou shalt have no other
gods before me!"

Carnelian bracelets at her wrists matched those Shatha wore
on his upper arms. His brilliant yellow robe was sashed and
cowled in scarlet. Across his chest, sapphires outlined the
serpent form of the god El. Both priest and quedesah wore
amulets about their necks. Hers hung from a scarlet cord and
was partially hidden by the neckline of the gown.

Slowly, they walked to the front of the platform. Heavy lines
of kohl were drawn under their eyes in the accustomed tradition of warding off visions of evil. The crowd roared fresh
approval. Shatha and Rahab accepted it with arrogant nods.

For an instant, Joel thought she looked directly at him. But
he couldn't be sure. Under the ritual paint, a wooden expression masked her face. Her eyes held a cold, uncaring look.
Or was it a look of hatred?

Nahshon approached the priest and quedesah. From the

golden pouch, she once again plucked a handful of the powdery substance and began to sprinkle it over them.

The priests of the leavened loaves and the grapevines, and the herdsmen-priests all came down from the altar and went about the sacred grove sprinkling the sycamores and the tamarisks with the milk of the slain she-goat.

At the same time, all the other priests joined the temple maidens among the crowd to begin collecting tribute. In Jericho, nothing was given without a price. Except for himself, all the crowd gave quickly and freely now for what was yet to come. As the tribute collection ended, all the noise, all the music, all movement in the crowd also ended. Some mysterious cue had frozen the frenetic crowd into total silence!

Astonished, Joel turned. All, save for himself, were kneeling! Every eye was transfixed on Shatha and Rahab with harsh, earthy anticipation. A shower of sparks poured from the torches and flashed and shimmered against the statue of Astarte, creating an illusion of voluptuous movement. The silence deepened, activating a sensuous emotional undercurrent that confirmed the intent of the crowd's anticipation and matched his own sense of apprehension.

A leathery drumbeat broke the silence. Music mingled with it.

Nahshon replaced the four-horned incense pot on its stand and began dancing a weaving pattern around Jericho's consort and courtesan.

Shatha's eyes glittered with arrogant possessiveness. His lips parted in a sardonic smile.

Impatience pushed the crowd onto its feet. "Balu! Balu!" they shouted. "Balu! El is mighty! Shatha is mighty! Shatha will conquer!"

In a commandingly deliberate pantomime that would fulfill the crowd's demands, Shatha moved toward Rahab.

A tremor shook Joel at the thought of the blasphemous consummation about to take place.

"Thou shalt not commit adultery."

Torchlight flamed around consort and courtesan, danced between them, and cast their shadow-play up onto the pulsating statue of Astarte. An earthy groan of approval swept the chanting, impatient crowd. They pressed forward.

A temple maiden clutched at Joel's arm. He shoved her away, his eyes riveted on the scarlet haze of moving figures before him.

"And the land is defiled."

Men took maidens and left their wives to priests and neighbors. Men took men. Brothers took sisters. Women took women. Fathers took daughters. All in the sight of Astarte in the sacred grove! Lust for the sake of lust.

Aching with passion unrelieved, Joel watched Shatha, like a conqueror presenting the spoils of war, pick up Rahab and hold her out to the lusting throng in the pagan grove.

Rahab turned her head and stared directly down at Joel. With a swift gesture, as if in defiance of Shatha, she dislodged the amulet at her throat so that it dangled from its scarlet cord in full open view.

For the second time in recent days, Joel saw the familiar, and now all too meaningful, second ram's horn ring! Unbearable bitterness choked him as he stared in disbelief.

10

To the east of Jericho, on the banks of the River Jordan, was a different kind of grove; one in which Joel had found refuge many years before and had remembered with an odd mixture of terror and sweet nostalgia. Only recently, he had rediscovered it. It was situated only a few yards north of the fords used by the caravans coming into Canaan from Midian and Moab. On two occasions, he and Hejaz had managed to elude the watchful eyes of the khan's household and had hidden in this place among the reeds and willows to count the caravans laden with goods for Jericho's treasure houses.

Northward, the Jordan plummeted through a deep, rocky cleft on its plunge to the Dead Sea. The chalky marl of Moab to the east across the river could be seen through the lacy green tangle. The river was wider here and flowed more smoothly. Reeds and watergrasses mingled with poplars and willows to form this shelter so secure from prying eyes. Only when the snows melted from the northern mountains and joined spring rains to bound down the Jordan's watercourse did this natural alcove change its peaceful garb or disclose its covenant of secrecy.

In the stillness of first dawn, he could hear the distant roar of the Jordan's cascading turmoil. After the tormenting revulsion of the Canaanite ritual, and the discovery that Rahab and the free-spirited girl who had saved his life so long ago were one and the same, he instinctively sought its refuge once again. This was the place she had hidden him years before.

114

For as he had plunged out of the temple's sacred grove, an awesome realization shattered him. He owed the debt of his life to Rahab, the Harlot of Jericho!

He moved deeper into the grove of willows trying to calm himself, trying to reassert reason though his head still pounded with the scarlet haze. How could he repay such a debt? If he did repay it, it would be at the expense of his obligations to Pharaoh. But even worse, it would be at the expense of his obligations to Rechibidan! Pursuit of those obligations to the throne of Egypt had, in fact, caused him to rediscover this place. He turned, glancing about, stifling the bitter gall that rose in his throat.

This had been a place of safety and of solace. What irony that he should be here again under such a circumstance. The first time he had come as an escaping slave and had felt the Lord had forsaken him. For years he had ignored the Lord because of it. Now, it was as if the Lord had propelled him to this place again.

He sank wearily to his knees, his mind reconstructing the events that had so quickly changed his view of life. So absorbed was his concentration that the quick, light footsteps coming up behind him, and the small gasp of surprise escaping from Rahab, went unheard.

For a long moment, she stood watching him, startled at his humble, kneeling position. It was the posture of slavery. But the longer she watched, the more aware she became of a powerful grace, an aura of freedom about his submissive pose. An indefinable force seemed to sustain and exalt him with authority.

A curious sense of relief went through her. She was glad he had come to the ritual. She had caught sight of him the moment she stepped onto the altar platform with Shatha. His yellow tunic, brilliant as Shatha's ceremonial robe, reflected torchlight like a warning signal. And she remembered thinking that only Pharaoh's rabiser would flaunt Jericho's ritual by wearing the Canaanite's sacred color.

She remembered something else, too — the intensity of her own feelings in reaction to the emotions that showed on his face during the ritual — dismay, disbelief, shock, the agony of fascination, angry disgust, and the torment of revulsion and bitter denial.

At first, the intensity of her own reactions to his facial expressions had surprised her, then puzzled her, and finally, worried her. Fah! she had told herself, why should she care what the Egyptian thought?

But it was his last look of utter condemnation that had sent a clamor of denial pounding through her and had pushed her to deliberately dislodge the talisman to full, open view.

He had reacted as she had hoped. No longer did she need to wonder about his identity — nor he about hers.

She gently fingered the ram's horn ring that still hung from the scarlet cord about her neck. Long-slumbering memories stirred again and fully wakened. Images of almost-forgotten hopes roused themselves, and she realized anew that the impression made by the fleeting hours spent so long ago with this man in search of freedom had never been erased. Neither had she ever fully understood the depths of her own feelings about that experience. Practical as she was, she had no answer for why she should feel these things so strongly.

Joel, still kneeling in front of her, still unaware of her presence, stirred uncertainly. He began to speak in a halting fashion as if trying to remember long-unused words. And yet she knew he only spoke out loud to himself.

"O mighty giver of the Law, You, who are supreme in the hearts of men, and in the history of my people, hear my plea. My heart is troubled. Reason turns its face from my mind."

Stunned at the poignancy of his tone, Rahab felt the tide of her memories and her sentiments rising.

"I need to understand this affliction. As with an unquenchable fire, you have once again enslaved me with the hardest of circumstances."

The yearning intensity of his voice caught at her and wrapped itself completely around her heart. She felt naturally drawn to him.

For a moment, she tried to imagine his eyes smiling as they once had. She tried to recapture the memory of the full, strong mouth lifted at the corners in a sign of pleasure. It was impossible to think he would not smile again in the same way he once did. It was painful to consider the possibility that they would never again share unspoken trust.

"Why do I look with favor upon — and owe my life to — this woman who reviles the love meant to exist between man and woman and who leads others to acts of abomination?"

Shock wrenched at her. He understood nothing about Jericho, about the ritual, or about her. The eastern sky steadily brightened. Branches of acacias thrust their feathery spikes skyward seeking the hard, orange-colored light.

Humiliation flamed through her. He was not talking to himself. He was praying! He was Hebrew! The discovery seared her brain, traced a scathing path through every fiber of her being. Tears of humiliation blinding her, she plunged through the grove.

But she had run only a few yards when he caught up with her and roughly pulled her to him.

She struggled, but his hands were strong.

His eyes searched her face as if he sought a different person. "Does it matter to you so much that I am Hebrew?"

"Does it matter to you so little that I am a quedesah?" Her lips trembled. "You made no mockery of me when I freed you!"

"I didn't know then. Anymore than you knew I was Hebrew."

"Would it have made a difference?"

He hesitated.

Fresh anguish coursed through her. She pulled away. "You needn't answer, Hebrew! I can see that it would."

His face darkened.

She plunged on, hurt and angry. "You accuse me of wrong-doing because I lead my people in the things they understand and believe."

"What you do *is* wrong!"

"In whose eyes? Your unseen god's?"

"In mine," he said flatly.

"Why should you care, Hebrew? I once told you I sought freedom. But you — you urged me to return."

Pitiless, his eyes bore into her. "You would not have paid the price for freedom, Rahab."

She turned away.

He followed her. "You said you had your reasons for returning, just as I had mine for fleeing. Yes, I did urge you to return — to your family. But not to the degradation I saw last night!"

The look in his eyes had turned hard as obsidian. She trembled and pulled the sheer mantle close about her shoulders.

"To be back in Jericho is an irony," he said harshly. "It's an amusement of fate. I should rejoice in it! As Pharaoh's rabiser, I can make Jericho pay for everything — everything!"

Rahab bridled.

He walked away.

By all sense, she should hate him more than ever. She should scratch out his eyes here and now, even though he prowled in front of her with such tigerish intensity. But a dreadful montage was forming in her mind and held her rooted to the spot. Superimposed in it were the mirage-like figures of the Hebrew and of Shatha. A dreadful tremor went through her.

He turned, glaring at her with the same look of abject disgust she had seen earlier. "Your ritual is a defilement. You worship yourselves, not gods. You twist ceremonials to fit your own conveniences and to satisfy your lusts!"

"Are Egyptians so different?" she shot back. "Or for that matter, the Hebrews?"

His eyes flashed with that peculiar spark. "Yes. They are different."

"Fah!"

"They are Jehovah's chosen people."

"Chosen for what?"

"For the purposes of God, not of themselves."

She gave a scornful laugh. "They have the same cravings and hungers as Canaanites. They're just as touched by the thorn and just as unprotected from the khamsin. They drink from a bitter cup just as do Canaanites. They are no different."

"Oh, they're different," he asserted, striding toward her. "They care about the inner qualities of a man. From what I've seen, you Canaanites don't. That's the difference."

She stiffened. The words were uncomfortably like those her sister had used. "There is no difference," she insisted. "With

Canaanites, Egyptians, or Hebrews, it is an eye for an eye — vengeance to one's enemies."

"Wrong again!" he said, coming closer. "To Hebrews, an eye for an eye means equality before the Law — not vengeance."

"What equality?" she snapped in surprise. "And what law?"

"Jehovah's Law," he said without pausing. "The poorest shepherd has rights equal to those of the richest prince before His Law."

Disturbed by the words and irritated at her own reactions to his nearness, she moved away. She snapped a twig from a nearby willow and twisted it in her fingers. "Laws are measured by the size of a man's purse, and so is equality. But you should know that, rabiser!"

"When we met before, the questions of equality and heritage were not important to us."

She tossed away the willow twig. "Egyptian tax-collector was not your title either. Nor did you mock me when first we met."

The look on his face softened. "I pray for you — and for myself."

She bridled. "I don't need your prayers."

"Oh, I forgot," he laughed sneeringly. "You have Shatha, haven't you?"

An aching and unanswerable hurt went through her.

"Tell me something, priestess. With all that you have, including Shatha, why did you come to this place? Why aren't you in bed with your consort?"

She could neither answer nor withstand his dark, probing look. She turned away.

"I know why you came," he pursued. "And it has nothing to do with tribe or clan, customs or practices." He gripped her arms, and determinedly turned her to face him. "Be honest with me, Rahab. That day you ran by the prison and I called out to you — you still remember it, don't you?"

She couldn't answer. Her heart hammered in her breast at his touch.

"When I called out to you from that prison, you paused for an instant like a wild, free spirit that dared not be stopped lest the soaring wings of flight dissolve. Indecision was written in your face. You were afraid if you stopped long enough to help me, you'd be captured. For one shattering instant, it was like seeing my own soul struggle. I desperately feared you would ignore me. And yet you made your choice as quickly as a bird's wing makes one full motion. You freed me from an abominable death."

Her heart skipped a beat.

"Do you realize what I'm saying?"

Willows soughed and the sun seemed fearful to burst from dawn's lingering clouds.

He touched her chin and lifted her face, forcing her to look at him. "What I'm saying is that I owe you the debt of my life. It makes me responsible for what you do with yours. You know this. It's why you came here to find me."

Scarcely daring to breathe, she studied the depth of the look he fixed on her.

"I am in your debt, Rahab of Jericho. And I make this solemn vow to you — not as a Hebrew, not as a Pharaoh's rabiser — but as a man. I shall find a way to repay the debt I owe you."

Disturbed at the softness his words aroused in her, she stood very still. It was as if she could touch time with her fingertips and assess destiny's changing intent for them both. Familiar landmarks in her life would vanish. New values would replace old. All was change. What lay beyond was unknown, and she feared it.

"Do you believe me?"

She sank down onto the ground. "I'm not sure I can. You mock the solemnity of Astarte's festival. And I do not believe in your — your — Jehovah."

He came and sat beside her. "Do you believe me?"

She shook her head. "We are different, Joel ben Dishan. We are enemies — sworn enemies. How can you possibly vow repayment such as this to an enemy?"

"You were not my enemy when you set me free. And even if you had been, it's Jehovah's Law that I repay the debt."

She straightened in surprise. "You speak as if he is your personal god."

"He is."

"What foolishness."

"He is also your personal God."

"But I don't believe in him!" she gasped.

He shrugged. "It doesn't matter. He is still active in human affairs — even yours. And He is a God of love and of justice."

She threw back her head and laughed aloud. The sound carried tinsel-thin through the clear morning air. "Justice? Love? Where is the justice — or the love — of a god who decrees death for women and children of Ammon and Bashan? Where is the justice of needless slaughter of thousands and the burning of towns?" She paused, waiting for an answer but not really expecting one. "Why don't you answer, Hebrew? Is it that you can no more answer for your god than I can for Astarte?"

He threw a quizzical look at her, but said nothing.

She got to her feet. "A god is just only when the sacrifice offered is sufficient. A god loves only when appeased in the proper way." Dawn was coming quickly now; pink and gold rose up beyond Moab's hills. "You're kind to be concerned for my future, rabiser — especially since you're so disapproving of my present."

Frowning, Joel stood up. "You mistake my purpose."

"Not more than once," she replied.

He shrugged, but pinned her once again with a deep, probing look. "A woman is much like a new clay jar for olives, Rahab. At first, the oil and preserving salt penetrates the vessel and gives a taste of earth to the olives. But after much use, the jar ceases to tell what it is made of. Is the same true for a woman like you?"

She glared at him, despising the intent of his meaning. "Stiff-necked Hebrew!" She walked away, heading out of the grove.

"You're a mockery, priestess. You know it."

She whirled about.

"You're a mockery because you lead, yet you don't believe. Not even the ritual paint last night could hide how you really felt about that ceremony of lust and about Shatha. You're a mockery. You really are a harlot!"

Fury tore at her. She threw herself against him, slapping and scratching. "I am no harlot! I am consecrated!"

He pinned her arms in a vise-like grip. "Whoring is not consecration."

"Blasphemous Hebrew! I should have let them kill you!"

He gave a scornful laugh and pushed her away.

She turned and ran toward the familiar protection of Jericho's staunch double-walls.

She was breathless and aching in body and mind by the time she reached the protection of her father's house. In blinding brilliance, the sun presided over the second day of the festival. The sounds of noisy crowds of celebrants in the courtyard harshly bruised her ears. The whole idea of the Festival of Harvest now was a misfit with her state of mind and heart.

Disillusionment had left her trembling. She leaned against the steamy wall of the entry-gate waiting for the sensation to pass. What a fool she had been to seek out the rabiser just to reassure herself of his identity. How childish to imagine that any vestige of closeness might remain between them after so many years and so many changes in them both. The willful impulsiveness that sent her chasing off to recapture a long treasured relationship had, instead, made her a captive of three devastating discoveries. He considered her a harlot. He was Hebrew. And he believed in the one invisible god, Jehovah.

She pulled the ram's horn ring on the scarlet cord from around her neck and with a despairing sob, stuffed it deep into the folds of her garment. Only her family could be trusted. Only they could offer comfort and solace. Nothing really mattered except her family. She must never again forget that who she was and what she did was important to their safety and protection. So it had always been, and so it would remain.

Quickly crossing the courtyard, she slipped into the shadowed coolness of her family's private chambers. A servant appeared to remove her sandals and wash her feet in the nearby basin.

From the terrace, her father called to her, and with her mother following, came toward her. "We've been concerned about you." His eyes were sternly questioning.

"You look tired, my daughter," her mother remarked. "Where have you been?"

"Walking."

"Alone?"

With a pang of conscience, she was slow to reply. Instead, she stepped out of the footbath, allowed the servant to dry her feet and take her mantle. Then, entwining her arms with those of her parents, went to a couch in the center of the main room. "I am very tired and hungry. Is there food, my mother?"

After instructing the servant to fetch a platter, Mozni went and sat down next to her daughter. Peridia, however, remained standing, displeasure in his eyes. "It is neither wise nor the custom for women to roam about by themselves," he said. "Particularly women of high station like you. Where have you been?"

She shrugged, not able to bring herself to tell him about the rabiser. Not yet. All that had happened was still too fresh, too upsetting.

"You have not answered me."

"I'm sorry, my father," she evaded with a heavy sigh. "Last night's ritual upset me. As soon as I could, I ran from the temple and from the city itself. I walked, trying to calm myself, trying to think and sort out my unhappiness. I wandered much further than I intended. That is all. I have not been harmed. No one saw me." She shrugged again, this time with weariness. "And certainly, I did not mean to worry either of you."

Peridia's look of displeasure did not waver. A muscle tensed in the square line of his jaw. "You *were* seen."

She straightened.

"That shouldn't surprise you. The absence of a high priestess does not go unnoticed. When a quedesah leaves the temple during the time of festival, tongues wag. Eyes become alert and prying, and the — " He stopped abruptly as the servant returned with a platter of food.

Mozni took the platter, set it on a low table beside the couch, and dismissed the servant. "You are too impetuous, my daughter," she softly scolded, reseating herself on the couch.

"You always have been," Peridia agreed, turning toward her. "Even as a child, your wild impatience got you into trouble."

123

"We have been fearful for you often," her mother added gently. "But last night, the fear was stronger. I suppose it was partly because of all this talk of the Hebrew threat."

Rahab stared at the platter heaped high with fruits, cheeses, meats, and breads, her hunger vanishing. "Again, I'm sorry I worried you. I sought only a brief escape."

"Escape?" her father charged. "Escape from what? You talk as if you have no freedom."

Wearily, she shook her head and sank back onto the couch. "You don't understand."

"Yes, he does understand, my daughter," Mozni said, placing a gentle hand on her arm. "But, you must understand that freedom is not a thing you can touch or hold in your hand and admire. It's a matter of living within the limitations of circumstance. None of us has complete freedom, but this household has more than most."

"But my mother, I just wanted to —"

"Your mother is right!" Peridia cut in.

He made a sweeping gesture that encircled them and the rich elegance of the room. "None of us carry the marks of bondage on our skins. We all come and go as we please. We have food, clothing, jewels, a fine house, influence, and wealth. Yet you risk losing it to satisfy some whim called a brief escape. Escape from what? Escape to what?"

She went sick inside.

"You have done a foolish thing. Much as I despise Shatha, I still respect the power he wields. And I fear for your safety because of this escapade."

"Three times during the night, he sent messengers to inquire about you," Mozni said.

Rahab straightened in surprise.

Peridia squared around to face her directly. "Do you not know that Nahshon followed you to the grove beside the Jordan crossing for your meeting with the rabiser?"

The earth seemed to tremble like sand shifting to unburden its own weight and carrying her with it. Fear pounded up inside her.

"It's bad enough to see you allied to that arrogant fool Shatha," Peridia rumbled. "But at least until now, you've been smart enough to hold him in check, and it has protected you in many ways."

"Whatever your reason for meeting with the rabiser," her mother injected, "Nahshon is making something very dangerous out of it. She is claiming you consorted with the Egyptian!"

With a blazing denial, Rahab came to her feet. Tears of frustration and angry protest blinded her, but not before she saw the stone-hard accusal in her father's eyes. She turned away.

"Is Nahshon's story the truth?" he demanded.

"Patience, my husband," Mozni insisted. "Don't force her to dishonor you with hurtful words."

"The dishonor is done!" he said angrily. "It is only the danger that is yet to come."

She went limp inside, remorse mingling with fear. How could she explain? What could she say? How could she tell them? How could they understand what was in her heart?

Courtyard sounds filtered through the room and rasped against the waiting silence. Finally, when she found the will to speak, her voice sounded unreal and far away. "I did not consort with the rabiser. I did not lay with him. But I did go to the grove beside the Jordan hoping to find him there. I met him there before."

Peridia's robes made a heavy rustling sound as he moved in abrupt shock. Mozni sharply drew in her breath.

"It was once, and it was a long time ago. How and when doesn't matter. I have known him forever. Not as a man. But as a feeling. He has been a deep whispering constantly in my soul. I have known him from the beginning of my life."

She moved to a wide low chest set with silver and brushed her hand along the gleaming richness of its surface. "When I am alone, whenever I stand quietly, unbusy, untormented by Shatha's demands, I hear the whispering song deep inside me. It is a quiet, persistent voice urging me to search for answers to questions I cannot even put into words."

A desolate sense of misery overwhelmed her. She stared across the lavish comfort of the room, blind to its opulence. "The quiet persistent voice asks of me, 'Who am I?' 'Why am I?' It wracks me with discontent. I grow restless. Even the air around me trembles with my uncertainty. It teases me with yearning. And always, always, it haunts me with the longing of hope unfulfilled. My soul's whispering mocks me, just as the world mocks itself. Is this not a kind of slavery? An even greater mockery made me seek him out. An even greater kind of slavery sent me to him."

She walked slowly toward the open doorway that led to the terrace and stared out at its beauty with no sense of enjoyment. "Once, long ago, for a brief moment, I knew real freedom of spirit and shared it with another human being. I wanted only to grasp it once more."

Tears glistened in her mother's eyes, matching those she herself fought to hide.

"When you share your heart with us — " Peridia's voice broke. With a heavy sigh, he sank down onto a chair. "I — uh — when —" He looked away, straightened slightly and cleared his throat. "When you share your heart with us — " His voice broke again. He made a fist of one hand and slammed it against the side of the chair. "The alliance with Shatha is a sorry bargain. In every way. I — I'm — truly regretful."

"And what of the Egyptian?" Mozni asked gently. "What are his feelings toward you, Rahab?"

Weariness reclaimed her. She shook her head and groped in the folds of her garments for a linen square to wipe away the tears welling up once more.

Her mother came to her, embraced her, and led her back to the couch.

"What he feels about me," Rahab murmured, finally regaining her composure, "may not be as important as the discovery of who he really is."

"What do you mean?" Peridia asked.

With one hand she dabbed again at her eyes. With the other, she drew forth from the folds of her garment the odd-looking ram's horn ring and held it dangling from the scarlet cord in clear view.

Her parents' reactions were immediate and identical — stares of astonished recognition.

Cautiously deliberate, Peridia got to his feet and came to her.

126

With an outstretched hand, he cradled the ring, scrutinized it, then glanced at her quizzically. "Does this mean you think the rabiser is a Hebrew?"

She nodded.

Her parents exchanged a look of wonderment.

"The same Hebrew," Peridia exclaimed, "that gave you this ring so many years ago?"

Again she nodded. "In fact, I know it to be true."

Shaking his head at the ironic coincidence, he withdrew his outstretched hand and rubbed at his chin with stubby trader's fingers. An expression of thoughtful calculation entered his eyes as he walked away to consider the effects of this newest development.

"My main concern," Rahab offered, "is whether Nahshon also knows his true identity."

Peridia hunched his shoulders. "It does not matter. Hebrew or Egyptian, he's still Pharaoh's rabiser and, therefore, still a threat to Shatha."

"But for the future, my husband," Mozni inserted softly, "if such a fact was widely known, it could make a difference."

Rahab and Peridia both turned in surprise. It was unlike Mozni to offer political suggestions.

She blushed, but did not hesitate. "To protect you from Nahshon and Shatha, I do not think we should openly discuss the rabiser's nationality. I know nothing of politics, but I know how dangerous Nahshon can be."

A new admiration for her mother swept through her. Her father, too, obviously accepted the wisdom of the gentle little woman seated on the couch. "Then it shall be as you say." He turned to Rahab. "But I shall want to visit with the rabiser about this so that he too understands the potential danger to you and to this household."

"There will be no difficulty in that, my father," she nodded. "He has already vowed to repay me for saving his life so long ago."

At the entry way, Ahabina suddenly appeared and gave a hurried bow. Rahab tensed, wondering how long Ahabina had been in this part of the khan and if her sharp ears had overheard any part of her confrontation with her parents. "Master! Mistresses! The high priest approaches through the courtyard and the venerable seeress is with him!"

"Excellent, Ahabina, excellent!" Peridia responded with abruptly cordial authority. "Go quickly to tell his eminence that the household of Peridia is honored." Ahabina bowed again and vanished through the entryway.

"Well, well," Peridia muttered, turning to Rahab and Mozni. "Now we shall see how well the seeress has told her story and how his Supreme Arrogance has reacted to it." He walked toward the entry, then paused and winked at Rahab. "Flee, if you like, my child. This old head can still be devious, too."

She flashed a grateful smile, but shook her head and resettled herself on the couch beside her mother. Across the room, they could hear the usual exchange of welcome and greetings being curtly shortened by Shatha asking in an imperiously accusing tone, "Does my quedesah bid me welcome also, or is she still absent from the khan?"

"She has welcomed you for many years as have we all, noble Shatha," her father responded, admirably holding back the edge in his voice. "The household of Peridia is honored, doubly honored, since Jericho's seeress has also come." The response was inaudible. With a broad wink to her mother, Rahab rose quickly and went toward the entry. She stopped abruptly and made a deep bow to the astonished Shatha.

He cast a sharply critical glance toward Nahshon, whose widened eyes made it obvious she had not expected Rahab to be present.

Rahab inquired in a careful tone, "You have need of me, my lord?"

Recovering quickly from his astonishment, he came closer and took her hand and roughly squeezed it.

She steeled herself, refusing to show any reaction to the vise-like grip. She stepped aside and motioned for them to enter the main room.

Shatha ignored the proffered hospitality, but he did release her hand. "You left the ritual so quickly, I was concerned. I sent messengers to inquire why. But their reports were unsatisfactory. So I came myself to see about you." He glanced reproachfully at Nahshon. "But it is obvious you are neither ill nor absent — as I was told."

"Nay, my lord. I am not ill."

"Then tell me, my quedesah, why did you leave so quickly? And where have you been?" His tone was unctious.

She knew better than to trust it. "For a walk," she declared flatly.

"It must have been a very long one," Nahshon put in with quiet challenge. "Where did you walk? Your consort's messengers searched the town."

Peridia moved closer to Rahab and protectively slipped his arm around her waist. "She was concerned for Shatha, honored seeress, as we all are. She was attending to a matter quite important to his welfare."

The surprise Rahab felt matched the astonishment on the faces of Shatha and Nahshon.

"It seems my daughter," Peridia went on in a proudly authoritative tone, "spied the rabiser at the festival. She also saw him leave unescorted — alone — without benefit of any of our guards. It worried her greatly. She was fearful that harm would come to him in some way and that you, Shatha, would then pay the penalty of Pharaoh's edict!"

Shatha's eyes narrowed dangerously. Nahshon paled and nervously glanced up at the priest, then quickly probed Peridia's face.

But Peridia went on without hesitation. "So she roused a household guard to accompany her and followed the Egyptian. He wandered clear down to the grove near the fording place at the Jordan. She had the guards concealed in the underbrush while she herself confronted him about his careless manner."

She could scarcely believe her ears. Her father's lie was masterful. A tumble of emotions flashed across the faces of Shatha and Nahshon.

Peridia shifted his weight, frowned heavily, and without giving anyone a chance to question his story, he admonished, "You are fortunate, Shatha, to have a quedesah so loyal that she will risk your displeasure, and even endanger herself, in your behalf!"

In unison, as if they were puppets pulled by a single string, Shatha and Nahshon followed Peridia's proud and protective gesture toward Rahab.

Fearful that she would give away her father's masterful ploy, she paced away a few steps. As she did so, she noticed the white mantle Shatha had given the temple maiden draped over a small table in the entry. She had ordered Ahabina to retrieve it just before the ritual. Strange she had not noticed it before. Had Ahabina purposely left it there after announcing the arrival of Shatha and Nahshon?

She also realized that either Shatha or Nahshon could have brought the mantle. Either way, the disposition of Shatha's playmate must be known to them. No wonder they were so upset at not being able to prove she was with the rabiser! She picked up the mantle, rubbed her fingers over its sheer linen surface, and held it out to her consort. "I have also had your favorite garment washed and mended, my lord. It had an odd tear in it, as if a knife had been thrust through it."

She held the mantle out to him. "I thought perhaps you would want to wear it for tomorrow's tribute session," she added, smiling up at him in open challenge.

The slate-gray eyes darkened. "You are ever considerate of my needs, quedesah," he said in a thin voice. Anger ridged his face but he contained it. He turned, salaamed to Peridia, and strode from the entry. Nahshon trailed after him.

Rahab watched them go, knowing the stand-off would be short-lived. She wondered what her consort's next thrust would be, and whether or not she would be able to cope with it alone. Only Peridia's quick wit had saved her this time. She turned to him and kissed him gently on the cheek.

11

It was the third and final day of Jericho's Festival of Harvest. In-gathering of the tribute-tax was taking place. Members of Jericho's khazianu, assembled in King Balaar's palace counting rooms, were impatient for this final important act of the festival to be over and done with.

At best, it was always a long and bitter contest between khazianu and citizens. The eventual outcome was always foreordained. Each side knew it. Fellaheen and bedu, town-dwellers and landowners, all classes of citizens, haggled and schemed to get off as lightly as possible. The khazianu, expecting such behavior, demanded more tribute than they knew they could get. Only a narrow margin was ever reserved for humor or for a joust of wits.

But today, no such margin existed at all. The annual charade of demand and acquiescence was like an evil wind that lays a sickness on the land. Sixty men had already been hauled off to prison or to the slave-huts, or had been condemned to the burial pits for "failure of just yield." Rahab had long since tired of the affair, unnerved as much by personal anxiety as by the harsh judgments being decreed.

Shatha was on a rampage. His judgments were abrupt and cruel. He was implacable to the pleas or explanations of hapless taxpayers who aroused his displeasure. So far, he had decreed death three times as often as had Jericho's king. And in pronouncing each decree, he had stared with absorbed attention at the amulet of Astarte in his hand. It was the same amulet he had torn from its golden chain and brandished so victoriously at the palace dinner for General Birsha a few nights earlier.

In contrast to Shatha's judgments, King Balaar assessed judgments with long-term calculation, his rheumy old eyes set deep in the creased, withered face, seemed to envy each man the years still left and measure his value in terms of future productiveness for the province of Jericho. But not Shatha, Rahab thought with dark disapproval. His eyes pierced and probed each citizen for immediate worth and satisfaction. She knew, too, that he still chafed over her disappearance from the ritual. He had patently ignored her and her father during the entire session.

Across the way, beyond the royal dais, sat the rabiser. His mood seemed as implacable as Shatha's mood was cruel. His dun-colored tunic, unadorned except for the badge of his office, made him appear older and hard. Rahab silently cursed the careless impulse that had driven her to him in the riverside grove. Even now, she refused to let her eyes drift too often in his direction, lest their gazes meet.

Scroll in hand, he added yet another entry to the exacting amount that would be Pharaoh's share of the tax being declared. A short dagger bristled from the leather girdle at his waist. His Nubian friend was fully armed, and so were the six Egyptian men-at-arms flanking them.

A shepherd approached the royal dais. In his arms he carried two pure white sheep. A tiny gasp of pleasure escaped from Rahab. In all of Canaan, nothing was more acceptable as a gift. The snow-white wool from the animals could be woven into immaculate apparel of exquisite beauty and rarity. The sheperd bowed to the king and explained that he had eighteen other animals just like the two in his arms. All twenty were to be given. Since lambing, all had been carefully tended and covered to protect them from manure and road-dust. They were a real prize!

In open appreciation, King Balaar nodded, accepting the gift.

Pleasure glinted, too, in Shatha's eyes.

But as the shepherd attempted to bow again to the king, one

of the sheep panicked and struggled to escape. In the ensuing disorder, one sheep slashed the other with a hoof. Blood trickled from the wound, marring the pure white flank with a crimson stain.

A groan of disappointment went through the assembly. When the animals were finally recovered and order was restored, Shatha bluntly announced in a tone of heavy disapproval: "The offering is spoiled by carelessness. Bury the shepherd — and all twenty sheep with him!"

A protest rose from the assembly. Anger whipped at Rahab. General Birsha set his mouth into a firm, hard line and made no move to have the astonished shepherd seized by the guards. Yanshuph's boyish face was pale. Peridia's square jaw quivered with disgust. And into Joel's eyes sprang revulsion. Only Nahshon seemed to approve the high priest's abrupt and ruthless judgment.

"Take heed, Shatha!" King Balaar wheezed in warning. "The judgment is too harsh!"

"My lord," Shatha defied in a half-whisper, "the fellaheen only understand harshness. The shepherd was careless. Carelessness is a punishable act."

"Nay! It will not be so in this case!" Balaar's voice grew loud. "In this case, the — "

A court messenger abruptly appeared at the old king's shoulder, interrupting his words.

Shatha, leaned forward. "Take note, rabiser. Carelessness is punishable in Canaan."

Rahab's heart thumped at the veiled threat.

Joel's even reply challenged it. "You mean an eye for an eye, high priest?"

"An eye for an eye," Shatha snapped. "You will also note that Canaan does many favors for Pharaoh. The case of the shepherd here is one example."

"How so?"

"By decreeing death to this careless fool, I have saved your Pharaoh the trouble of housing and feeding yet another slave."

Joel's face hardened. "And you also withhold yet another portion of the tax that is rightly due to my Pharaoh!"

"That is a pity!"

"It is also unwise!"

Shatha's face reddened.

Rahab tensed. The candor was too blunt.

"Such magnificent wool is a rarity," Joel went on. "Pharaoh would find such a gift quite acceptable — perhaps even acceptable enough to affect certain royal edicts."

Rahab gasped at the public mention of the edict. The assembly looked puzzled.

Shatha's anger flared openly. "Don't presume, rabiser, to advise me of my relationship with Rameses!"

"I presume nothing," came the flat rebuttal. "I note only that you have once more reduced the amount of tax due to Egypt."

Shatha's next response was aborted. King Balaar turned back to the assembly as the court messenger hurried away. He held up his hand and proclaimed, "I, king of Jericho, revoke the high priest's judgment of the shepherd."

The assembly roared its approval. Pained surprise flushed Shatha's face.

Balaar raised his thin, blue-veined hand to quiet the assembly. "I further proclaim that this in-gathering of tax is at a close. Those who still have tax to declare will do so at the palace counting house. Clear the hall!"

Rahab looked to her father for an explanation of the unexpected pronouncement. He shrugged, puzzled and curious, but made no move to leave the hall. Nor did any of the other of the khazianu. It was obvious that Joel, too, intended to stay. He handed the scroll of accounts to Hejaz and motioned him toward the palace counting house. Three of the Egyptian men-at-arms went with him. Three remained in close guard over Joel.

As the palace guards cleared the citizens from the hall, Shatha leaned forward and asked angrily, "What is this foolishness? The tax session is not —"

"Do not further resist me, Shatha!" Balaar commanded. "You may despise my age and covet my power, but we may yet need to stand together."

From the far end of the hall, the court messenger, accompanied by two other men, pushed through the departing crowd and approached the royal dais.

Rahab recognized one of the men as Tegush, the Amalekite trader. Had he not been wearing the same dirty, orange-striped trail robe, though, she would not have known him. He was clean-shaven. The straggly beard was gone. But she found something else even more of a curiosity. The Amalekite's appearance brought Joel upright. For a moment, she thought he was going to rush to his feet and accost the trader.

"What is the news you bring, Tegush?" King Balaar asked immediately.

"Once again, your majesty, I bring news of the Hebrews."

Joel leaned forward, rigidly attentive.

"My courier here," Tegush went on, acknowledging the man with him, "has crossed and recrossed the Hebrew encampment in the plains of Moab many times recently. His reports are of great importance to Jericho."

"Must we listen to this," Shatha fumed. "Exaggerations — exaggerations all about a band of beggars!"

Balaar silenced him with an imperious gesture.

"The Hebrews are more than a band of beggars, priest," Tegush contradicted. "There are twelve tribes. The people number far more than all the inhabitants of the entire province of Jericho. Their power and their ability to fight is equally impressive, for they are led by the Lord God Jehovah."

A murmur went through the khazianu.

"The Hebrews have prevailed against all of Jericho's neighbors," Tegush went on. "Ammon, Bashan, Moab, and now, Midian. They have prevailed even though the kings of Moab and Midian sought out Balaam, the mightiest of seers, and beseeched him to curse the Hebrews."

Nahshon abruptly stirred and focused her heavy-lidded eyes on the trader. "Balaam?"

Tegush nodded.

"Did he perform the curses?"

"Nay, seeress, he did not."

"What did the kings of Moab and Midian do when he refused their requests?" King Balaar asked pointedly.

"They were affronted, of course. But Balaam is an all-powerful seer in the lands to the east, so again they asked him. They told him that the Hebrews were powerful, that they had defeated Og of Bashan. Three times they asked him to perform the curses, and three times he refused."

Nahshon and Shatha exchanged puzzled looks.

Rahab trembled.

"What were Balaam's reasons for refusing?" Nahshon asked.

"His reasons were these. He said to them, How shall I curse whom God hath not cursed? How shall I deny whom God has blessed? He then said he had received a commandment from the Hebrew God not to curse the chosen people. And — because of that — he would not curse them!"

Stupefaction filled the faces of Nahshon and Shatha.

"Say on, Tegush," King Balaar commanded.

"Balaam also told the kings of Moab and Midian that the Hebrews will rise up like a great lion and eat up the nations that are their enemies."

The words trailed ominously across the assembly. The khazianu shifted uneasily. Shadows had spilled into the palace as day waned, and attendants started lighting the braziers. The first sputtering smokiness from them added to the sense of gloom that invaded the mind and caught at the heart.

King Balaar sank back in his chair. "Always it is the same. Always, there is this same news of the power of this Hebrew god."

"Aye!" General Birsha emphatically agreed. "It is the same as the reports from our northern neighbors. We must arm! We must prepare ourselves!"

"To what avail, General Birsha?" Tegush asked calmly. "Who shall live when God does these things?"

Shatha shifted menacingly. "Those are dangerous words, trader. You're a fool to say them in the presence of this company. The Hebrew god is a mockery! And Balaam, the seer, is a coward!" He turned toward the worried khazianu. "And we are cowards if we believe this lying tongue from the trail!"

Fire sparked in the Amalekite's eyes.

Shatha charged on. "There is no richer province than Jericho. Wealth is her safeguard — wealth that appeases the gods of Canaan and releases their power among us. Those gods are the most powerful, just as the seeress of Jericho is the most powerful of all the seers. She sees no blessing for the Hebrews." With a look of arrogant certainty, he dared anyone to contradict. "If Balaam won't curse the Hebrews, Nahshon will!"

Immediately, she agreed. With eyes widened, she straightened in her chair and proclaimed, "I will not only curse them, I will stop them! Hebrews are neither giants nor gods. They are men. Being men, they are as strong and as weak as their passions dictate." She fingered the talisman at her throat and looked directly at Shatha. "A man who seeks pleasure often forgets to seek war."

A thin laugh rippled up from some of the khazianu, but Tegush was not impressed. "Midian has already thought of that, seeress. The women of Midian were sent to entice certain Hebrew princes and captains to seduce them. They did so. And the vengeance of the Lord God was quick and stern. His wrath flamed up against the houses of the guilty. On both sides, Hebrew and Midianite, many houses now lie in ashes."

Rahab felt the quick catch of fear in her throat and remembered Joel's words — "Whoring is not consecration."

"Thus has come to pass everything that was prophesied," Tegush added in a matter-of-fact tone.

"And what might that be?" Nahshon asked with malevolence.

"There is a fire gone out of Heshbon. A flame from the city of Sihon has consumed Arad of Moab and the lords of the high places of Arnon. Woe unto thee, Moab and Midian, thou art undone!"

"This is a prophecy?"

"So it is written and spoken in all the lands east of the Jordan. Don't you, as the powerful seeress Shatha proclaims you, know of these prophecies?"

Shatha flared at the sarcastic accusal, and angrily rose to Nahshon's defense. "Are you schooled in the priesthood, trader? Or is your courier who stands there mutely at your side? Have either of you ever experienced the revelations of the mystics?"

"Nay! I know only that which I see and that which I hear!"

"You waste our time. Lies — that's all you bring — lies."

"Hold, Shatha!" King Balaar ordered.

But Shatha would not be stopped. "My lord king, you're being sidetracked with lies about prophecies and seers. I know this man! He is not to be trusted. Only a few days ago he turned over an entire load of goods to the rabiser in order to evade his rightful taxes owed Jericho!" If Shatha expected a sign of agreement from the khazianu, it did not come. He plunged on. "The Midianite god Chemosh is the cause of Midian's defeat by the Hebrews. And he's an unimportant god — one without the powers of Astarte and El." He turned, gesturing toward Rahab and Nahshon. "Right here among us we have the most powerful representatives of the unconquerable power of Canaan's gods and goddesses. On this very dais is enough power to halt the Hebrews!"

In spite of herself, Rahab was reminded of another thing that Joel had said to her in the riverside grove — "As quedesah, you are a mockery." She looked at him. He was watching her with an unwavering gaze. A tracing of cold fear went through her.

"Listen no more to Tegush." Shatha implored. "He is an ignorant man of the trail!"

Tegush came close to the dais. "It's true, priest. I am a man of the trail. So is my courier. It's also true that neither of us is schooled in the ways of Canaan's gods. But schooled or not, I give this to you as a solemn vow. I can, I will, and I do witness for the Hebrew God." He slowly turned and looked at each face with deliberate challenge.

Joel straightened.

Tegush said it again. "I can, I will, and I do witness for the Hebrew God. I have seen the power of His hand. It is shown through the actions of men who believe in Him — men like Moses and Joshua, son of Nun, who is to succeed Moses as the leader of the Hebrews. They are men of principle and of discipline who obey the one true God.

"They lead the Hebrew people in obedience. When the punishment for whoredom with Midian was done, Moses assembled the twelve tribes and recounted to them the laws given by the Lord God Jehovah. He reminded them that only through obedience to God's Laws can victory be theirs.

138

"He also reminded them that the day soon would come when the Lord God would open the way for them into the land of promise. All who had seen the miracle of the parting of the Reed Sea in the escape from Egypt are now dead. Besides himself, only two now live who were of that first generation of the exodus — Joshua, son of Nun, and Caleb of the house of Dan."

Intensity burned in the eyes of the Amalekite. No one in the room could doubt his sincerity; all were transfixed at the truth of his words. "Moses then reaffirmed that God had predestined the survival of Joshua and Caleb. Joshua was to lead the people. Caleb was to help him.

"When Moses finished reminding the people of all these things, he went up from the plains of Moab onto the mountain of Nebo, to the top of Pisgah, which is against Jericho. From there, he looked upon the land of promise. From the River Jordan to the Great Sea in the west, from the mountains of Syria in the north to the southern deserts, the Lord God Jehovah showed all this land to Moses.

"This land!" he emphasized with a downward motion of his hand. "This Canaan! This, your land, is the land promised to the Hebrews! From of old it has been said that Moses himself would not lead the people into Canaan — that with his death, the time for the people to take the land — under the command of Joshua — would be at hand!"

The peculiar spark in Joel's eyes was now a living flame. It matched the furious pounding that had abruptly overtaken Rahab's heart. She clenched the arms of her chair as if bracing for the news that she knew must now surely come from the Amalekite. Snatches of conversations recently heard flashed through her mind: The land is theirs since the time of Abraham. Moses will never enter. Joshua will lead them. The Hebrew God has no images. He comes and leads them in a pillar of fire. He demands strange obedience, but if He is obeyed, even though the Jordan flows full, He will lead them across!

With a decisive gesture, Tegush moved yet closer to the dais. His voice grew more intense. "The Word of the Lord God Jehovah is straightway in its purpose. And His purpose is the drive of destiny. The Lord will not be put aside. The time is at hand. Within a moon's waning, though the River Jordan flows full, the Hebrews will cross into Canaan!"

Grotesque shadows thrown out by the flickering braziers marched across the walls of the palace.

"The time is at hand. According to the Word of the Lord, the Hebrews have shaved their beards in mourning for Moses, dead now in the land of Moab."

The sound of the trader's voice hammered across the hall, pulsated against the flickering shadows, echoed from the marble floor and the inlaid walls like a funerary chant, until, at last, it faded into mournful, bewildered silence.

At the mention of death, Joel touched his hand to his ear in the Hebrew custom. He then turned and gazed at Rahab as if asking her to measure deeply the truth of the trader's words.

She resisted, glanced away, and fought against new fears rising inside her. She wanted neither to lose her wealth, her family, or her life. But to accept the Hebrew god for herself was out of the question.

Shatha broke the bewildering silence. "Raca! You're a fool, Tegush!" He held the amulet of Astarte in his fist and shook it at the trader. "This — this is the true power. Here! In my hand! No invisible power can challenge this seen power. This unseen god you believe in lived only in the imagination of Moses. But since Moses is now dead, the god of the Hebrews is dead, too!"

"Nay, priest!" came the quick, hard reply. "He is from everlasting to everlasting. He lives in the hearts of men and shows Himself through their actions!"

"Mouthings of a child!"

"They're wiser words than yours, Shatha. You covet and take that which is not yours."

Shatha's eyes went black with hate.

"Your gods are false!"

"Blasphemy!" Vengeful anger pounded in the veins of Shatha's neck. He came to his feet. "Astarte curses you, Amalekite! El curses you!"

Tegush stepped closer. "You lead the innocent to idolatry. You commit adultery, fornication, thievery, and murder in the name of false gods!"

Fear hammered at Rahab.

"It is you who are dead, priest — *you!*"

In a spasm of rage, Shatha's hand flashed out, hurling the amulet at the Amalekite.

Tegush dodged, but not soon enough. The amulet hit his forehead a glancing blow, then dropped and shattered. Precious stones scattered wildly across the marble floor.

Rahab gasped in horror, and an animal fear streaked the faces of the khazianu. Before them all, Jericho's high priest stood guilty of Canaan's grossest crime — the destruction of a religious figurine. Rahab began to tremble.

Stunned, terrified silence pressed down, and an awful astonishment gripped the figure of her consort. Sweat beaded his brow. He glanced about wildly and sought her, as if begging for reassurance and for forgiveness. She turned away. To behold him now was to behold doom itself. Shaking uncontrollably, she pressed back against her chair.

Tegush brushed at the blood on his forehead. "You mock your own futility, Shatha! You claim power and yet you stand there shaking with fright before a bit of broken clay and stone. The hand of God touches even you, priest of Jericho!" He laughed with knowing scorn.

Shatha straightened abruptly, turned with a jerky swiftness, and in a single stride was at the edge of the dais. He grabbed a spear from a startled guardsman and sent its deadly shaft hurtling toward the Amalekite trader. The time his aim was true. The spear caught Tegush squarely in the chest.

With a scream of agony, he fell back against his courier, then slipped to the floor. Life fled from him even before blood stained through the dirty orange-striped robe and seeped onto the marble floor. A dark pool formed around the shattered amulet.

12

The news that Shatha had killed Tegush in a fit of fearful rage spread through Jericho with the speed of fire through dry grain.

Reactions were immediate and mixed. Nearly all of them focused on the personalities involved, rather than on the larger issue that Jericho would soon encounter destiny with the Hebrews.

"The Amalekite provoked our high priest!"

"That rotten trader — he sold goods to the rabiser!"

"I hear the quedesah acted like she believed what the trader said about the Hebrew god. Can you believe it?"

"Shatha should never have broken that amulet of Astarte. He will pay for it!"

"High time he made retribution for something!"

"I think the priest did the right thing!"

Jericho's children made a game of the slaying. But festival visitors looked at it as a more serious omen. Many of them hastened their departures from the City of Palms. Consequently, Jericho's shopkeepers viewed the whole affair as bad for business.

To most of the khazianu who were present, Shatha's actions represented a climactic piece of evidence for their growing suspicions about his power and about his understanding of just how strong a power led the Hebrews.

The threat of an invasion by the Hebrew people finally had become real to them. Almost to a man, they were now persuaded that General Birsha had been right all along.

King Balaar instructed the general to dispatch Yanshuph to the northern provinces to seal the bargain for the mercenaries and to return with several regiments as soon as possible.

Peridia sent couriers (his most trusted couriers) to the merchant-princes in other provinces, urging them to boycott trade with the Hebrews.

General Birsha took personal command of defense preparations in and around Jericho. Her walls were to be strengthened. Breastworks were to be thrown together around the watering-places beyond the walls. Sentries were to guard them at all times. The local garrison was to be readied for the expected arrival of the northern mercenaries.

Sentries patrolled the city walls day and night. Watchguards were doubled at the gates. And by royal decree, the gates now were closed and barred securely at sundown each day. Sentries were also assigned to watch all traffic coming and going at the fording-places of the River Jordan. They were to report any unusual activity at once.

King Balaar then sent yet another plea — this one truly an impassioned plea — to an old friend, Rameses the Second, Pharaoh of Egypt and all her provinces. Men-at-arms were what Jericho needed. To make sure that Pharaoh understood the seriousness of the situation, the plea for help was accompanied (at Peridia's suggestion) by a heavily-ladened caravan of tribute-tax, including twenty pure white sheep.

The preparations for amassing the huge caravan had been undertaken with great stealth in order to conceal it from Shatha. The idea had been suggested to him, but he had flown into such a rage that the subject was dropped. For all intents and purposes, the high priest, from that time forward, was to be allowed to think that his authority had prevailed.

The caravan, however, was gathered in a surprisingly short time and went off to Ramesseum with Ali ben Azi personally conducting it.

Pharaoh's rabiser was absent now from the frequent secret meetings of the khazianu. It was assumed by all that he, too, had accompanied the huge caravan to Egypt. Rahab knew better. Though he had not told her, she knew where he was going. She had not even seen him since Tegush fell dead before them all. But in her deepest heart, she knew, without question, that he had gone to his own people.

She did not blame him. What hope was left for him here? Ruefully, she acknowledged she had been right when she told him he would never be able to repay the debt he felt he owed her for saving his life. Most likely, she had seen the last of him.

As might have been expected, Shatha's reactions in the aftermath of killing the Amalekite were most strongly influenced by the factors bringing the greatest reassurance to his ego — the expressions of support from Jericho's citizens. When reports were brought to him that street gossip supported his action, he set about at once to exploit them.

A new, larger, gaudy amulet of Astarte appeared about his neck on a huge, golden chain. Daily, he counselled with Nahshon. Publicly, he let it be known that he and the seeress were performing incantations that would guarantee to make Jericho more productive and favored than ever in the eyes of Canaan's powerful gods and goddesses.

At Nahshon's insistence, he asked Rahab to aid him in renewing the vestiges of his priestly power by holding special audiences for the citizens and by accompanying him on daily walks through Jericho's streets in a show of supremacy and solid union.

"Our presence will be reassuring to the people," he had told her. "They know there is no greater power than wealth — and we are wealth! Smile at me and be obedient to me — as a woman should!"

Her immediate reaction was one of total rejection. She feared him more than ever. She recognized a parallel between her revulsion for his arrogance and cruelty and her own waning confidence in the supremacy of Canaan's gods. She now admitted to herself that her world was to be shattered as surely as the broken amulet had been. She would be foolish to have anything further to do with Shatha; he was a doomed man. All that he represented was doomed. If she was to save her wealth, her family, and her own life, she must stay away from the high priest.

Surprisingly, however, her father and King Balaar urged her to comply with Shatha's request. Their urgings were based on three important facts: Shatha had a sizable, well-paid (and thus, loyal) temple guard; Rahab was the only one who could gain access to the temple treasury without arousing suspicion; and Jericho's khazianu now had great need to know, in advance, if Shatha decided on some subversive action to deter the defense preparations for the City of Palms.

"Far better to stalk the lion than to be its unwitting prey," they had told her.

She finally agreed to do it — but with the understanding that strict limits would be set on how much time she would have to spend with Shatha, and where. And she insisted that a trusted cordon of palace guards be with her at all times.

Shatha agreed. And so it was that day after day she went through the motions of being his supportive quedesah. To her unremitting surprise, the high priest stuck to the limits of the bargain, including the one that allowed her to return each night to her own chambers at the khan. This, more than any other, was the greatest proof that the shattering of the amulet had genuinely shaken the arrogant priest.

Daily, they paraded the streets amid cheering throngs. Every third day, they sat in audience to hundreds of citizens and visitors who were presented with miniature figurines of Astarte, which were blessed on the spot by Nahshon.

The charade continued for fourteen days. Twice during that time she had tried to get into the temple treasury to inventory its contents for her father and the king. But both efforts had been thwarted. Shatha had doubled the guard with fully loyal men.

By the end of the second week, the confidence and arrogance of the high priest reasserted themselves. To be with him was suffocating — like being in a pall of smoke on a windless day. She had begun to wonder how much more she could endure.

The reprieve came sooner than expected. On the afternoon of the fifteenth day, a palace messenger pushed through the audience and rushed to Shatha announcing that he was urgently needed in the king's palace.

Without hesitation, and with no word of parting to her or to Nahshon, he rushed off. In turn, and with unbounded relief, she closed the audience and retreated to the sanctuary of her own chambers in the khan.

She felt drained, empty. It was a recurring condition. From the day on the rooftop of the khan when she first tried to analyze her dissatisfaction and even deeper stirrings of change, she had had no sense of real peace. The series of disturbing events that had followed that day served only to enhance her uncertainty.

She no longer found comfort in the power of Canaan's gods. She was not even sure she believed in them now — maybe she never had. She had long ago admitted that she did fear the Hebrews and their unseen god. Yet, she had no way to believe in this Jehovah, no way to find comfort in such a belief. Joel could influence, but the choice had to be hers.

She moved to the window and looked at the land. The barrenness of the freshly-harvested fields would soon be hidden by the Jordan's springtide. Marshbirds and waterfowl would soon darken the sky with their flight to cooler climes. And then would come the khamsin — east and south winds — that pitted the skin and blinded the eyes. The sense of change was not just in her restless soul. It was in the land itself.

A loud banging on her chamber door interrupted her. She turned, startled, then heard the arrogant, loudly-demanding voice of Shatha arguing with her father. She paused only long enough to light a brazier against the encroaching darkness and then went to the door. "Is that you, my father?"

"Yes, my daughter. The high priest has honored us with a visit. Come and join us in the main room before he breaks down your door."

As she opened it, Shatha broke loose from Peridia's restraining grasp. "Why were you so long in answering my knock?" he demanded. The smell of balsam rum was strong about him.

"Come, let's go into the main room," she parried, grasping his arm. Peridia caught the other one and steered him down the passageway into the family's salon.

"Is there nothing but carelessness in Jericho?" he muttered.

She glanced at her father questioningly.

"We've just come from a meeting at the palace," Peridia explained. "Your consort found the latest news as upsetting as

146

I did. But he expresses his displeasure in a different way."

They sat him down on a divan. "I repeat," he said in a baleful tone, "Is there nothing left to us but carelessness? A witless trader mocks us. Birsha prepares defenses against my wishes and turns the people against me. And now, our neighbors openly offend us."

Nervously, she looked at her father, wishing he would call the servants to take Shatha away. She did not understand why he had brought him here in the first place. But Peridia was walking toward the sideboard where a carafe of balsam rum was sitting. Rahab watched in astonishment as he picked up three cups, filled them, and returned with two of them, one of which he handed to her and the other to Shatha. He returned to the sideboard and picked up the third cup for himself.

"Cursed Amalekite!" Shatha muttered, gloomily staring at his cup. "Cursed Hebrews! And curse you, innkeeper!" He gulped at the rum and wiped the back of his hand across his mouth. "Curse you for even asking for my temple treasury!"

Rahab's eyes went wide.

"It's my right to ask for it," Peridia answered in a calm tone. "My daughter shares the wealth with you. Half of it is hers, and she has no reluctance to spend it in defense of Jericho!"

"It is not hers!" Shatha slowly staggered to his feet and stood wavering. "It is mine — all of it! — and I am Jericho's defense!"

The brazier sputtered and cast an evil shadow across his face. Weakness showed in the line of his mouth. Rahab put out a restraining hand, and Shatha staggered back onto the couch.

"Bad news comes in bunches, like flies around a freshly-killed animal." He look at her accusingly. "Do you know that your brother-in-law has come back without the mercenaries from the north?"

She glanced at her father for confirmation and found it in his grim visage.

"I told Birsha to go after them himself!" the priest asserted, fumbling at the buckle on his wide, jeweled girdle. "That boy, Yanshuph, was no match for the Elamites. Captain of the army!" He scoffed and threw aside the girdle. "They should listen to me — not a boy!"

Annoyance flared. "If they'd listened to you, they would

never have bargained with the Elamites in the first place. It was Birsha who insisted, and who succeeded. You were against it."

"What do you know of politics? You're a woman — and a meddling one at that!" He drank again.

Rahab got up and went to her father. "Why did you bring him here?"

"To draw off the guards from the temple treasury. We've summoned them to come after your consort. When they do, Balaar's men will transfer part of the wealth to the palace." Peridia gave a grim smile. "Be patient, my daughter. This visit of our high priest will not be without reward!" He picked up the carafe of rum and went to Shatha and refilled his cup.

"You've failed again, Peridia," Shatha accused. "You, your meddling daughter, and your whimpering son-in-law. Your boycott of trade with the Hebrews has been ignored; Yanshuph failed to bring back the mercenaries — and your daughter — " he sneered and pointed at her. "Look at her. She stays as far away as possible. Is this the way a courtesan should behave toward her consort?"

Peridia handed Shatha the freshly filled cup without comment.

"Are you listening to me, Rahab?" A new note of demand was in the priest's voice. Once again he struggled onto his feet.

"Yes, my lord, I'm listening."

"You're a failure, a careless failure." He drank from the new cup of rum. "Everybody in Jericho is now a careless failure — even the king. Did you know that doddering fool secretly sent the wealth of Jericho off to Rameses and now wants my temple treasure to refill his own empty coffers?"

"No, my lord, I did not know that."

He weaved toward her. "One hundred and fifty-five animals ladened with wealth have been sent as a begging bribe to the Egyptian pig. I had forbidden it, yet it was done." He stopped right in front of her, glowering down. "Did your careless meddling cause this, too?"

Involuntarily she backed away.

He followed her. "Was it your meddling?" he demanded again. "Or is it that you have found the rabiser suddenly too persuasive?"

This thrust caught her off-guard. She stared at his intense, accusing look.

"Why do you not answer me, quedesah?"

"Because it's a foolish question, priest!" Peridia warned, coming toward them.

Shatha ignored him. "Why do you not answer me, quedesah?"

"Because you are right, my lord!"

Astonishment went through the drunken, bloodshot eyes. Peridia halted abruptly.

"You are right, my lord." She chose her words slowly and with immaculate care. "You are right when you say I know nothing about these affairs of state. It is, as you said, not my place to know of such things. I have been almost constantly at your side since such political actions were decreed."

Suspicion narrowed his eyes. He rocked unsteadily and sipped again at the cup of rum.

"I know nothing of such things, and it pains me to hear you say I am careless."

"Your humility is remarkable," he answered waspishly. "It is also unusual — strangely unusual!"

"All of Jericho acts strangely these days, my lord." She walked away.

Shatha turned to face Peridia. "Is it your daughter's carelessness that causes your household to be plagued by such a grievous attitude these days?"

"The attitude of my household," Peridia shot back, "is that of any loyal Jerichoan."

"*No*, innkeeper. It's an attitude of failure!" He followed after Rahab. Unsteady as the rum had made his footsteps, it had not subdued his arrogance or suspiciousness. "I'll prove to you this household has an attitude of failure. First, you failed to make suitable tribute to Rameses and caused him to send another rabiser to Jericho. Then, your father's attempted boycott of trade with the Hebrews failed. Then you ran away from me at the ritual. Now Yanshuph fails to bring back the northern mercenaries. And, along with that news, I also learned you had sent a new caravan to Rameses. You still have not told me who is responsible for that shipment of treasure." He grabbed her arm and jerked her around toward him. "Was this last shipment of treasure your meddlesome idea?"

"She knows nothing of that," Peridia said. "You were told the details earlier at the palace. Rahab knows nothing of it."

"I think she does!"

"She knows nothing, I say!"

"And what of the rabiser?"

"Does he know nothing of it, either?"

"Back off, Shatha!"

"Does the rabiser know nothing of it, or is it that you have struck a bargain with that vulture?"

"Fah!" She wrenched out of his grasp. "The rum addles your brain."

With astonishing quickness, he threw down the rum cup and grabbed her again with a vise-like grip.

A cry of pain escaped from her.

Cursing, Peridia rushed toward them.

"Don't lie to me!" Hatred blazed in Shatha's eyes. "You have struck a bargain with the rabiser!" His grip tightened. He swung her around, blocking Peridia's bull-like rush.

She struggled wildly against his grip, but it was useless. From the corner of her eye she saw her father charge in from the side. With one furious backhanded blow to Shatha's head, he knocked the priest off-balance. Reaction to the impact sent her to her knees before Shatha released her. Then, as if in slow-motion, she saw her consort's body drop woodenly to the floor. Heart pounding, she stared down at his unconscious form.

"I should not have brought him here," her father muttered, breathing hard. "It was foolish to involve you. Are you hurt, my child?" He bent down to help her get up. "Are you hurt?" he asked again, searching her face.

She could only shake her head. Words would not come.

Her father bent down again and knelt over Shatha's body. His stubby trader's fingers searched for the pulsing neck vein. "He lives."

"Worse luck!" she gasped, finding her voice.

Her father glanced at her fearfully.

"He will retaliate. I fear for you!"

The sounds of running feet came from the entry hall.

Rahab turned as two of the household servants appeared. Their curiosity changed to abrupt alarm when they saw the priest's body.

Quickly, Rahab explained that the high priest had had too much rum and had fallen and hit his head. "An escort of temple guards has been summoned. But go quickly and tell them to hurry." As the servants did her bidding, she turned again to her father.

"That's quite a simple story, but they seemed to believe it, my daughter. I wonder if Shatha will when he comes to?"

"We must see to it that he does, my father!"

By the time she returned to her own chambers once again, twilight smudged the western sky. Her weariness was so heavy that she sank onto her couch and was almost immediately enveloped in sleep.

Some hours later, she stirred. Night had fully vanquished day. Moonlight shimmered through the windows, and a small flame flickered in a tallow-oil lamp nearby. She stretched, feeling much refreshed. In fact, it was several seconds before it occurred to her that she had not lighted the tallow-oil lamp. She lay quite still, wondering at it. Slowly, she became conscious of the feeling that someone was in the room with her. She strained to hear even the slightest sound. There was none. But the feeling persisted. Her pulse began to pound. "Ahabina? Are you here?"

"No, Rahab," came the hushed reply. "It is Joel."

She jerked upright.

He came toward her from the shadows, and sat down on the edge of the couch.

"What are you doing here?" She moved the lamp to better see him. He was dressed as he had been when she last saw him on the day of Tegush's murder. His dun-colored tunic was still adorned only with the badge of his office. The lamplight burnished the open planes of his face and laughed in the reflected strength of his eyes.

"I'm glad you're happy to see me," he said brashly.

"Who said I was?" she countered.

"It's written on your face."

"Then I shall have to teach my face to be more truthful." His closeness was disturbing, and she was having trouble looking at him. The ram's horn ring still hung about his neck on its silver chain. "I thought Jericho was finally rid of you, rabiser."

He laughed softly. "Still you fight me, eh, proud one?"

"I shall always fight you. You are Jericho's enemy."

A half-smile played across his mouth. "I'd like to be her friend."

"Perhaps you can be," she said cautiously, "if you have brought news that Rameses will send men-at-arms to us."

He hesitated a moment. "But — I have not been to Egypt!"

"Then where have you been? Hiding, like some frightened woman? That's what they've been saying in the streets."

He gave a soft laugh.

"Where have you been?" she repeated.

"With my own people."

She sat up straighter. "Did Tegush speak truly of their intentions?"

"Yes, he spoke true. My people will march on Jericho very soon."

A stricken feeling went through her. "Then why did you come back? You were free! Why did you come back?"

"To help my people," he said candidly. "And — to repay a debt."

Misgiving thrust at her. "To a harlot?"

"To a friend."

She searched his eyes and found only sincerity.

He shifted his position, leaned closer to her, and protectively took her hand. "Rahab, listen very carefully to what I have to say. Jericho is dead. It has been placed 'under the ban.' Herem! Herem means dedicated to Jehovah. It means utter and total destruction of every building, every weapon, every piece of merchandise, and treasure, and of every human being!"

Her heart stood still. She dared not even breathe. Desperately, she searched his face for a hint of relief, for some tiny clue that he could be mistaken. But his eyes sparked with the terrible intensity of truth.

"The signs have been many," he pressed. "The Lord God Jehovah has commanded it because of Jericho's wickedness and idolatry. Joshua, our leader, has proclaimed it."

Fear, sharp and stabbing, raked her, matching the intensity of his look. All the stories she had ever heard about the overwhelming power of the Hebrew god flashed through her mind: the parting of the Red Sea, the provision of manna and quail, water from a stone, the pillar of fire, the fiery serpents and the rod of brass, the victories over Arad and Sihon and Og, the refusal of Balaam the seer to curse the Hebrews, and the punishment for those disobedient and disbelieving. Herem! Dedicated to Jehovah — if not by voluntary acceptance — then through complete annihilation. Just like Ammon and Bashan, like Amor, Moab, and Midian, Jericho would be destroyed by the hand of the Hebrew god.

"To keep my vow to you, in repayment of my debt, I am offering you your life and the lives of your family. Two men wait for me in the grove by the river. They wait for a sign from me before they enter Jericho. Will you help me to get them into the city and keep them hidden while they are here?"

"Spies?" She pulled away from him, aghast that he was asking her to betray her own people.

As if reading her mind, he said quietly, "There is no betrayal involved. You cannot betray something you don't believe in."

She trembled.

"In your decision lies the fate of your family and its wealth." He named off the members of the household one by one, including servants and slaves. "Will you help me to help my friends? Or will you sacrifice yourself, your family, and your wealth in a vain hope to defy Herem?"

Her heart hammered up. Lamplight caught at the ram's horn ring hanging from its silver chain about Joel's neck and shadow-played across it as if urging her to realize that destiny had brought them together long ago for a purpose far beyond the scope of man's understanding.

The irony of Shatha's false accusation only hours before clashed with what Joel was now asking. She laughed sardonically. If she struck a bargain for the safety of herself, her wealth, and her family, she would be the traitor Shatha had already accused her of being. On the other hand, what did she still owe to Jericho?

"Time presses us, Rahab," Joel urged. "My friends must come into Jericho tonight. Will you help them?"

"How can I be sure they will save my household?"

"You have my word."

"And what of your friends? Will they, too, give their word?"

He nodded.

"Can I consider their word a 'true sign?'"

He gave a gently chiding laugh. "What real choice do you have, Rahab?"

She trembled. "What signal are you to give your friends?"

"I am to send Hejaz for them."

"And where is he?"

"Hiding in the weaving rooms."

"Then no one in the household knows of your return?"

"I hope not. Secrecy about this whole matter is an absolute necessity. In fact, secrecy will be part of the bargain. Will you help?"

She straightened again, pushed at him to make him move, and got to her feet. He was right, of course. What real choice did she have?

"Will you help?" he repeated.

She turned, looked at him, and nodded yes.

He came toward her to embrace her. She backed away. "If secrecy is a part of the bargain, we'll have to do something about your clothes." She turned and went to a nearby chest, rummaged through it, and pulled out a coarse, homespun robe. She had made it for Shatha as a trail robe. He had refused to wear it. It was plain and caused him to look like a bedu, he had complained. She tossed the robe to Joel. "This will hide your rabiser's clothing."

He put the robe on, but because he was so much shorter than Shatha, it drooped and sagged tent-like.

In spite of herself, she grinned. She went and adjusted the robe by pulling it up over his head in cowl fashion. She got a wide sash belt from the chest and tied it around his waist. She stood back and gave a nod of approval. "Now we'll go. There is an inner passageway leading from here to the weaving rooms. Immediately next to the weaving rooms is a storeroom that is seldom used. It is directly beneath your quarters."

"Yes, I know the one you mean."

"In it is a door that leads outside the wall of the city. You can dispatch Hejaz from there, and he can bring your friends into the khan the same way." Picking up the tallow-oil lamp, she led the way down to the weaving rooms. Hejaz appeared from the shadows, and followed them to the storeroom door.

The door would not open easily. Its leather hinges creaked with dryness before finally giving way. As it swung open, a rat scuttled out. Rahab stifled the cry that sprang to her lips, then led the two men into the storeroom.

At this particular location, Jericho's double-built walls narrowed so that the intervening space was only about five feet wide. Thus, the inner wall of the city was actually inside the storeroom. It supported a stairway that led up to the khan's roof. The city's outer wall had a doorway cut into it and so was situated immediately in front of the hidden stairway.

She explained the peculiar construction to Joel and Hejaz and cautioned them not to let the two strangers go up onto the roof in the daylight lest they be discovered by some member of the household. They should be safe enough as long as they stayed hidden in the storeroom.

Loosening the leather thong that held the bolt-bar in place on the outer door, she pushed it open. Moonlight dazzled after the darkness of the storeroom. Canaan's loamy soil stretched out bleak and empty beyond the blue-black shadows of the wall. Only the silhouette of a sentry atop the east gate marred the emptiness. Far away, the grove by the river was only a smudge in the moonlight. Beyond, rose the mountains of Moab and the Hebrew encampment. But within the first hundred cubits of the wall, the land appeared flat, desolate, and very open.

A night bird screeched. Rahab paused, wondering how any man could find enough cover in the scattered thorn bushes for safe escape. For an instant, she considered the idea of sending Hejaz out the south city gate. But that was foolishness. They would have to go through the city streets to get to it. Besides, time was running short. As it was, Hejaz would have to hurry to get the men back into the khan before daylight.

Joel gave the Nubian final instructions, and the towering black man melted noiselessly into the shadows outside the wall. It was as if the land had swallowed him up. Incredulous that one so big as the Nubian could vanish so completely, she whispered, "Where is he?"

"There," Joel pointed. "Rolling, now crawling, and now rolling again. He keeps to the depressions on the face of the land. Don't fret. He will not be seen."

She did not doubt that. Though she strained her eyes, she could spot nothing at all that moved. She wondered if the Hebrews would come upon Jericho in this same way, silent as a lion, unseen as the wind. A tremor went through her. She carefully closed the door and set the bolt-bar so that Hejaz could open it from the outside.

She turned to Joel and gave instructions to hide the strangers in the storeroom. "I will also make sure they are fed," she assured him. "And," she finished, "tell your friends to be careful of the shopkeepers. They have sharp eyes for strangers."

Joel nodded and followed her back as far as the weaving rooms. "I ask yet another favor of you."

She glanced at him warily.

"Carry this with you." The flame from the tallow-oil lamp glinted on a small dagger. He held it out to her. "Carry it for your protection."

She hesitated, but he insisted and pressed the dagger into her hand. "It can protect you in ways that I cannot."

She closed her fingers over the weapon. The cool metal warmed quickly to her touch and gave her a sense of power.

"Be very careful," he whispered, turning back toward the storeroom to wait for his friends and Hejaz.

A funny little thump went through her heart as she turned and retraced her way to her own chambers.

13

Rahab slept very late the following day. She roused only when Ahabina brought word that the rabiser had returned to the khan and that his man, Hejaz, was waiting to speak to her. Agreeing at once, she pulled on a robe and dismissed Ahabina.

Hejaz quietly and quickly conveyed a three-part message. First, Joel had decided it was wiser to let it be publicly known that — as rabiser — he had returned. Second, he had decided to house the two spies in his own quarters at the khan rather than in the storeroom. He had reasoned it would be easier to protect them there during the nighttime hours. Third, he wanted Rahab to come to his quarters to meet the spies, but only when she could do so without being observed.

The wisdom of Joel's decisions was clear. She thanked Hejaz for bringing the message and assured him that she would go to meet the spies at the first opportunity.

After an evening meal with her family, she pleaded weariness, returned to her own chambers, and allowed Ahabina to help her prepare for bed. For some reason, Ahabina was slower than usual. Rahab carefully controlled her impatience, fearing that the slightest deviation in her normal routine would arouse the slave-woman's suspicions.

At last, apparently satisfied that her mistress would be comfortable for the night, Ahabina set a small tallow-oil lamp near the sleeping couch, smothered the flames in the wall braziers, and took her leave.

Rahab waited for several minutes to make certain that Aha-bina would not return. Then pulling on a homespun robe, she carefully made her way to the rabiser's quarters to meet the Hebrew spies.

They were standing with Joel and Hejaz at a table covered with drawings and maps. As one of the rabiser's guards stood aside to let her enter, all four men quickly turned. Hejaz, ever alert, drew his dagger; then, with a sheepish grin of recognition, replaced it. Joel came toward her.

"I was not followed," she volunteered, anticipating his questioning look.

He grinned and said to the spies, "You see, my friends, I told you she was quick-witted!"

Both men nodded and appraised her with careful scrutiny. Their appearances differed from her expectations. She was rather disappointed. They were ordinary. Both were a little taller than Joel, and they were obviously the products of constant companionship with sun, wind, and sand. But they did not seem to be imbued with any special god-like qualities or even with any unusual human qualities. Their appearances were similar to a thousand other fellaheen.

One of them was an old man, maybe old enough to be her grandfather. And certainly, to her way of thinking, he was much too old to be a spy.

"This is Caleb, Rahab." Joel spoke in a tone of great respect. "He is a close and trusted friend of Joshua, son of Nun, our leader. They have been friends since boyhood. In fact, Joshua and Caleb were among a group of twelve spies sent to search out the land of Canaan by the great leader, Moses, more than forty years ago."

"That was before any one of you were born," Caleb chuckled in response to Rahab's surprised expression. "And you are no doubt wondering why an old man like me is sent out again now as a spy! Eh?"

She fumbled. Color rose in her face.

Joel rescued her. "The truth of the matter is that on that spy mission forty years ago, Caleb and Joshua were the only two who urged Moses to march forward then and capture Canaan. But Moses refused. The Lord Jehovah had not yet proclaimed the time for the capture of Canaan."

Her eyes went wide with disbelief.

Caleb chuckled again, but without rancor. "It must be hard for this pretty lady to understand the importance we Hebrews place on obedience to Jehovah, Joel. Sometimes, it is hard for us to understand it ourselves."

She warmed to his unexpected humility. It would have been so easy for him to brag about obedience to an unseen god and make her feel like a foolish child.

He went on to explain: "Forty years ago, Joshua and I — in fact, all the people — were told that our time was yet to come. Joshua and I trusted that word and were patient."

"And their trust and patience have been rewarded," Joel inserted. "Of all the men who were over twenty years of age forty years ago, only Caleb and Joshua still live. They alone were given the promise that they would see the capture of Canaan."

With a nod of his head, Caleb confirmed Joel's words. "The promise of God *is* coming true. Joshua leads our people under the command of Jehovah, and I am appointed to help him. That is why I am here. All of God's promises will be fulfilled."

His eyes sparked now with the same peculiar intensity she had so often noticed in Joel's eyes. She glanced at the younger spy. His eyes also reflected the same expression. It was a look she was beginning to associate with a sense of trust.

Joel turned, laughed, and slapped the younger spy on the shoulder with brotherly affection. "This is Salmon, Rahab. He is nephew to Caleb and a friend of my youth with whom reacquaintance has been a joyous event."

She appraised the young spy more carefully. Quiet determination grooved the wind-cut planes of his face. There was a strength about him that even Joel could not match. He seemed to possess a solid princely authority; yet it was softened by an easy smile and a voice of gentle manliness.

"We appreciate your help, Rahab." He bowed in acknowledgment of Joel's introduction; then he turned and indicated the maps and drawings on the table. "My friend was just showing us some of the work he has been doing as rabiser while here in Jericho. But it now appears his own people will best appreciate it."

She moved closer. The drawings were all about Jericho —

her fortifications, her great double-walls, her watering-places, her grain bins, her treasure houses and storerooms, the palace, the temple, Nahshon's house, the Street of Shops, and the khan.

Grudging admiration seeped into her mind.. She had been right. He had not, as Tirzah had so strongly believed, just drawn and sketched to amuse Reba. He had successfully used the child as a foil—oh how successfully! Everything of importance in Jericho was faithfully reproduced in deft charcoal strokes.

Alongside the drawings lay a series of maps. Well-delineated, they platted the surrounding countryside as far to the northeast as Adamah, where the high clay bluffs of Canaan and Moab came close together and narrowed the course of the River Jordan.

She glanced at Joel and slowly shook her head with reluctant respect. Had she needed additional proof that Canaan's gods would forsake Jericho to a greater power, these maps and drawings seemed somehow to be the final evidence.

Salmon reached out, grasped her hand and led her toward a bench beyond the table. "Joel has told us a great deal about you, Rahab," he said, sitting down with her. "And he has told us of your promise to him that you will hide us while we're here."

She nodded.

"We need you to also make that promise to us."

His directness appealed to her. These were the words of a man of substance and practicality for whom second-hand bargaining was not considered good enough. She approved. "Your openness is pleasing. Especially so, since I, too, require a direct promise from you — a promise that my family will be spared and protected when your host marches against Jericho."

Salmon straightened. A smile broke at the corners of his mouth and he glanced over her shoulder toward Caleb. "Is this a woman we can deal with, my uncle?"

"I believe we can," Caleb chuckled. "This is no child seeking a 'true sign,' though I do believe she would like to ask for one. But instead, this is a woman who understands that our word — our vow — is our bond. Undoubtedly, she also understands

160

that in return we must be able to trust her word — her vow."
He leaned toward her. "You take no offense at this testing of
your trustworthiness, do you?"

She gave a light laugh to cover the realization that, in truth,
she did not take offense. In fact, she felt no enmity at all toward
either of them. For some strange reason, she trusted them.
They impressed her as men destined by an unseen force, and
she wondered if this was what Joel meant when he had said his
friends were men of faith preparing for a holy war. The idea
that war could be holy struck her oddly. "I'm in no position to
quarrel with destiny, honored Caleb." She chose her words
carefully since they were strange to her lips. "Joel has told me
that Jericho has been placed under the ban. And he has told me
that this proclamation of Herem is not of human origin, but
rather, that it is a proclamation of your unseen god Jehovah."

"That is true," Caleb confirmed, shifting around to more
directly face her. "But as a Canaanite priestess, is this an idea
you can accept and believe?"

With a rueful smile, she shrugged. "I have to accept the
possibility of such an idea. If for nothing more than as a matter
of logic, I would have to accept it."

Both men assessed her with patient silence.

She stood up and moved about the room. The truths dwelling in the depths of her mind weighed heavily. "It is said your
god Jehovah proclaims Herem in order to destroy deceit and
wickedness and idolatry. I know that in Jericho these things
exist. And I know, too, difficult as it is to face, that Jericho's
people will refuse to turn from such things." She hesitated,
reconsidering her own reluctance to admit that anything could
be more important than possessions and wealth until she was
threatened with the possible loss of her family. She spread her
hands in a gesture of futility. "So you see, I must, as a matter of
logic, accept the possibility of the idea of a god-proclaimed
Herem. How else can deceit and wickedness and idolatry be
destroyed?"

She turned again toward the spies who were watching her
intently, and her heart gave a funny thump as she realized the
look in their eyes reflected the same understanding that was in
Joel's eyes.

Sighing heavily, she returned to the bench and sat down

next to Salmon once again. Caleb followed. "All the inhabitants of this land faint because of you," she said slowly. "We
have heard long ago how the Lord God Jehovah dried up the
Red Sea when your people came out of Egypt. Most recently,
we have heard what you did to the Amorites and how you
utterly destroyed King Sihon and King Og.

"When people heard those things, their courage began to
flee. Some have moved away to other provinces. Some have
sought refuge in rum. Some have pretended to ignore all the
reports. Others have killed to contradict them and paraded
about in a show of disdain to disprove them. But many others
already believe, as I do, that no man can prevail against your
Lord God Jehovah."

So naturally had the words finally come, she did not realize
she had made a profession of faith until she saw the looks of
astonishment on the faces of the two spies. The realization was
embarrassing. "Fah! I talk too much."

Joel grinned. "But not without good cause! There is much to
be said about the Lord God and His power."

"Aye!" Caleb straightened. "You know, Rahab, after the
death of Moses, the Lord God Jehovah spoke to my friend
Joshua and told him to arise and take the people across the
Jordan. He told Joshua that wherever the people should place
the soles of their feet, the land would be theirs to be divided
among them as an inheritance, as promised to our fathers of
old.

"The Lord God Jehovah also told Joshua, 'There shall not
any man be able to stand before you all the days of your life. Be
strong and of good courage. Be not afraid. Neither be dismayed. The Lord your God is with you wherever you go.' This
is the power that leads us."

The words echoed deeply inside her, invaded to the very
marrow of her soul. She was carried along on a drift of thought
that seemed to have its natural beginnings in her soul, as if it
was an expression of self far deeper than teachings or customs
had ever before revealed to her.

Caleb got up and paced across the room with his hands
clasped behind him. "After the Lord spoke with Joshua, then
Joshua commanded the officers of the people to pass through

the host and command the people, saying, 'Prepare victuals for yourselves. Within three days, you shall pass over this Jordan to go in and possess the land which the Lord God has given you to possess.' And the people agreed to do all that Joshua commanded."

Rahab stirred in surprise. "Three days?"

"Yes," Caleb reaffirmed. "Even now the tribes await our return. Then the tents will be removed from the place of the acacia trees in the plains of Moab, and we will await the signal at the Jordan's eastern shore."

"But — the river —" Rahab protested in a low tone. "The river is at flood stage."

Salmon leaned over and with an easy smile protectively placed his hand on hers. "We follow the command of the Lord. Who are we to outguess Him? Besides, that is not our concern. Our concern, and yours, is a matter of exchanging vows. The vow we need from you, Rahab, is that you will hide us safely during our stay here — and most importantly, that you speak to no one about this."

She looked down at his strong, sun-weathered hand still clasping hers and wondered why she did not want to pull away from him.

"Do we have that vow from you, Rahab?"

She nodded. "And do I have your vow that my family and all my household will be spared and protected when your host marches on Jericho?"

"You do. You do have our word on it." Salmon firmly pressed her hand.

She turned and questioned Caleb with a look, knowing before she did so that his vow was the same as his nephew's. "So be it. I hide and protect you and say nothing, and you spare this household on the day of doom."

She rose to her feet, acknowledged the bows given by both Hebrews, and smiled at Joel. "It is as you said, Joel ben Dishan. I thank you for it. And consider your debt repaid."

He grinned and walked her toward the door where Hejaz was surveying the passageway and the courtyard below. "It is safe for you to go now, quedesah," he murmured. "But go quickly."

14

For three days, the Hebrew spies went about the business of observing Jericho's condition and the mood of her people. Surreptitiously as a vagrant breeze, they came and went each day from their hiding place in the khan. Rahab marveled at the apparent ease with which they were performing their dreadful task.

At the same time, she inwardly shrank at the awful portent of their actions and at her part in them. Now, when her beloved Jericho approached its struggle with death, she was turning her back.

From the beginning, the choice had been made for her. She knew it in her bones. A power greater than that of Canaan's gods was moving across the face of the land, usurping Astarte's holdings, castrating the minds and hearts of her people, and destroying their will to resist or to change. And as human representative of Astarte, she was being used as a fulcrum for the destruction to come. The presence of the spies and her secret bargain with them proved that.

In despair at the devastating irony, she laid aside a bolt of newly-woven linen and looked sadly about the weaving rooms. She had busied herself here in an effort to occupy her mind with something other than thoughts of the spies, and had pushed the slave-women for more and more production. This day alone, she had kept them at the looms since early light.

What an exercise in futility! The Hebrews would attack before the beautiful goods could be finished and shipped to Jebuz and Tyre. Jericho would lie dead long before the payment for them could be returned.

Heavy at heart, she motioned for Ahabina to call a halt to the day's work and dismiss the slaves. She got to her feet, walked to the doorway, and looked out across the courtyard. Travelers were filling up the place. How many of them, she wondered, were aware of the destruction to come? The cooking fires blazed against their trail-weary faces and projected shadows of their figures in long distortions up the libn walls to the second story.

Her mind turned to Joel. He had been as tense over the presence of the spies as she. But he had covered his tension by acting out the role of rabiser with overt deliberateness. He went about the city prying and probing into storerooms, grain bins, treasure houses, and shops under the guise of preparing another shipment of tribute-tax. He had met with her father and led him to believe that his recent absence from Jericho was the result of a hurried journey to Ramesseum. When Peridia asked about the Pharaoh's reaction to the huge shipment of goods sent to pay for mercenaries, Joel shook his head and replied, "Pharaoh is in no mood to help you. He has neither forgotten nor forgiven the violent temper of Jericho's high priest."

With a heavy frown of disappointment, Peridia had muttered that he, too, had neither forgotten nor forgiven. "I should have killed him for assaulting Rahab."

"Apparently, you almost did, innkeeper," Joel rejoined. "The high priest has not been seen since the night you struck him down. Street talk has it that he's recovering from a severe fall. The seeress Nahshon attends him."

Rahab gave a weary sigh, stepped out of the weaving room doorway, and walked slowly across the courtyard toward her family's private chambers in the main building. It would not matter whether Nahshon's ministrations helped Shatha. The high priest's destiny was too intermeshed with that of Jericho's. Whatever was done to heal him now would be to no avail.

A sudden commotion near the gate made her pause and turn, then freeze in fear. A squad of palace guards had entered the gate and were swiftly spreading out in a search-pattern.

They rousted the khan's guests by roughly seizing them, jerking them to their feet, and loudly questioning them about their identities.

Fear darted through Rahab. She glanced up toward Joel's quarters, praying that Salmon and Caleb had not returned from this day's search of Jericho. She also prayed that Joel had successfully hidden them if they had returned.

The search in the courtyard grew more strident. Angry, resentful protests surged up from the travelers, catapulted into the air, and reverberated against the walls. Fighting broke out. Pack animals, on the verge of panic, moved restlessly against their tethers and kicked up swirls of dust that mingled with the smoke from the cooking fires.

Beyond the melee, she suddenly spotted the two Hebrew spies entering the gate. Salmon's tall figure was unmistakable. Panic tore at her. Such boldness was insane! No matter how powerful their God, such boldness was insane! But as if invisible to all but her, the Hebrews slipped unnoticed around the squabbling and fighting and vanished into the storeroom where the hidden doorway led outside the walls.

A sense of awed relief started through her but was aborted as quickly as it began. For now, the young captain of the guards was bearing down on her, his boyish face contemptuously officious.

She straightened, bracing herself to divert him and put a stop to the search of the khan in some way. In any way, she thought with desperation. Her bargain with the spies depended totally on their safe return to the Hebrew encampment.

The young officer was directly in front of her now. Ignoring all formalities, he bluntly ordered, "Fetch the men hiding here. King Balaar commands it!"

She forced herself to delay a response and instead gave him a scathing toe-to-head look. "Who are you to address Jericho's quedesah in such a way?"

The young officer faltered. A tinge of surprise flickered through his eyes making it obvious that he had not recognized her.

He hesitated only a second, but it was all she needed.

"Speak up!" she now commanded. "Who gives you the right to order your quedesah to do anything? And tell your men to stop that!" She pointed imperiously to the agitation of search-and-resist going on behind him. "You insult the house of Peridia with such nonsense. Stop it at once, I say!"

"Do as my daughter says, young man," Peridia confirmed, coming up quickly to join her. "Call off those guards!" His voice rumbled menacingly, and he stared down the explanation springing to the lips of the young officer.

"Call them off!" he repeated more stridently, stepping toward the officer.

The young man retreated, hesitated yet another moment, then turned and shouted an order for the search to stop.

As the noises of the confrontation began to subside, Peridia asked angrily, "What is the meaning of this insult? Why are your men rousting my guests?"

"He accuses us of hiding spies!" Rahab explained, grateful that her father's intercession would buy extra time for the spies to slip out the hidden doorway and take their leave of Jericho completely.

"King Balaar sent me, honorable Peridia," the officer explained, finding his voice again. "It is reported that two men traveling without animals or baggage have been seen here at the khan."

"And that makes them spies? What rot! Many men travel without animals or baggage."

The face of the young officer reddened.

Peridia bore in. "Even if there should be spies in Jericho, they would not dare stay here. My loyalty and friendship with our great King Balaar is well-known. The king, above all, knows of my loyalty to him. Yet you insist that he sent you?"

The look of embarrassment on the young officer's face deepened. He made a conciliatory gesture. "It is because of your allegiance to your king that the spies would choose this place, honorable innkeeper. They would reason it was a place above suspicion."

But the conciliation came much too late for Peridia. His blue eyes, so startlingly like Rahab's, continued to hold the hardness of scornful disbelief. "Your incursion and your rudeness

167

to my guests is the act of someone other than King Balaar. It has all the earmarks, in fact, of someone like the high priest. And your accusations are dangerous."

To break the strained silence that ensued and to rid the khan of the soldiers as quickly as possible, Rahab decided on an overt move. She laid her hand on her father's arm. "I wonder, my father —" She hesitated with uncertainty as if trying to recall some unimportant incident. "I wonder if the two men seen by the slaves this morning could be the same men sought by this officer?" It was an outright lie, but the effect was apparently believable.

Her father looked at her with puzzlement.

The young officer's eyes fairly danced with redeemed pride. "Your slaves saw two men without animals and baggage?"

She nodded slowly and carefully gauged the pace of her words. "Let me see. Yes — that was the talk in the weaving rooms this morning." She made a helpless gesture. "I guess it's not really that important, is it?"

"When were they here? And where did they go?"

With eyes downcast, Rahab pretended to think for a moment longer. Then shrugged. "They were here before midday, I think, and apparently didn't stay long. It was so unimportant. They were penniless bedu."

"You're sure your slaves saw these men leave the khan?" the officer pressed.

"You need not doubt your quedesah!" Peridia cut in sternly. "She has no reason to help or to hide spies!"

She felt a stab of guilt. She looked around, wishing she could confide in her father. One day she could explain it all and he would understand. But not now.

"Go after these men," Peridia ordered. "They may already be well beyond the walls by now."

"Yes," Rahab added quickly. "Go at once. Overtake them before they reach the Jordan."

The officer bowed. "My apologies to you both." He salaamed, turned, barked an order to the squad of palace guards, and followed them out of the courtyard.

Rahab sagged as relief swept through her. She leaned against her father and thanked him for coming so quickly to quell the search and all the commotion it caused.

He grasped her gently by the arms and held her out so he could look directly into her face. "I have seldom seen you so frightened. Why? Does it have anything to do with the fact that the rabiser is Hebrew?"

"Many things are frightening these days, my father," she parried, avoiding his look. "My concern was for the insults to your guests. Just look at them. They still are smarting from the rousting by those soldiers."

He released his grip on her and turned to view the disgruntled travelers.

"Go to them, my father," she urged, unwilling that he should pursue any discussion of Joel and the spies with her any further. "Go to them now. Reassure them."

He glanced at her with a curious smile. "Very well, my daughter. But you go talk to the rabiser. Make sure he isn't hiding any spies in this khan!" She trembled, watched the squat, solid figure of her father walk toward his guests, then turned and hurried up the stairway to Joel's quarters.

He met her just inside the door. Hejaz stood behind him. Their faces mirrored a mixture of worry and admiration. "You handled it well," Joel whispered.

She gave a small laugh of nervousness. "It may not yet be over. My father is convinced that Shatha sent the soldiers. If he's right, they will come again." She glanced nervously over her shoulder. Her father still mingled with his guests in the courtyard below. "We've got to get Salmon and Caleb out of that storeroom quickly."

Joel exchanged a quick look of surprise with Hejaz, then asked in astonishment, "You mean they are here? Now? In the storeroom?"

She nodded and moved past Joel toward the window. "We must get Caleb and Salmon out of Jericho tonight. Whether they are ready to go or not, we must get them out tonight. The danger for them and for my family grows greater with each passing moment."

"I'll send Hejaz to fetch them from the storeroom and bring them here. They will be safe. Shatha's soldiers will not dare intrude on the rabiser."

With a shake of her head, she turned to him. "That won't do. Shatha's soldiers may not dare intrude, but my father will. He

169

already suspects you are hiding the spies here in these rooms. When he finishes reassuring his guests, he will make a search of his own. These quarters, and the storeroom, will be the first places he will look."

Joel appeared to pale a bit.

Rahab went to him and whispered, "Send Hejaz to fetch Salmon and Caleb and take them up to the roof through the hidden stairway." She turned directly to Hejaz. "When you get them on the roof, hide them under the stalks of flax that are drying there."

He nodded.

"Will your father not search the roof?" Joel questioned.

She shook her head. "It's the one place in the khan he never goes. When all is settled below and the household sleeps, I will come to you on the roof."

Joel accepted the instructions and grasped her hand. "The free-spirited girl of so long ago has become a woman of courage and faith," he whispered, pulling her close and embracing her.

A tremor of emotion raced through her. How easy it would be to give way to the protection of his arms, how very easy, indeed. But this was neither the time nor the place. Regretfully, she steeled her emotions and slowly pulled away from him. "I must go, rabiser. And so must you and Hejaz." She quickly turned and left the room.

15

In the interval of time that followed, Rahab's mind chafed with impatience. The boldness with which she had instructed Joel and Hejaz to hide the spies on the roof was now matched by a desperate uncertainty about the way their eventual escape actually could be accomplished.

Alert eyes were now everywhere, inside the khan as well as out. Her father had, indeed, searched the storeroom and Joel's quarters. As they now sat at the evening meal, he reported he had found nothing in either place, and that probably he owed the rabiser an apology for intruding.

The risks of getting the spies out of Jericho had increased enormously. Secrecy was a major part of the bargain. She must not fail. Failure would extract equally enormous penalties from the Hebrews and from Shatha. She felt sure it was Shatha who sent the soldiers to search the khan. The more pressing question was 'why'? Had it been simply a trumped-up ruse in retaliation against her father? Arousing King Balaar's suspisions against him would be as harmful to Peridia's pride as the earlier physical assault had been to Shatha's pride. Or was it that someone in the household with alert and watchful eyes became suspicious of the two strangers going in and out each day from the rabiser's quarters?

The latter possibility worried her the most, since secrecy of the whole bargain was uppermost for success. In fact, it was as important as figuring out how she was going to help the spies escape.

She toyed listlessly with the food in front of her and sank deeper into preoccupied silence.

Her mother finally noticed it. "Do you feel ill, my daughter?"

With a thin smile, she pushed away the food. "Oh — it's just that I am very tired."

"Why don't you retire?"

"Yes, Rahab," her father agreed. "It has been an upsetting day. Go on to bed. I suspect that the rest of us will follow very shortly."

After what seemed an interminable wait in her own chambers, she was satisfied that the rest of the khan finally had retired for the night.

The hour was at hand. She slipped into a mantle and made her way to the roof. Moonlight hop-scotched with restless clouds and teased the slumbering land with quick-silver light and moody darkness. At the city gates, torches flickered uneasily. Sentries paced tensely above them on the top of the wall. Closer at hand, the weaving looms and their palm-thatch covering lurked as a darker shadow-mass against the reluctant sky. Crouching alongside them, indolent and mute, were the dyepots and a supply of scarlet sashes left over from the festival.

Beyond, rows of flax hid human contraband. The idea taunted her. The fact that something as harmless as flax could be used as a weapon of protection for Jericho's mortal foes was almost laughable, yet she dare not indulge the humor right now.

Joel and Hejaz suddenly materialized beside her from the shadows. She stifled a gasp of fear. If the Hebrew attack came with the same stealth, Jericho would surrender out of sheer fright.

Joel clasped her arm with a comforting steadiness and led her toward the stalks of flax. Hejaz leaned down, pushed aside the stalks, and whispered, "The woman has come at last." He pulled the older spy, Caleb, up onto his feet.

Salmon scrambled up, brushing impatiently at his robes. "High time. The roaches also hide in the flax." He turned to her. "I am more glad than ever to see you, Rahab."

"What's the plan?" Joel asked. "Do we take them back through the storeroom?"

"No," she responded on reflex, still not sure how to effect the escape. "No, the storeroom is no longer safe. It is being watched by my father's servants. He is most upset over the soldier's accusation that you are here." She gestured toward the dark land. "You could not use that door anyway. Your pursuers prowl east of here toward the Jordan."

"We know that!" Salmon exploded softly, brushing hard at his robes again. "But how do we get off this infested roof?"

"We've been watching the torches of our pursuers," Caleb inserted. "It helped to pass the waiting time."

"Aye," said Hejaz, "we thought you'd decided not to come at all."

She bristled, a retort hot on her lips, but Joel's hand stayed her. "You can see the torches for yourself."

Salmon came close and pointed. "Jericho's soldiers prowl like jackals. They spread out by ones and twos then rejoin the pack to move forward again. My uncle and I will have to be very careful even after we're off this roof."

"You're sure the storeroom is not safe?" Hejaz pressed.

"I mistrust it."

The Nubian gave a muttered oath.

She ignored it and looked at the pile of scarlet sashes left over from the festival. What she was thinking was absolute madness. She wasn't even sure the idea would work. But it would be one way to try. Then her part of the bargain would be done.

"We're running out of time, Rahab. What do you want us to do?" Salmon urged in a tense voice.

Still, she hesitated, reconsidering the plan of madness once again.

"Send Hejaz down to scout the storeroom first," Joel prompted. "Even if your father's servants see him, they'll think nothing of it."

She shook her head.

"That's too sensible!" Hejaz said with uncharacteristic sourness. "I think the quedesah plans to march your kinsmen boldly across the courtyard!"

Rahab turned away in irritation, walked to the edge of the roof, and peered down. The base of the wall was some thirty to forty feet below.

"Have you no sense of urgency?" Hejaz prodded.

"Ease off, Nubian!" Salmon defended. "She's just as nervous as we are. She has just as much at stake — and maybe more!"

"My kinsman is right, Hejaz," Joel agreed, following Rahab to the edge of the roof. In a low tone, he warned: "If you have in mind what I think you do, it's foolishness. They cannot jump from here. The walls are too high."

She made no response but glanced back to the pile of scarlet sashes. There were enough to do what she had in mind. The fact that they symbolized the only way of life she had ever known was now unimportant. She had already exercised her freedom of choice to turn her back on that life as a matter of survival. From the folds of her gown, she pulled the ram's horn ring and the scarlet cord from which it was suspended.

Suddenly the clouds breached, spilling moonlight over the roof. Instantly, all five of them crouched down to avoid detection. Close beside her, Joel whispered, "The ring still stands for freedom, Rahab. You will not regret what lies ahead. My people will accept you and your family as you accepted me so long ago. But tell us what to do, and tell us now!"

She slipped the cord over her head and adjusted the ram's horn ring in the hollow of her throat. A strangely loving look swept over Joel's face.

Salmon came to them. "The moon has gone behind the clouds again. Tell us your plan, Rahab."

She stood up. "One moment, Hebrew. I must be certain in my mind that it will work."

"If we don't depart this open roof soon, your Canaanite friends will tread upon our necks," Salmon insisted. "Tell us your plan."

"I'll tell you her plan," Hejaz put in acidly. "She expects you to crawl down that wall like an ant!"

She flared. "I expect neither that nor your Nubian insolence!"

"Patience!" Joel commanded. "Keep still, Hejaz. This is no time for quarreling."

Rahab walked to the pile of sashes, picked up one, and handed it to Salmon. "These sashes are very strong. Try one. Tug on it." He did so. "They are woven on my own looms. Tied together, they will make a rope strong enough to bear a man's weight. Tie enough of them together, and they will serve as your door to freedom from the window in a small room just beneath us. That is my plan."

The tension between them now eased. All four men squatted down and with quick, deft thrusts began to tie the sashes together.

She walked away a few paces. The final pangs of conscience about what she was doing picked at her. Across the sleeping courtyard lay the city where beauty and squalor, wealth and poverty, and all that was in between, were linked by anonymous night. Houses and shops, narrow streets and watering-places, the plaza with its sentry of sacrificial trees all cowered under the dark fold of heaven. All seemed indifferent to the shattered reflection of the torches guarding Astarte at the front of Jericho's temple. Rahab found the view unreal, yet threatening; unwanted, yet courted by perversity of custom and the enormity of what her actions this night truly meant. By the time the men finished tieing together all the sashes, she was trembling.

She motioned for them to gather up the length of rope and follow her down to the small, ugly, prison-like room in which she had first housed Joel and Hejaz. Once there, they secured one end of the rope around a battered chest and pushed it solidly against the wall under the room's one window.

"It is done!" Rahab said, tossing the free end out the window. "You will descend to freedom on the scarlet ceremonial sashes dedicated to Astarte." Sarcasm flared in her voice. "Rather fitting, don't you think?"

Salmon came to her, took her hand, and as gently as possible reminded her, "A power greater than yours has ordained these things. We shall report to Joshua that all the inhabitants of the City of Palms, save one, are faint-hearted and have no spirit in them."

Tears sprang to her eyes.

He brushed at them with a finger. "We shall also say that truly the Lord has delivered into our hands all this land because of what Rahab of Jericho has done for us."

Rahab pointed with a trembling hand toward the Jebuz road. "Go that way, to the west, for a short distance and then turn north into the mountains. Hide yourselves for three days until the soldiers quit their search. And afterward, go your way. Thus, my promise, my part of the bargain with you, will be fulfilled."

"And our part of the bargain will also be fulfilled, Rahab," Salmon reassured her. He still held a short length of the scarlet rope in his hands. "Our lives for the lives of your family."

"So be it," Caleb confirmed. "But remember, Rahab, your family must be with you inside the khan. Whoever goes out into the street takes his blood upon his own head. We will be blameless. You understand?"

She nodded.

"And also remember that if you utter a single word about this, the bargain is off!"

"I understand."

He turned, bade farewell to Joel and Hejaz, climbed through the window, and descended the scarlet line.

Salmon saluted Hejaz and gave Joel a farewell embrace. "The Lord be with you, old friend, and thank you for all your help. I shall see you soon."

"The Lord be with you, my kinsman."

Salmon now turned to Rahab, searched her face with open interest, and held out the short piece of scarlet sash. "Bind this piece of line in this window of your house so that our people will know it is to be untouched, and the people who are in it are to be spared."

She looked at him in surprise.

"When we first met," he gently reminded her, "you wanted to ask for a 'true sign' that we would keep our vows to you. Let this, then, be that 'true sign.'" A quick smile filtered across his face. "I will see you again, Rahab of Jericho. You are a woman of great courage. I will want to see you again."

As her fingers closed around the familiar sash, she felt a new and unfamiliar sense of trust. As Salmon disappeared through the window into the hovering darkness, she heard herself murmur, "The Lord go with you, my Hebrew friend!"

With the spies gone, Hejaz quickly recovered the line of sashes from the window and haltingly apologized for his rude impatience earlier. "I was confused. I was near panic. That's seldom happened to me. But I was truly near panic."

"If it's any consolation," she returned, accepting his apology, "I was near panic myself."

He bowed deferentially, then pointed to the piece of sash she was still holding. "Shall I bind that in the window for you?"

She glanced at it and smiled slowly as she handed the sash to Joel.

Without hesitation, he took it and carefully anchored it to a small iron brad sunk into the libn wall just outside the narrow window. "There!" he said, satisfied that the sash was secure. "Now we all have a 'true sign,' and I have repaid a very old and very important debt!"

So the two men returned, and descended from the mountain, and passed over, and came to Joshua the son of Nun, and told him all things that befell them:

And they said unto Joshua, Truly the Lord hath delivered into our hands all the land; for even all the inhabitants of the country do faint because of us.

And Joshua rose early in the morning; and they removed from Shittim, and came to Jordan, he and all the children of Israel, and lodged there before they passed over (Joshua 2:23-24;3:1, KJV).

This movement of the Hebrew encampment to the east bank of Jordan was closely followed by Canaanite eyes. Reports of it were sent quickly to Jericho's king and her khazianu.

The reaction was understandable, but deadly. Now grasping at any straw, the khazianu grossly misinterpreted the meaning of the Hebrew action. They deemed the new encampment to be evidence that an immediate attack would not occur. In fact, some members of the khazianu argued that the Hebrews had changed their minds about entering Canaan.

Practicality, they said, supported such views. The river was on a rampage of spring flooding, thereby making an immediate crossing impossible. Several weeks would have to pass before a successful fording could be accomplished. And by that time, the Hebrews would have lost interest in Canaan. Pasturage on the east bank was ample, perhaps not as lush as in the plains of Jericho, but ample. It would be much simpler for them just to stay where they were.

Such reasoning found great popular support. Shatha, still recovering from his injuries, took full credit for the apparent halting of the tribes. He sent a message to King Balaar and the khazianu, proclaiming, "It is a sign against the Hebrews. They fear the power of Canaan's gods. Nahshon's incantations are successful. The prayers of your high priest have caused the Hebrews to reconsider. Astarte prevails! El prevails!"

Peridia and General Birsha had different ideas. They saw the Hebrew's latest move only as a temporary delay. They regarded it as an extra bit of time in which to better fortify Jericho's defenses, to add to the already-bulging food supplies stored up against a long siege, and in which to make another plea for help from the northern provinces and from Rameses.

Peridia sought Joel with the request that he return to Egypt, and, as rabiser, personally lay Jericho's case before the Pharaoh.

Joel refused. Regretting that the request forced him to duplicity, he made a counter suggestion that he go instead to the Hebrew encampment and attempt to bargain with them. Whether out of a sense of surrender to the inevitable, or out of a genuine belief that the suggestion was valid, Peridia accepted the ruse. By doing so, he gave Joel a legitimate reason for going in and out of Jericho at will during the ensuing days.

General Birsha, on the other hand, ordered Yanshuph to take a small squad of soldiers and return to the northern provinces immediately. Then, in order to rally support among the khazianu for his assessment of the latest Hebrew move, he invited them to accompany him and his captains to the west bank of the river and see the enemy for themselves. All went, except Rahab and the rabiser.

The khazianu beheld the Hebrew encampment. It was enormous. Its tents pock-marked the plains of Moab for almost a full league, and the flocks numbered in the tens of thousands. It was an awesome spectacle.

To General Birsha's consternation, however, the effect on the khazianu was the reverse of what he had expected. Impressed as they were by the size of the encampment, they came away less fearful of the Hebrews' ability to make war. No sentries guarded the east bank in front of the encampment, they said; no men-at-arms and no weapons were visible.

Neither had they seen any evidence of a supernatural, all-powerful presence among the Hebrews. The Ark of the Covenant and its tabernacle, which was reported to be his dwelling place, could not be seen anywhere.

And so, they returned to Jericho reassured that what their own eyes had seen was what they should believe, namely, that the Hebrews were nothing more than a large horde of peaceful-looking bedu with many tents and many animals.

They announced their conclusions to one and all upon their return. The city went wild. Pent-up anxieties burst into a jubilation of relief. The city gates were thrown open. Wall sentries left their posts. Bedu and fellaheen spilled out of their houses and shelters and swarmed through the streets urged on by the siren song of false security.

Not even the spring rains dampened the jubilation. Rather, the people exulted in them as yet another sign that there was nothing to fear from the Hebrews; for the rains soaked into the loamy soil, filled up the low places, and formed fresh, clear pools in the wadis. Cisterns ran to overflowing. The Plain of Jericho gorged itself as fully as did the citizens in the City of Palms.

Shatha sent a message to Rahab: "I shall once again parade before the citizens in our streets and hold audiences for them at the temple. You will accompany me."

She refused, using illness as her excuse.

But the people needed no one to lead them in their celebrations or to tell them that their high priest had turned away the threat with his powers. All over the city, orgies of excess ensued and became yet another testimony to man's infinite capacity for self-satisfaction and self-deceit.

For three days, whoredom and idolatry prevailed. On the third day, the walls of the city literally trembled, as if the earth itself suddenly sickened at the debauchery. But Jericho's gyrating humanity did not feel the tremor in the earth. They were too obsessed with what they believed to be a reprieve from destiny — from Herem.

During these same three days on the east bank of the Jordan, a contrasting belief in destiny held sway. The Hebrew tribes were preparing to move forward in accordance with the commands of the Lord God Jehovah.

The officers went through the host; and they commanded the people, saying, When ye see the ark of the covenant of the Lord your God, and the priests the Levites bearing it, then ye shall remove from your place, and go after it.

Yet there shall be a space between you and it, about two thousand cubits by measure: come not near unto it, that ye may know the way by which ye must go: for ye have not passed this way heretofore.

And Joshua said unto the people, Sanctify yourselves: for to morrow the Lord will do wonders among you.

And Joshua spake unto the priests, saying, Take up the ark of the covenant, and pass over before the people. And they took up the ark of the covenant, and went before the people.

And the Lord said unto Joshua, This day I will begin to magnify thee in the sight of all Israel, that they may know that, as I was with Moses, so I will be with thee.

And thou shalt command the priests that bear the ark of the covenant, saying, When ye are come to the brink of the water of Jordan, ye shall stand still in Jordan.

And Joshua said unto the children of Israel, Come hither, and hear the words of the Lord your God.

And Joshua said, Hereby ye shall know that the living God is among you, and that he will without fail drive out from before you the Canaanites, and the Hittites, and the Hivites, and the Perizzites, and the Girgashites, and the Amorites, and the Jebusites.

Behold, the ark of the covenant of the Lord of all the earth passeth over before you into Jordan.

Now therefore take you twelve men out of the tribes of Israel, out of every tribe a man.

And it shall come to pass, as soon as the soles of the feet of the priests that bear the ark of the Lord, the Lord of all the earth, shall rest in the waters of Jordan, that the waters of Jordan shall be cut off from the waters that come down from above; and they shall stand upon an heap (Joshua 3:2-13, KJV).

The dawn came with uncertainty. Rain-bearing clouds intermittently moved across the heavens. Flights of birds shattered the dubious daylight with whirring wings and anxious cries. The wild game that came to drink from the overflowing river approached cautiously and did not linger.

The sentries who remained at the fording-place noticed these things and began to feel a curious tenseness. Nervously, they paced back and forth trying to peer through the early light at the Hebrew encampment. Something unusual was stirring. But they sensed it more than saw it, for the light was against them.

The fording-place was situated where the chalky marl of Moab's heights broke apart and spilled into gentle downward slopes toward the river. For a league or more, the land flattened out into the plains of Moab, as if from the beginning of creation it had awaited a procession of history. It was across this openness that Jericho's sentries continued to peer. Their tensions grew. They grumbled among themselves and cursed the task of having to be at this place.

And then, as the day came more fully awake, they could see movement in the Hebrew encampment. The Hebrews appeared to be packing up. In disbelief, they stared and began arguing among themselves about the reason for it. Did this mean the Hebrews were moving back deeper into Moab from which they came? Or did it mean they were moving forward toward the river?

"You're a fool, Achad!" shouted one of the sentries. "How can they move forward? There's nowhere to go but the river!" The others agreed, pointing to the rampaging flood waters.

"All right — all right — " Achad shot back in agitation. "But look for yourselves, donkeys. They are moving in this direction, and one of us will have to report it to the king."

"At this time in the morning? Not me!"

"Nor me!"

The argument quickly heated up and erupted into a scuffle. The scuffle exploded into a surly fight. By the time their tempers had cooled and they again surveyed the east bank of the river, the Hebrew host was moving steadily and surely toward them.

"Look at that!"

"They're mad!"

"They'll have to stop. That water is fierce!"

But the host continued moving forward. In the vanguard was not a single man-at-arms. Nowhere could they see a single lance or spear. Nowhere could they see swordsmen or foot-soldiers with slings and stones. Instead, with sure and steady purpose, a procession of priests led the host. The men of B'nai Konath came first. Across their shoulders they carried long, golden staves inserted through golden rings, which in turn upheld a large, square object covered with a shining cloth of purest blue.

The sentries stared in absolute dismay.

"What kind of trick is *this*?" one of them demanded.

"What kind of *army* is this?" Achad bellowed.

"A womanish army!" sneered another.

"Aye," the fourth agreed, "No self-respecting man would burden himself with that kind of baggage."

"They act like they're proud of being ladened like donkeys," Achad said scornfully, pointing to the staunch, clean-shaven men carrying the strange object.

"Wrong, Achad! No donkey walks like *that*!" the first sentry hooted, pointing to the men at the front of the object. They were walking backwards and facing the object as if it had some unearthly power, as if it was the symbol of the presence of a supreme being, one so mighty that none could turn away.

A freshet of breeze whipped at the shining blue cloth. For one flashing instant, the object was revealed to their scornful eyes. Carved from a single block of wood and lined inside and out with the purest gold, it held two stone tablets. This was the Ark, the Ark of the Covenant!

Transfixed, the sentries stared at the strange, open-sided box. Its pure gold roof was carved with cherubim that faced each other across the interior space. Their wings were protectively spread over the area that symbolized the resting place for the divine presence of Jehovah, the Shekhinah. This was the symbolic heart of Hebrew belief. It was the evidence of the presence and power of their unseen God. His commandments, as given to Moses, were written on the two stone tablets.

Stunned as they were by the sight of the Ark, something else stunned them even more. Since the strange object was leading the vanguard, it represented an army advancing to war guided by the power of trusting obedience, rather than by the might of arms. The idea terrified Jericho's sentries. They were so overwhelmed that they literally reeled under the impact.

How could they report these things to King Balaar, General Birsha, and to the high priest? Shatha would accuse them of madness, Balaar and Birsha of lying and disobedience. And yet, plainly before their disbelieving eyes, the advance of reverence continued. Other Levites followed the Ark carrying golden cruses of oil, holy vessels, basins, fire-shovels, a magnificent seven-branched candelabrum of gold, and the shewbread on its golden platter. Each of the items was borne separately on the shoulders of the men in the advancing column.

Next came the elders of the tribe of Levi: Eleazar, the high priest and Joshua, son of Nun, commander of the host, with his ministers and aides, heralds, trumpeters, and signallers. Behind them came the B'nai Gershon transporting the Tabernacle of the Ark on six wooden carts pulled by twelve oxen.

After this, an interval of some two thousand cubits separated the sacred vanguard from the rest of the host. It was as if the Hebrews dared not press too close to the Holy of Holies, lest they presume upon the greatness of Jehovah.

And now, for the first time, Jericho's sentries caught sight of the Hebrew men-at-arms. In strict military order marched forty-thousand men from the tribes of Gad, Reuben, and half the tribe of Manasseh. Their numbers alone were more than the entire population of the province of Jericho. Unencumbered by families and possessions, they strode along bristling with lances and spears, stones and slings, knives and cudgels. Right behind them, marched the armed men from the tribes of Judah, Issachar, Zebulun, Simeon, Ephraim, Benjamin, Dan, Asher, and Naphtali.

Behind the men-at-arms, under a billowing cloud of golden dust that hovered in the sky like a protective cloak, came the old people, the women and the children, and pack animals laden with baggage, folded tents, household items, and the tens of thousands of herd animals.

Closer and closer, they approached the river. They showed no hesitancy as they moved toward the tormented waters bounding down the Jordan's watercourse toward the Dead Sea. If they feared the swollen currents, their fears did not show. If man's extremity is truly God's opportunity, the stiff-necked invaders would soon testify to such divine anticipation.

Jericho's astonished sentries stood like stones as they watched the priests who bore the Ark reach the water's edge, and without so much as a pause, step into the raging torrent.

But to their even greater astonishment, the waters abruptly began to quiet. The noise of the rushing torrents softened. The sentries cast fearful looks at each other. It was as if the high clay bluffs near Adamah, where the river narrowed, had fallen in upon one another; as if the earth had trembled and quaked, demanding that the waters subside. It was not possible!

And yet, it was happening. Somehow, the river had been given relief from its swollen burden of melting northern snows and springtime rains. The sentries glanced sharply northward with horrified looks, half-expecting to see some supernatural being astride the high clay bluffs, contorting them into a gigantic and miraculous obstruction. The Hebrew priests continued to move through the water to the very middle of the river. Feet, ankles, and knees submerged, yet they neither lost their footing nor were they swept away! Instead the water grew more and more gentle.

It clung to the whiteness of their linen tunics and splashed and sparkled against their sun-weathered arms. It seemed to drain away and disappear as the priests reached the very middle of the river and halted to form a protective cordon for the vast host of people who were now to pass over Jordan.

Abruptly, the sun breached errant clouds and bathed the priests and the Ark with a golden glare. The shining blue cloth covering the Ark reflected the sunlight with blinding brilliance.

That the waters which came down from above stood and rose up upon an heap very far from the city Adam, that is beside Zaretan: and those that came down toward the sea of the plain, even the salt sea, failed, and were cut off (Joshua 3:16, KJV).

Jericho's sentries panicked; one was struck dumb, another fled in terror; the third writhed on the ground, whimpering and moaning like an injured animal unable to rise and soon to die; the fourth, too afraid to stay and too shocked to run, sank to his knees and tried to pray.

But he had nothing to pray to. No marvel such as this just

seen could be accounted to Astarte or any other of Canaan's gods. Mesmerized, he stared as the procession of Israel began to pass over Jordan on dry ground. On and on they came, with believing eyes ever turned toward the Ark of the Covenant held on high by the priestly cordon. With trusting feet, they marched straightway across the river and into the land of Canaan.

Tribe by tribe, they came. Banners and standards fluttered against Canaan's sky in a salute to the grace of the promise of God. For several hours they came, until at last, all had passed over safely. With that accomplished, twelve men, one from each tribe, on command from Joshua as Jehovah had decreed, picked up twelve stones from out of mid-Jordan and carried them to the place of their first night's lodging in the land of Canaan. There they were set up as a memorial to Jehovah's greatness.

As a similar sign, Joshua took twelve stones and set them in the middle of the river where the priests had stood. When all was done, the waters of the river returned, plummeting fiercely down the watercourse and overflowing its banks once again.

Thus, the Lord exalted Joshua in the sight of all Israel. They stood in awe of him as they had stood in awe of Moses.

Only after witnessing all these things did the last of Jericho's sentries struggle to his feet and make his way to Jericho's king and general and high priest, and to all the people of the city.

The reaction was catastrophic. Jericho simply gave up.

Not one stone had yet been hurled at her gates. No assault had yet mounted her walls. No firebrand had yet spread its flames through her grain bins. Nor had a single Hebrew warrior come close to her.

But the Whore of Canaan, once so proud and independent, once so grasping and possessive, left her wealth unheeded and unguarded and laid down upon a bed of self-inflicted defeat to await the final, merciful act of utter destruction — Herem!

17

The marvel of the Jordan crossing occurred on the tenth day of the month. But even though Joshua was a known and respected warrior, he ordered no assault. For eleven days, no attack came.

After the passing of the first two days, Jerichoans cautiously came out of their houses and shelters. They took to their rooftops to view the Hebrew encampment less than three leagues south and east of them. The campfires could be seen at night.

"Maybe Joshua has lost face with his people," they surmised, trying to explain to themselves the lack of action.

"Maybe they've changed their minds. There's plenty of room for them down there on the plains without attacking Jericho."

"Nahshon and Shatha have prevailed!"

"Aye. Once more, they have influenced Astarte to smile on Jericho!"

Though they said these things, it was with only surface conviction. The accumulated reports over recent months, climaxed by the marvel of the Jordan crossing, could not easily be put aside. The longer the Hebrews delayed, the more puzzled and jittery became Jericho's citizens. They were quarrelsome, tense, and fearful.

Spies were sent out. They returned with rather heartening news. "The Hebrews neither look nor act like warriors. They are undergoing some peculiar ritual."

Once more, the people of Jericho clutched at false hopes. They were ignorant of the fact that the ritual was that of circumcision, a ritual that represented 'freedom from bondage' and was an immediate prelude to a holy war of conquest.

After the two monuments of twelve stones were set up in honor of God's miraculous halting of the Jordan's waters, Joshua called for the rites of circumcision. Neglected during the years of desert wanderings, the rites were now necessary. It had not only hygienic importance; it was symbolic of "the rolling away of the reproach of Hebrew slavery in Egypt."

Now that they had fulfilled the penance of forty years of wandering and had at last reached the land of their forefathers, they were called on by the Lord to sanctify and purify themselves from every trace of bondage. A new generation was among them. Thanks must be given by all for the fulfillment of God's promise. Rededication as a free people about to claim their inheritance was their first sacred duty in the land of Canaan. The rite of circumcision and the celebration of the Passover both must be accomplished before any attack against Jericho could be mounted. It was the command of Jehovah.

As one day followed another, the very stillness of the Hebrews became more unnerving to Jerichoans than an all-out attack. The waiting was unbearable. Some citizens packed up and fled. Of those who stayed, many did so out of mankind's peculiar unwillingness to believe that total destruction can become a reality. Jerichoans had no capacity to grasp the idea that an ageless wisdom led the world, rather than their gods and goddesses of stone.

They shored up their false hopes of survival by reminding themselves that the double walls surrounding the six-and-a-half acres of the city were staunch enough to protect them.

"Besides," others said, "Nahshon's magic will send a plague on the Hebrews. She makes spells daily." And still others were certain that Shatha's power had caused the Hebrews to undergo their strange ritual, and that he would do even more to delay, and finally, halt the invaders.

Shatha encouraged that belief among his people. In fact, he even thought it was true. From the moment he had heard about the Jordan crossing, he had ordered Nahshon to produce a continuing series of her most powerful spells against the invaders. At the same time, he began offering up special — and grotesque — sacrifices to Astarte: bats wings and the head of a snake; the entrails and fetus from a pregnant camel; the head and genitals of a male jackal. The fact that the Hebrews had not moved closer to Jericho convinced him that he and Nahshon were succeeding.

But on the tenth day after the crossing, two couriers brought reports of an astounding nature.

An angel of the Lord Jehovah, the Hebrew god, had visited Joshua!

The full assembly of Jericho's khazianu did not believe it.

"But we saw it and heard it!" the couriers insisted. "From our hiding place near the Hebrew encampment, we saw it and heard it." The words tumbled from their mouths in a spate of excitement.

"The angel stood before the leader Joshua as a warrior with sword drawn! Without fear, Joshua walked toward the angel and asked him, 'Are you with us, or with our enemies?' The angel replied, 'I am captain of the army of the Lord God Jehovah, and I am now come.'"

Shatha exchanged a look of dismay with Nahshon. The priest's face still clearly showed evidence of the blow from Peridia. The rest of the assembled khazianu were transfixed by the couriers' report.

"Then Joshua fell on his face to the earth and worshipped the angel and asked him, 'What are my Lord's commands to his servant?' And the captain of the Lord's army — the angel — told Joshua to take off his sandals because the place where he was standing was holy!"

Shatha exploded. "Holy, did you say holy?"

The couriers nodded.

Shatha's slate-gray eyes narrowed in scornful skepticism. "And did this Joshua do such a humiliating thing as to go barefoot?"

"Aye, great priest," the couriers replied. "Aye, Joshua obeyed the Lord's angel. He removed his sandals then and there."

Shatha threw back his head and gave a hard laugh that ricocheted through the palace.

Confused and fearful now of Shatha, the couriers looked for

reassurance from the khazianu and found nothing but astonishment and perplexity. Only Nahshon remained impassive.

Shatha laughed again and with an arrogant gesture told the couriers to leave. They protested that there was more to tell, but he was adamant. "Begone, I say! You waste our time!" The couriers scattered, jeered on by the harshness of Shatha's scornful laughter.

King Balaar and the khazianu reacted differently. Ignoring the high priest, the king rose to his feet with harsh instructions for the city to be shut up once more. "None is to go out. None is to come in. Double the sentries and prepare to man the walls. Khazianu, you are dismissed." He turned to General Birsha and Peridia and said, "Come with me to my privy counsel rooms."

Immediately, all did the bidding of the king and left the hall. Shatha and Nahshon were left to themselves. He turned, expecting her to enjoy and agree that his view of such a nonsensical story was right. Instead, he found another contradiction. And this one sobered him.

Nahshon warned against making light of the report. "Angels are real," she said solemnly. "As a high priest, you know that. As a seeress, I know it." Balefully, she went on to remind him of the number of times over the years that reports of angelic visits had come to them. "We have always had to make very special rituals to Astarte to keep our people from panic over such reports."

Peevish that she did not agree with his view, he swung up out of his chair. "You, of all people, should not fear such foolishness."

Deliberately, slowly, she got up and went to him. "Fear, my prince, has nothing to do with it. The truth of the report can be to our advantage in several ways."

He hesitated. A muscle tensed in his jaw.

"So far we have stopped the Hebrews with our spells and incantations. And the people know it. This new report of the angelic visit gives us a chance to now put forth a special offering that will rid us of the Hebrews entirely."

He probed her with a hard, questioning look.

She moved closer to him. "It would be of special pleasure to Astarte if we were to offer Rahab to her as a special sacrifice!"

190

The hard, questioning look slid from Shatha's face and was replaced by a look of surprising indecision.

Nahshon cajoled him with an evil promise. "To use Rahab as a sacrifice would be just retribution. The house of Peridia has insulted and humiliated you. It has physically abused you. It has promoted the king's attempts to rob your treasury. Astarte expects you to exact a just retribution for those things." Her heavy-lidded eyes burned with fanaticism. "What better way to appease Astarte than to offer Rahab in sacrifice?"

Shatha stood perfectly still, probing the fanaticism in Nahshon's eyes and seeing also the glint of malevolence that went beyond concern for the goddess Astarte. It made him hesitate even longer. Whatever else Rahab might have done; however she may have scorned him in recent weeks; whatever he suspected about her relationship with the rabiser, he still found her the most gratifying of all women. None else matched her fire, or, for him, her beauty. If he did as Nahshon was suggesting, she would be mutilated and of no further pleasure to him. He had no reservations about hurting her — or about punishing her — but in a different way. Mutilation? That idea repulsed him.

Nahshon had moved quite close. She placed a blunt finger on Shatha's face and slowly traced the mark left by Peridia's blow. "What better way to exact retribution?" she whispered. "What better sacrifice to the resurgent power of Astarte?"

"Nay, seeress!"

"It would not be hard to get her away from the khan," Nahshon pursued in a sympathetic tone. "Ahabina will help us. And your temple guards can kidnap her."

"Nay!" He jerked the seeress's hand away from his face and gripped it hard. "She is now too well-guarded by the rabiser's men-at-arms. I want no trouble with them. Rameses' edict is still — " He turned away.

Nahshon waited, sensing from the set of his shoulders some new suggestion was forthcoming.

"Yes — of course — " He faced her, fresh, cruel arrogance in his eyes. "There is another way. An even better sacrifice for Astarte — the supreme sacrifice! We will do that when the proper time comes."

While Shatha and Nahshon continued to stand in Jericho's

palace plotting human sacrifice for their goddess of stone, Joshua, son of Nun, had called together the Hebrew people on the plains of Jericho three leagues south and east.

"The Lord God Jehovah has spoken," he proclaimed to the host of the people. "And the Lord has spoken thusly:"

> I have given into thine hand Jericho....
> And ye shall compass the city, all ye men of war, and go round about the city once. Thus shalt thou do six days.
> And seven priests shall bear before the ark seven trumpets of rams' horns: and the seventh day ye shall compass the city seven times, and the priests shall blow with the trumpets.
> And it shall come to pass, that when they make a long blast with the ram's horn, and when ye hear the sound of the trumpet, all the people shall shout with a great shout; and the wall of the city shall fall down flat, and the people shall ascend up every man straight before him (Joshua 6:2-5, KJV).

And thus did Joshua relay to the people the commandments of the Lord God Jehovah. Joel and Hejaz heard his pronouncement first-hand. They were standing in the forefront of the host with Caleb and with Salmon. As soon as Joshua had finished speaking, Joel turned to Salmon and said, "The time has come. We must ask Caleb to remind Joshua of the bargain with Rahab.'"

With a paternal chuckle, Caleb told them it wasn't necessary. Joshua would remember. "But if it will settle your impatience, then come," he relented. "Come and see for yourselves the integrity of my old friend."

Joshua was a big man, remarkably strong, sinewy, and unstooped despite his eighty years. But it was the expression in his eyes that was most remarkable. A piercing, visionary keenness was combined with the gentle humility of discipline and obedience. When he caught sight of Caleb, his face creased into an immediate smile. He came toward them, arms outstretched in a magnanimous gesture of affection. "Ah, my true friend, what say you of this day? This, the first day of Passover, the day when we begin to make siege on Jericho. Is your heart as full of praise for the Lord as mine is?"

Caleb returned the embrace of friendship and then indicated

Salmon, Joel, and Hejaz. "All four of us welcome this day, Joshua, though for different reasons. Now, take young Joel here — "

Joshua cut him off with a hearty laugh. "I suspect he has come so that you can urge me to remember the vow you made to the woman called Rahab. Am I right?"

Caleb chuckled. "Your memory is as keen as the timing of the siege."

"It is no less than your valor in searching out Jericho for us," Joshua responded. "Nor could it be any less than the valor — and the faith, perhaps — shown by the woman in Jericho." He turned to look directly at Joel. "From the look of relief on your face, young man, I surmise you hold that woman in even greater esteem than I."

Joel reddened.

"You are quite serious about her, aren't you?"

Joel nodded. "She is the only woman I ever wanted to marry, sir."

Salmon and Hejaz glanced at him in surprise.

"In fact," Joel went on. "Once she and her family are safely among my own people here, I plan to talk with her father about the possibility of arranging a marriage."

Hejaz gasped in open astonishment. Then, with a wide grin, he slapped Joel on the shoulder and uttered a whoop of congratulations.

Caleb joined him. "She is a very beautiful and spirited young woman. I don't blame you, Joel — or any other young man — for wanting to take her to wife."

Salmon remained strangely quiet. Disappointment flickered in his eyes as he turned away and stared off toward Jericho.

"When the time is proper," Joshua offered, "I will add my blessings to such an arrangement. I owe much to you and the woman for safeguarding my old friend, Caleb, and your kinsman, Salmon, on their scouting mission. Be assured, Joel ben Dishan, the vows made to the woman in Jericho will be honored."

Joel bowed in appreciation as Joshua encircled Caleb's shoulder with his arm. "You, old friend, must stand with me as I give the signal to begin the siege of Jericho."

From inside the khan, the first blast of the Hebrew trumpets was barely audible. It was a thin, reedy sound almost like the screech of a distant owl calling from the thick balsam forests. And it faded as quickly as the call of an owl. Had Rahab not been at the window of the small, ugly, prison-like room to check on the scarlet sash tied just outside, she would not have heard it at all.

The sound came again, a bit more full in tone and a bit more sustained. But, even so, it did not match the description of the signal Joel had told her to expect. It came again — more full — more sustained. Now, with hands cupped over her eyes against the morning sun, she peered out into the distance toward the Hebrew encampment.

Haze veiled the view, but the trumpet sound came more distinctly. A quiver went through her. The destiny of change had begun its confrontation with the settled past. What was it Joel had told her — six days they would march and then attack on the seventh?

The sound of the trumpets came more steadily now, and more stridently. On the heels of it came other sounds — the sounds of clamoring curiosity and the fascination of dread from the people of Jericho. All over Jericho, they were hurrying to windows and rooftops for a firsthand view of the enemy. Ever louder, ever more persistent, the trumpets sounded.

She hurried from the small, ugly room and carefully locked its door against any intruder who might accidentally discover the scarlet sash fluttering outside the narrow window like a rivulet of blood.

Reaching her own chambers, she joined Ahabina who stood close by one window, alert and listening. The slave's scarred face was immobile as a carving. Beyond, on the fields so recently shorn of their fruits and grains, marched the Hebrew vanguard. Forty-thousand men of the tribes of Reuben, Gad, and half the tribe of Manasseh were compassing the city. Lances and spears glinted in the sun. But — except for the careening blasts of the trumpets — they all marched in absolute silence.

Behind the vanguard, in glistening white linen vestments, came the priests blowing seven ram's horn trumpets. For the first time, Rahab could see that the trumpets were, indeed, fashioned from the horns of the ram — the same as her ring! It was a precious moment of singular understanding — one which would sustain her in many ways.

Instinctively, she reached to touch the ring suspended at her neck on its scarlet cord.

The trumpet sounds blasted and reverberated against Jericho's walls. A gasp escaped from Ahabina. She clapped her hands over her ears. Awesome fear glazed her eyes.

The Ark of the Covenant, symbolizing the presence of the Hebrew God, now came into view. Its shining cover of purest blue so dazzled that the golden sun seemed to shine from it, rather than on it. Golden staves, inserted through golden rings, supported the ark. It was borne on the strong shoulders of the men of B'nai Konath. The men at the front walked backwards to face the ark in praise and reverence.

Rahab remembered what Joel had told her, and shuddered. "The Lord God Jehovah moves with the people of Israel. He leads them. His presence is a living spirit among them." The vision of reality shimmered before her, and beneath her fingers, the ram's horn ring vibrated warmly.

Behind the Ark of the Covenant came the men who bore the holy vessels and all the trappings of the tabernacle. These were the elders of the Levites. They were followed by the six carts on which all the trappings of the tabernacle were placed. Twelve oxen pulled the six carts. Next, came Eleazar, the high priest, and then came Joshua, son of Nun, commander of the host. Joel's description had been very clear. And now that she saw the Hebrew leader, she immediately recognized him. He strode in regal confidence in the midst of his captains and other officers. But she did not see Joel. She hoped she might. Behind the officers came still other men-at-arms following as a rear-guard.

There were upwards of seventy thousand warriors. Yet, in all that host, not one sound was uttered as they compassed the city. The trumpets only continued to proclaim the message of disaster.

Beside her, Ahabina made a curious animal sound. She glanced around and discovered that the slave was staring in confused astonishment at the ram's horn ring suspended on the scarlet cord at her neck. It was as if the slave had never seen the ring before. Yet, that was foolish. She had seen it many times over the years. For an instant, Ahabina's reaction was strangely amusing. But as the slave's look changed from confused astonishment to hard accusal, Rahab suddenly realized that her body-servant now recognized the true value and significance of the ring. Fear pierced her.

Reflexively, she dropped her hand, leaving the ring to full view. Again, Ahabina's expression altered. This time to a dangerous anger.

"You have betrayed us. The spies were here! You have betrayed us all!"

Rahab's heart hammered. So this was the informant! Her mind reeled toward the edge of panic. Secrecy was part of her bargain with the spies! Safety for all of them was but a few days away. Ahabina must be silenced!

Forcing herself, she stepped toward the slave instead of away from her and demanded, "What did you just say? What insolence did I just hear?"

But Ahabina did not back off. "You have betrayed us. You did hide the Hebrew spies!"

"Liar!" She threatened, slapping her full in the face. "Ingrate!"

Ahabina reeled.

Rahab pursued. "Liar! I'll have your tongue cut out!"

The scar on the slave's face writhed viciously. With a swift movement, her hand went into the folds of her garment and reappeared with a short, sharp dagger.

Rahab halted, fear tearing at her. It was the dagger Joel had given to her on the night the spies arrived at the khan.

Outside, the ram's horn trumpets continued to blast forth the larger message of destruction. The sound bludgeoned the walls and the room itself trembled.

Ahabina's eyes went wide with terror and pain. The hand holding the dagger seemed to falter as she threw her free hand against her ear, against the sound.

Unhesitatingly, Rahab threw herself onto the taller woman and pushed her down to the floor. In a frenzy of panic, she knocked the dagger loose. It flew across the room, glanced off the top of the dressing table, and buried its deadly point into the polished bronze mirror nearby.

The Hebrew trumpet sound enveloped the chamber, pulsated, crashed around with devastating certainty. Ahabina rolled on the floor, clutching at her ears, and moaning like a wounded animal.

Rahab scrambled to her feet, rushed to the door, and flung it open to yell for Joel's men-at-arms. They came very quickly. Hejaz was with them.

Breathless from the exertion and the fear, she ordered Ahabina's imprisonment. The men-at-arms gathered up the half-crazed slave-woman and carried her out. Rahab sank onto the nearest couch and shook uncontrollably. Death had never been so close!

Hejaz knelt in front of her, holding out a cup of wine, and helped her to sip at it. Soon her trembling eased, and she sank back onto the couch and described to him what happened.

"She must be silenced," Hejaz advised. "It is dangerous now for all of us to let her live. I will do it for you, my lady!"

She straightened and then shook her head. "I can't kill her. I just can't kill her!"

18

For six days, the Hebrews compassed Jericho. Always in the same pattern; always for just one encirclement; always just as the Lord had commanded it be done.

Once a day, the Hebrews assailed the City of Palms with the presence of the Lord God Jehovah, symbolized by the Ark of the Covenant and by the tabernacle; with the uncompromising call of the ram's horn trumpets; and with the relentless human silence from more than seventy thousand warriors.

The silence bellowed, accused, and condemned more loudly than seventy times seventy thousand. Only one other could match it; that was the silence hovering inside Jericho itself. Minds were buried in awesome fear created by the war of nerves. If weeping and wailing and gnashing of teeth was done, it was done in Jericho's deepest heart of hearts. Not even the sound of crying babies cluttered the coppery silences of these six days or disturbed the inky stillness of the nights. When Jericho stirred at all, or sent her women to fetch water from the springs, she moved on slippered feet of fear and spoke only with gestures. It was as if the City of Palms attempted to confuse its encircling enemy into believing that the city had been deserted.

But from the house on the wall, the scarlet sash still fluttered in every errant breeze, a symbol that this one household sought rebirth based on a human vow. But only one inhabitant knew that.

"If someone would just shout!" Tirzah exclaimed irritably.

"A whisper would even be welcome!" Mozni agreed with unaccustomed nervousness.

"Why do they just march around and around? Why don't they attack?" Tirzah cried. "Why don't they say something? Or yell? Or — something!"

"Patience, my sister," Rahab fumbled. "Patience is all we have."

Her mother and sister had looked at her with such beseeching eyes that she turned away, fighting down the impulse to tell them everything. "Patience is all we have," she repeated, "and safety is all we have to hope for. Especially for her —" She pointed to the child playing near them.

When the seventh day dawned, the first peal of trumpets came earlier than usual. Rahab sat bolt upright, sleep draining away immediately. The blast of the trumpets was more continuous. And while it seemed impossible, it was more terrifying in its intensity. The sun was coming up hot and brilliant, almost a savage brilliance. And already, the golden air was supercharged with a dreadful anticipation.

Hurriedly, she dressed, brushed at her hair, and glanced into the polished bronze mirror, warped now from the impact of the sharp dagger. Her reflection came back to her distorted, unreal. She shuddered at how closely it resembled the scarlaced distortion on Ahabina's face. She turned quickly away and grabbed up a mantle.

Joel's instructions had been clear. Hejaz had reminded her of them just the previous evening. "Everyone who is to be saved must be inside the khan."

She slipped the mantle over her shoulders and went about the khan checking to see that all the household was accounted for. They seemed to be. And all seemed mesmerized at the sight of the enemy's march on this day. She hurried along, checking the slave quarters and the quarters of the household servants. All there seemed to be in order, too.

By the time the fourth encirclement had begun, she went up to the small, ugly room. The scarlet sash still fluttered outside the narrow window in mournful salute to the marching host. She looked out, finding herself fascinated by the march. The all-pervading silence had now transferred itself to the beasts of the field and the birds of the air. Nothing moved on the plains of Jericho except the relentlessly silent host. Only the ram's horn trumpets broke the muteness.

She turned away from the window and started to check on Ahabina imprisoned in the storeroom. But as she reached the top of the courtyard stairs, she saw her father and Yanshuph rush across the opening and out through the gate in the direction of the palace. Panic caught at her. They must not leave — not now!

Wildly, she ran to find Hejaz, and together they chased after Peridia and Yanshuph. They caught sight of them entering the palace. Hejaz started to hurry ahead and stop them, but Rahab caught his arm. "Wait. Those are Shatha's guards at the door, not the king's."

The sound of the trumpets proclaimed that the fifth encirclement was about to begin. Joel had said that the attack would come on the seventh encirclement. "This way!" She led the Nubian through a little-known passage that linked the palace to the temple until they came to a door leading to the privy counsel chambers. "We must be very careful — especially me. Women are not allowed in this part of the palace. But there is a heavy drapery where we can hide, until you go in and get my father and brother-in-law."

As they stepped into the stuffy confines of the drapery enclosed area, the sounds of arguing came from the privy counsel. Peeking through the drapes they could see twenty or so of the more prominent khazianu. The king and Shatha were flanked by temple guards. That meant that Shatha was now — somehow — in total charge.

King Balaar stood up and calmed the argument before him. In a tired and weary voice, he said, "Jericho's heart is cut out by this unrelenting march of human silence. But we must not let Jericho die without some sign of resistance!"

The khazianu looked away from each other. Fear was too personal. It hovered too closely to each of them.

"Today, the trumpets are louder and more demanding for surrender. No doubt they will soon make their attack."

Rahab trembled with fearful impatience.

"But we must do something!" The king waved a hand in futility. "There have been two courses of action suggested —

200

one by General Birsha and one by your high priest." A flicker of last hope swept across the faces of khazianu, but vanished when Balaar went on to say, "Neither course of action finds my approval." He coughed and cleared his throat. "The two-thousand men-at-arms that the great Rameses sent to us have turned tail and fled back to the Nile."

The khazianu murmured disappointment. Despair etched the faces of Peridia and Yanshuph.

Balaar nodded sorrowfully. "Yes, Rameses did heed our pleas. He did accept the last great shipment of tribute we sent, and he did send two thousand soldiers to us. But when they saw the host of the Hebrews yesterday —" He made a scattering gesture and let the disappointment fill out his meaning. "Now, General Birsha thinks we should do the same. He recommends all citizens flee this tomb and leave the city an empty husk for the invaders."

The Hebrew trumpets could be heard blasting urgently, as the khazianu again began to argue over the suggestion.

Rahab could hardly contain herself. She glanced at Hejaz and started to send him around to fetch her father and brother-in-law. But at that moment, Peridia stepped toward the dais and addressed his old friend King Balaar. "Our reaction to this suggestion of the noble general is the same as yours; we do not like it. It is the act of a cowering jackal to sneak away in the face of battle. We will stand with Birsha's garrison, small though it may be. If there remains one spark of spirit among us, it must shine forth now, even in the face of certain defeat!"

"It will be lost in the blackness, my old friend," Balaar said with a weak smile. "Such a tiny spark cannot blind this enemy!"

"I agree," Peridia conceded. "But defeat lies not so much in the hands of the Hebrews, as in the spirit that dwells among the Hebrews."

A dark rankling spread across Shatha's face.

"The present danger," Peridia went on, "is not the usual warfare that we know how to fight. If it was, then General Birsha's suggestion of temporarily fleeing might be useful. But we're facing a different kind of war. By their very tactics over these last six days, the Hebrews give evidence that the City of Palms has been 'placed under the ban.'"

Rahab's heart caught in her throat.

"If this is so," her father proceeded, "none of us shall escape, even though we attempt to flee. We have no choice left but to stand and fight and meet the enemy like men of honor. We must force the attack and get it over with."

Tears sprang to Rahab's eyes. Yanshuph placed a proud hand across Peridia's shoulders. General Birsha regarded him with respect, and King Balaar contemplated his old friend with sadness.

Shatha leaned forward, his yellow ritual robe brushing ominously against his chair. "There is a more effective way still left to us, innkeeper."

Rahab tensed.

"Tell Peridia about my suggestion, King Balaar," Shatha urged in an oily tone.

The old king went pale.

"Very well, then," Shatha picked up. "I will tell him." He turned toward her father. "The time for men like you has passed, innkeeper."

"You mean we are like Jericho — defeated by our actions and customs?" Peridia lashed back.

"No. I mean that power is strength — the power of wealth and men-at-arms who are loyal — and the power of persuasiveness with the gods of Canaan."

"And what has this to do with your suggestion to save Jericho from the Hebrews?"

Shatha lolled against this chair with such arrogant confidence that a puzzled look of concern flashed across Peridia's face. He had expected argument, but Shatha looked positively benevolent. And that was dangerous!

"The answer to our problem is quite simple," Shatha announced. "The only way to avert Herem is to offer a ritual of supreme sacrifice to Astarte, the ritual of child sacrifice!"

Rahab felt herself sway as a smothering sensation gripped at her. Hejaz moved closer to steady her. His stern look warned her to make no outcry. She watched fearfully as lines of horror etched themselves into the faces of the khazianu. Each of them had children and grandchildren.

Shatha leaned forward now. Impersonally, he enumerated

the requirements for the sacrificial victim. It must be the child of a high-born family; a first-born child, preferably a boy. "However, there is an exception in this situation." He purred like some giant cat ready to spring. "Special circumstances face us now. So, we need a special requirement. Nahshon, our seeress, has decreed that this sacrifice must be a girl-child!"

Open relief flashed onto the faces of those who had no girlchildren. But a peculiarly agonizing expression filled the faces of Peridia and Yanshuph.

"Because of the great danger," Shatha went on as if giving a lesson in routine barter, "we must make the perfect sacrifice to Astarte. We have found such a child." He stood up, the yellow robe swaying insidiously about his tall figure. "This particular child will not only appease Astarte, but will, as well, repay a debt."

The Hebrew trumpets gnashed and wailed against the stunned silence.

"This particular child will pay the price of the betrayal of Jericho!" Shatha glared directly at Peridia.

Rahab staggered. "O God! No! No!"

Hejaz firmly held her and restrained her from breaking into the room. His strong hand clamped hard over her mouth.

"Some days ago, two spies were harbored within this city. They were Hebrew spies. A special guard was sent to apprehend them, only to be told they had departed. Later, it was discovered that the spies were hidden and protected in a well-known Jericho house. For what price, I don't know!"

Peridia's face hardened.

"The price however," Shatha went on quickly, "doesn't matter. The scale will be balanced. At this moment, the favored child of sacrifice is in the temple and the ritual has begun." His eyes glinted savagely. "She is the perfect child. We cannot fail. For the child is the kinswoman to the beautiful and deceitful quedesah of Jericho — the betrayer of Jericho!"

Shock staggered the assembly. King Balaar came to his feet. Peridia and Yanshuph lunged forward and threw themselves at the high priest. The khazianu scattered. General Birsha stepped swiftly in front of the old king, sword drawn protectively. Temple guards scuffled with Peridia and Yanshuph just long enough for Shatha to turn and run toward the draped exit where Rahab and Hejaz were hiding.

The Hebrew trumpets screeched and bellowed their closing notes of warning.

Rahab struggled free from Hejaz. "The priest is mine," she snapped. "But first, let him lead us to the child."

The Nubian drew his dagger. "I'll stop the guards if they try to follow the priest. And I'll bring your father and brother-in-law."

She nodded and pressed back against the wall as Shatha pushed through the draperies and rushed headlong out the side door.

With swift power, Hejaz yanked down the drape and trapped the guards that were rushing after Shatha. His dagger made quick and final work of them.

Unnoticed by her consort, Rahab turned and followed after him to the place where Reba was to be sacrificed.

19

The temple was deserted.

No hint of activity came from its rooms. Priests and maidens had vanished as if swallowed up by the earth itself. Only the unmitigated horror of a ritual child murder manifested its ugly presence along the dun-colored walls and writhed in the darkest corners.

Shatha disappeared through the black maw that led out onto the altar platform. Rahab hesitated, making sure that he did not reappear. She turned aside, and by a more direct route, hurried through the door used by the maidens during the festival.

Sunlight parched the arena of death. Reba lay on a ceremonial crib at the foot of Astarte's bejeweled statue. She made neither sound nor movement. Rahab realized that mercifully, they had drugged the child.

Ahabina crouched at one side of the ceremonial crib. How she had escaped from Joel's men-at-arms was unimportant, but the magnitude of her revenge jolted Rahab. She stood stock still, then saw the hollow, vacant stare of madness in Ahabina's eyes. A few steps away, Nahshon chanted incantations over a set of ceremonial knives.

Horror fastened on Rahab. Her skin crawled. She knew each hideous step of the ritual by heart: the disfigurement of face and body; the cutting off of fingers, toes, ears, and genitals. Each part of the act would be done with a different knife and with a different magical placation. Finally, the largest bronze knife would come plunging down, shattering the breastbone, rending the chest cavity — down, down into the heart of the child.

Nausea seized her.

Shatha emerged from between the legs of the statue, glanced about, saw her, and came to an abrupt halt. Evil twisted his face. "Does my quedesah return to me after all? Does the betrayer of Jericho come to assist in the placation of Astarte?"

Nahshon, hands suspended mid-air, ceased her guttural chant and turned at the sound of Shatha's voice.

"Vileness!" Rahab said thickly. "Deceit of wickedness! Murderer!"

"A sacred rite!"

"Murder! Vengeance!" She pulled out a dagger. Hejaz had returned it to her after retrieving it from the polished bronze mirror. "Murderer!" She started toward him.

"You will not kill me! You can do nothing but fail. You are careless! I've told you that before." The slate-gray eyes mocked her. He threw back his head and laughed. The sound of it flew up into the coppery sky, faded against the blowing of the Hebrew trumpets, and died into nothingness.

Behind her, she heard the arrival of Hejaz with her father and Yanshuph. Shatha saw them. His face distorted into a black mask of rage. He spun around and yelled at Nahshon. "Kill the child! We have no more time! Kill the child! Kill!"

Rahab's heart wrenched up into her throat. Peridia, Yanshuph, and Hejaz were rushing past her toward Shatha and Nahshon.

"Kill!" Shatha raged. "Kill!"

Rahab screamed and ran toward him as he wrested the knife away from Nahshon and raised it above the helpless child. But before any of them reached the tableau of vengeance, the knife in Shatha's hand faltered. For a long, tremulous moment, knife, hand, and arm were paralyzed in space. Sweat broke out on Shatha's clean-shaven head. The slate-gray eyes bulged in surprise and pain. Then, slowly — ever so slowly — like thistle drifting on the wind, the body of Jericho's high priest crumpled onto the platform, his hand still clutching the ceremonial knife.

It was Hejaz who reached the ceremonial crib first and saw

206

Ahabina crouching beside the priest. In her hand was the smallest of the ceremonial knives.

An agonized cry, torn from morbid depths, wracked Nah-shon. She sank to her knees and gathered the priest's lifeless body into her arms. Blood seeped from the wound and bound them together. Hejaz moved quickly to stand over her, lest she move in reflexive desperation against the rest of them.

Rahab stared at the scene, knowing she should feel some emotion. But she didn't. She felt nothing — nothing at all. An oppressive stillness settled over them. The sacred grove was hushed. The total silence vibrated with its own inescapable nature; abysmal as man's tortured soul; futile as his depravity that turns upon itself in gluttonous destruction.

The silence deepened and wrapped itself around them. Pervading, encompassing, the silence reached even up to the sky and hovered over all Jericho.

Rahab stirred, looking again at the child, aware of a subtle change coming over all of them. Yet the child had neither moved nor made a sound. Still, she had the curious sensation that an element of nature had shifted and re-laid its pattern on the earth. She glanced about.

Silence moved against silence.

Then, it came to her! "The trumpets," she gasped. "The trumpets! They no longer blow!"

"We must go quickly," Hejaz ordered.

"The seventh time," she blurted, remembering Joel's instructions.

Yanshuph and her father looked confused and started to question her, but Hejaz cut them short. "Back to the khan! Quickly now. Quickly. You'll understand soon enough!"

Rahab tore off her mantle and tossed it to Yanshuph to wrap around the child. "Hurry, please hurry. Now it is we who have no time!"

Yanshuph and Peridia wasted no time. They picked up Reba and moved off immediately toward the khan.

Rahab looked at Ahabina. The dark face, with its serpentine scar lacing the left cheek, stared blankly across the platform. A mixture of emotion whipped through Rahab and traced a twin path of pity and sadness through her. The awesome stillness began to vibrate.

"We must go!" Hejaz urged. "Leave the slave. You cannot help her!"

A tremor went through the earth. Rahab knelt down beside Ahabina and with hesitant fingers caressed the scarred face. "We shared much. Come with us. Let me try to help you."

There was no response.

"Come, my lady! We must hurry! My master's instructions were tha —"

The words were hurled from him as a rumbling, screeching blast of trumpets spewed forth and was joined by a tumultuous human shout — a human shouting so vast, so deep, so thunderous that it splintered her soul. In horror, she glanced about.

The walls of the open-roofed altar room seemed to sway, jarred by the roar of human voices. The ground trembled.

Hejaz grabbed her by the arms and jerked her up onto her feet. "Run!" he ordered. "Run! Run for the khan!"

She obeyed.

Seventy thousand throats boomed out the decree of destruction. Seventy thousand voices roared forth in obedience to divine command — pulsing, hammering, thundering. Peal on peal, the shouting came and shoved her along on its clashing tumult. A sea of sound, it broke and crashed — splitting, rending, tearing.

Destruction!

Devastation!

Dedicated to Jehovah!

It rumbled across the plains of Jericho, rolled and battered against the walls of Jericho, flung itself up into the coppery skies, and fell like a sledge on the cowering City of Palms. A new sound cut through the bludgeoning din — a plaintive and beseeching sound.

Rahab glanced around over her shoulder. Across the sacred grove, on the altar platform, Ahabina now stood upright, her hands outstretched in a helpless plea. Beside her, Nahshon still cradled Shatha's body. Compassion tore at Rahab. She stopped. The altar wall behind Ahabina began to move, shaken by an unseen hand.

With a hideous snapping sound, a cleavage appeared across the face of Astarte's statue. Temple doves by the thousands

208

swooped and fluttered from their nesting places high on the wall. Burnished against the coppery sky, they looked like giant black moths as they swooped and flew in and out and around the undulating statue. A side wall split asunder. Blazing sunlight stabbed at the great naked idol, and flamed over its lewd contours as the precious stones dropped from the eyes and the crown of sapphires disintegrated.

Piece by piece, section by section, the statue began to crumble. Stupefaction gripped Rahab. The final fulfillment of devastation occurred before her eyes. The face of the idol contorted into a hideous grimace of death.

"My lady! Hurry!" Hejaz implored. "You must come! Now!"

She could not move. The stones at the knees of the statue began to break apart, and the serpent-form of the god El, with its human head uplifted in praise of the loins, split and slid away into a gaping maw of torn earth. Altar, statue, and temple all writhed against each other and crashed down upon the altar platform.

Rahab shut her eyes, unable to endure any more.

A deep, heavy rumble overlaid the thunder of the Hebrew shouting. The earth jolted in demand for complete destruction.

"You must come, my lady!"

The ground shook, indignant and vengeful.

The Nubian's arms came around her, lifted her up, and sped with her toward the khan. Jericho's east wall disappeared. Chunks of libn flung themselves up and out, seeking escape from the angry earth. The temple crashed in upon itself, burying arrogance, treachery, and self-indulgence. The sky darkened. Clouds of dirt roiled up and were afraid to resettle on the convulsing land.

The shouting tumult increased and was joined by heaven itself so that it blasted, reverberated, and pummeled the City of Palms unmercifully.

Jericho's walls, staunch and unbreachable in Canaan's mind, bled with giant cracks. They quivered, swayed, tottered, crumbled, and fell down flat!

The City of Palms bellowed out its pain and screamed with the agonized pangs of unholy death.

The shouting tumult continued as Hebrew feet came swiftly

into the city. Seventy thousand swords and lances were drawn and poised to complete the divine command of utter destruction.

> And the city shall be accursed, even it, and all that are therein, to the Lord: only Rahab the harlot shall live, she and all that are with her in the house, because she hid the messengers that we sent....
>
> And they utterly destroyed all that was in the city, both man and woman, young and old, and ox, and sheep, and ass, with the edge of the sword (Joshua 6:17, 21, KJV).

It was as commanded. Except for those clustered together inside the main building of the khan, no one in Jericho survived. Above them, in the small, ugly, prison-like room, a bit of scarlet ceremonial sash still fluttered from the window.

The earth quieted. The trumpets and the tumult of human shouting ceased.

Abruptly as Herem began, so it ended.

All was silence across the plains of Jericho.

In the immediate aftermath, the silence of having been wondrously, miraculously spared hovered over all the survivors. Except for Rahab and Hejaz, they all clung together with uplifted and fearful eyes, still expecting to be destroyed. Then, they began to realize they were safe. Their faces mirrored disbelief that destruction had passed them by. It defied explanation. Suddenly, they began to embrace each other, and the music of the laughter of relief filled the main building of the khan.

Rahab wept openly.

It was finished.

Done!

Her family lived — and all its household. Her life was now her own. Nearby, Hejaz smiled at her. She touched his arm and thanked him. "Your arms and your heart are as strong as your master's vow. I do thank you."

"You are welcome, my lady. But you —" he grinned and shook his head. "You do take your time in moments of crisis! I thought you'd never leave that altar room, just as I thought you'd never find a way to get the spies off the roof!"

Her father and mother intervened to embrace Rahab. As Hejaz stepped out of the way, he glanced toward the open door. "My lady!" he called back to her, "Caleb and Salmon approach!"

"Who's that?" her father questioned.

"The Hebrew spies we hid here in the khan," she explained quickly. "It was our lives for theirs. That was the bargain."

Her parents exchanged astonished looks and watched her move toward the doorway.

She looked out anxiously, eager to see Joel, to share with him all that had happened in the final days. But only Caleb and Salmon were crossing the courtyard. Disappointment traced through her. "Where is your master, Hejaz? Didn't he plan to come with Salmon and Caleb?"

A worried look came onto the Nubian's face. He hurried out to intercept the spies in the courtyard. For several moments, they talked; then turned and walked together toward the main building.

From the look of Hejaz's face, Rahab knew something was wrong. "Your master, where is he?"

The Nubian stared down at the floor and did not answer.

"Hejaz! What's wrong?" she repeated. "Where's your master?"

Salmon came forward, took her hand and held it gently. "Your friend — and mine — is dead, Rahab."

Open-mouthed, she stared at the young spy. The chatter in the household stopped. Peridia came up and put his arm around her waist. "How?" he asked. "How did it happen?"

"By a freak of fortune, innkeeper." Caleb stepped forward and introduced himself. "Joel ben Dishan was of the tribe of Judah, as is my nephew, Salmon, here. In fact, they were boyhood friends and had just been reunited after many years. Just as my nephew rejoiced in finding Joel again, so did all the people of the tribe of Judah. They welcomed his return with all the fervor that a people can offer to one of their own who has returned from bondage." He hesitated, then coughed to cover the sudden break in his voice. "He was an exuberant young man. And he had some splendid plans in mind for you, Rahab."

Again, his voice broke with emotion. Salmon spoke up. "The fact is, innkeeper, Joel had plans to discuss arrangements with you to marry your daughter. He cared for Rahab very deeply."

A deep, sobbing sadness welled up inside her. Tears glistened in her eyes.

"With those plans in mind, sir," Salmon went on, releasing Rahab's hand, "Joel was putting together places of shelter for you and your household among our kinsmen. He was so determined that those places be ready that he continued to work on them alone during the days the rest of the men of Judah encircled the city. He had only his young Egyptian page to help him. At some point in their efforts, one of the lodge poles fell and struck them both in the head. Apparently, they both died instantly."

For a seemingly endless span of time, no one in the crowded room moved or spoke. Rahab fought with herself to understand the fickleness of fate, to grasp at some logical reason why such an uninvited, unwanted thing should happen. But she found no answers, and very little understanding. She knew only that never again would she experience the close, comforting strength or share the sense of freedom he had first offered her so long ago.

A moan of bitterness escaped from Hejaz. His great shoulders shook.

Glancing at him, Rahab suddenly realized that he, more than anyone, suffered the greatest loss. He was alone. She had her family. He had no one. She shrugged free from her father's supporting arm and went to Hejaz. Salmon followed her. Together, they led the big man outside and sat down on the steps to cry with him for the one true friend he had ever had.

Thus they remained, comforting one another, for some length of time. Then Caleb came to them and with quiet compassion said, "We must go, my children. Joshua has ordered the burning of the city." He pointed out across the courtyard toward the rubbled remnants of the temple. "Already, the torches have been put to the grain bins. We must go. We must go now."

So the family and the household of Rahab removed themselves from the devastation of the once proud City of Palms. Through the hidden doorway in the storeroom, they made their way out into the stillness and the safety of the plains of Jericho where Joshua would welcome them with sympathy and with esteem. There they would live out the rest of their lives in peace and plenty, and with the acceptance of a compassionate people.

Halfway to the Hebrew encampment — on a rise in the fertile land — Rahab stopped and looked back toward Jericho. The staunch, double-built walls were rubble. The palace, the temple, the treasure houses, the Street of Shops — everything was rubble.

Only the khan and the portion of the wall that supported the khan still remained. The small piece of scarlet sash still fluttered from the window.

The decree of destiny had been fulfilled. The Whore of Canaan was dead. Her heritage of self-indulgence and self-betrayal burned on a funeral pyre of its own making. All that would ever remain would be a warning to future generations.

A tremor went through her.

Salmon came close and put his arm around her, steadying and supporting her, and turning her away from the past. "A new life awaits you, Rahab. A new life awaits for Hejaz, too. It's the kind of life in which our friend, the rabiser, had the greatest of faith!"

And Salmon begat Boaz of Rahab; and
Boaz begat Obed of Ruth; and
Obed begat Jesse; and Jesse
begat David the King (Matthew 1:5-6).